3 9077 09466 2767

W9-AFG-786

NEW!

STOLEN by NIGHT

ALSO BY STEVE WATKINS

On Blood Road

Sink or Swim

Ghosts of War

The Secret of Midway

Lost at Khe Sanh

AWOL in North Africa

Fallen in Fredericksburg

STOLEN by NIGHT

STEVE WATKINS

SCHOLASTIC PRESS / NEW YORK

Library of Congress Cataloging-in-Publication Data

Names: Watkins, Steve, 1954– author.
Title: Stolen by night / Steve Watkins.
Description: First edition. | New York : Scholastic Press, 2023. | Audience: Ages 12 and up | Audience: Grades 7–9 | Summary: Despite her youth and her father's law enforcement ties, Nicolette becomes involved with the French Resistance during World War II, until one day she is taken from the streets of Paris and sent to a Nazi concentration camp, where she is determined to survive and bear witness to the atrocities she has endured. Includes historical note.
Identifiers: LCCN 2022059709 (print) | LCCN 2022059710 (ebook) | ISBN 9781338306071 (hardcover) | ISBN 9781338306088 (ebook)
Subjects: LCSH: World War, 1939-1945—France—Paris—Juvenile fiction. | World War, 1939–1945—Atrocities—Juvenile fiction. | World War, 1939–1945—Underground movements—France—Juvenile fiction. | Survival—Juvenile fiction. | Paris (France)—History—1940–1944—Juvenile fiction. | France—History—German occupation, 1940–1945—Juvenile fiction. | CYAC: World War, 1939–1945—France—Paris—Fiction. | World War, 1939–1945—Atrocities—Fiction. | World War, 1939–1945—Underground movements—Fiction. | Survival—Fiction. | Paris (France)—History—1940–1944—Fiction. | France—History—German occupation, 1949–1945—Fiction. | BISAC: YOUNG ADULT FICTION / Historical / Military & Wars | YOUNG ADULT FICTION / Social Themes / Prejudice & Racism | LCGFT: War fiction. | Historical fiction.
Classification: LCC PZ7.W3213 St 2023 (print) | LCC PZ7.W3213 (ebook) | DDC 813.6 [Fic]—dc23/eng/20230313

10 9 8 7 6 5 4 3 2 1 23 24 25 26 27

Printed in Italy 183
First edition, November 2023

Book design by Christopher Stengel
Photo © Shutterstock.com

For my grandsons Bobby and Reuben

BOOK ONE

OCCUPIED PARIS

1940

I

UN

Jules and I are flying on our fathers' old Favor racing bikes down roads and paths through the Bois de Boulogne, the great park across the Seine from the Eiffel Tower, sending pedestrians and slower riders diving out of our way. We can barely feel our frozen fingers, but neither of us cares. Two men in heavy overcoats throw themselves into thorny rosebushes and curse us loudly. Another stumbles into a shallow puddle. It's Armistice Day, 11 November, but it's no longer a holiday under the German occupation. I have changed out of my school uniform of pleated skirt and tights and blouse and jacket and into a pair of Papa's cycling pants and one of his old wool jerseys. I cut off a fistful of my long hair this afternoon before our ride and tucked the rest under my cap. Jules says I look just like a boy now, which pleases me. Perhaps I will be able to actually enter races for real, like him, and like our fathers when they were young. Perhaps if I pretend I'm a Nicholas instead of a Nicolette.

But today, the freedom of Jules and me tearing past each other in the park will have to do—playing cycle tag under the bare cedars and beeches and sequoias, past the winter gardens, the two lakes, the Grande Cascade, the windmill, the hippodrome, the empty red-clay tennis courts. We're fourteen and we're free, or that's what we tell ourselves—the bills flipped up on our Peugeot casquettes, our favorite bike caps, our faces bright red from the cold and the wind and the exertion.

Oh, to be out in the countryside instead of locked down here in Paris. What Jules and I wouldn't give to be in the Pyrenees, or the Alps, on the Tour de France, like Papa when he was young, riding solo, a touriste-routier, back when cycling was an individual sport and the peloton was banned. We have grown up hearing all the old stories from our fathers of the glory days of the sport, back when wooden rims were required on the mountain stages of the Tour for fear that hard braking would melt the glue holding tires on metal rims.

But that was a different France, and this is a different Paris. The Tour was canceled this past summer after the occupation. There was mass panic ahead of the Nazi advance back in June, with many leaving the city, fleeing to the south and Vichy, to the west and the Atlantic. On trains, in cars and flatbed trucks, on horse-drawn wagons, on foot, carrying everything they owned on their backs, piled in strollers, strapped to handcarts.

I remember watching from the balcony of our apartment and seeing an old woman sitting helplessly in the center of the avenue, sobbing, left behind or lost. No one stopped to help until Maman went out and pulled her to the sidewalk. Everyone else was too busy—holding the hands of the little ones, who were also crying, terrified, their faces contorted by fear and their parents' urgency to flee. Except some of the little ones were abandoned as well. Their faces blank, uncomprehending. They waited. The crowds swelled around them, threatened to trample them. People were shouting what everyone already knew: "The Nazis are coming . . ."

But Papa wouldn't let us leave. Maman begged him—she was from the countryside, she reminded him; we could go to her village—but he was stubborn, insistent. "The Germans are not coming to crush us, but to save us," he said. Maman kept quiet after that, but my sister, Charlotte, who is eighteen, argued with him, insisting we must fight. Papa would hear none of it. "This is our home," he snapped. "We will not flee like those cowards. It may well be good for Paris, for all of France, to have the Germans come in and clean house of all these trade unionists and communists and atheists who have been trying to undermine our institutions and destroy our traditions."

Charlotte stormed out of the apartment that day—as she has done many days since—to meet her boyfriend, Antoine. Maman assured me, as she always does, that Charlotte would be back, and that surely if we cooperated, the Germans wouldn't hurt us. In response, Papa stomped through the apartment, picking things up, putting them down forcefully. He did not stop until a figurine broke and Maman gave him a pleading look. A wingless angel now sits on the shelf.

We had read about the Nazi advance in the newspapers and heard about it on the radio—back before the newspapers and radio were banned. How the Germans broke through to take the Netherlands and Belgium in the north. And, to our despair, marched through our own defenses—the supposedly unbreakable Maginot Line between France and Germany, which was not unbreakable at all, as it turned out. The German army merely went around it, through the Ardennes Forest in their Blitzkrieg. Jules's father, a captain in the French army, was one of a million of our soldiers who surrendered to the Germans and who is still a prisoner of war, in a work camp somewhere deep inside Germany.

Our French flags, le tricolore, are gone. Everywhere now we see bloodred flags with black swastikas instead. Street signs in German. Closed shops. Soldiers goose-stepping through the city—thousands of them, giving their stiff-armed Nazi salutes. But Paris wasn't destroyed. The Germans only bombed two automobile factories at the city's edge. Nothing like what they did to Warsaw, to Rotterdam, to London. Our French army rolled over meekly. And now, five months later, many of those who fled from Paris have begun slowly to return, to register with the German command and the French Police Nationale, and to turn in their neighbors who dare to speak ill of Hitler and the soldiers of the Wehrmacht. There are eyes and ears everywhere.

Jules and I continue our wild ride through the park, laughing and shouting as we sprint to catch each other, practicing our pursuit racing. An elderly Police Nationale, probably assigned to the Bois de Boulogne because he's too old to be a true police, yells at us to slow down as we blaze past him. It is now late afternoon, with perhaps another hour of daylight left for us to ride, to embrace these moments of freedom. The gendarme pretends to give chase, and we pretend to take him seriously. With so few cars on the streets—most have been confiscated by the Nazis, and there is no petrol anyway—we leave the Bois de Boulogne on Avenue Foch and continue our race down the deserted Champs-Élysées as if on the last stage of the Tour.

But something isn't right. Lining the road and side streets are hundreds of Police Nationale in their blue uniforms and box caps and winter capes, carrying riot shields and clubs, while behind them in tight formation stand columns of heavily armed Wehrmacht soldiers, their faces set in grim masks.

We keep riding, now afraid to stop or even to slow down on the wide, empty boulevard. Until we reach the far end of the Champs-Élysées, and there, massed around the statue of the war hero Georges Clemenceau, is a crowd of young people, thousands strong, maybe tens of thousands, gathered to protest the occupation, something that hasn't happened in all these quiet months since the Nazis took over. We've seen the flyers, of course, like everyone at our schools, like everyone in the city, announcing that there would be speeches at the statue and then a march in open defiance of the Nazis and the traitorous Vichy government.

Students of France! On 11 November, we are gathering to honor the Unknown Soldier at the Arc de Triomphe at 5:30 p.m. for a Day of Memory. 11 November 1918 was the date of a great victory. 11 November 1940 will signal yet another. All students are in solidarity that France must live!

Charlotte argued with Papa about it at breakfast just this morning, insisting she was going; Papa, who works at the Police Nationale Central Office, ordered her to stay away. "You are being ridiculous," he shouted at her when she refused. "The Nazis will leave when they are ready to leave, and not because a handful of children threaten to hold their breath until they turn blue. Once we accept the reality of their greater military strength—and the new social order they insist must be followed—then they will withdraw back across the Rhine."

After the argument, Papa left for work. Maman left to help our neighbors, the Ashers, in their boulangerie down on the street. I left for school. Charlotte left for the Sorbonne, where she is in her first year at university. Or that's where she said she was going, anyway.

Still, I didn't believe anyone would be foolish enough to actually show up for the protest. Not even headstrong Charlotte.

Now Jules and I sit on our bikes, a short distance away, both of us amazed at the size of the crowd.

"Perhaps we should join them," Jules says, catching me off guard.

I stumble to respond. "But all the police," I say. "And the German soldiers."

Jules shrugs. "They seem to be only watching. Just in case. What can be the harm?" And then he adds, quietly, "We would honor my father by doing this."

What can I say to that, except to agree? And wonder if perhaps Jules steered us in this direction, planned for us to end up here all along. We hide our bicycles behind a nearby shop and return to work our way deep into the crowd so we can hear the speeches at the base of the statue—about Clemenceau, the Tiger, the old prime minister, the Father of Victory, who held fast against the Germans in the last war, who engineered the Treaty of Versailles, who kicked the German dogs out of our country, tails between their legs. About how we must stand strong now in the face of the occupation and march together to honor the spirit of independence. About how we are the manifestants, the ones who will raise our voices in protest, the leaders of what will surely become a mass movement to throw out the Nazis.

Wreaths woven from flowers and lace and sequins and bows are laid at the base of the statue. Some in the crowd wave fishing poles for the new hero General Charles de Gaulle, in exile in Great Britain, exhorting us nightly in BBC broadcasts to continue the fight. Some here have brought instruments, others have fashioned their own with sticks and trash can lids, and they begin to bang and play as the march begins.

I see someone I recognize from school—a quiet girl named Yvette—standing alone, holding the banned tricolore, and we wade through the crowd to join her. She recognizes me, too. "Bonjour, Nicolette." She has to shout the words. Soon we are taking turns holding the flag aloft and waving it proudly above the protesters. It is too loud to hear one another speak, but Yvette's wide smile tells us she's glad we have come.

The crowd swells around us, forcing us into one another, a mass of sweating, chanting bodies despite the November chill. I am thrilled to be here and find myself shouting slogans along with the rest. But I am frightened, too. Worried about the uniformed police and the Wehrmacht soldiers lining the boulevard, standing, waiting, perhaps ready to pounce. Early streetlights illuminate the side streets and the soldiers as the afternoon fades, and eventually Jules and Yvette and I are swept up as the crowd begins our march onto the Champs-Élysées, heading west past the massive stone columns and domed entrance of the Grand Palais, its windows now shrouded with swastikas, through the first traffic circle at Rond-Point, on toward the Arc de Triomphe, playing and whistling and singing "La Marseillaise" at the top of our lungs as if our voices and our presence here, our witness and our protest, will make a difference.

But we never make it. The police have no intention of letting us. It is as if we are fish, chased into a net. They let us make our way half the distance from Clemenceau's statue down the Champs-Élysées, within sight of the Tomb of the Unknown Soldier, cheered on by shopkeepers and citizens, absurdly proud of ourselves for making such a grand statement to the world, or so we hope. But in an instant, everything changes. Without warning, the police charge, their batons raised, descending on those at the fringes. Bodies go down in the street. Others try to flee but are boxed in, and they, too, are clubbed. For a second I think I see my sister, Charlotte, her red hair flying loose around her angry face as she fights to free others from the clutches of the Police Nationale. But as quickly as she comes into view, she vanishes again inside the melee. I try to pull away, to go to her, but Jules and Yvette are clinging to me too tightly.

And then suddenly the police are on us, too. We try to run, but there's no way to escape, nowhere to go. Fearless Yvette lets go of me and grabs a policeman's arm to keep him from swinging his club at Jules, but that only makes her a target. He turns on her, striking. She stumbles to her knees, tries to raise herself back to her feet, is clubbed from behind, blood spattering the back of her blouse. She falls again. Jules and I struggle against the crowd that now separates us from her, but two girls help her to her feet before we can get there. They wrap a scarf tightly over her wound and half carry, half drag her away.

Nowhere is safe. People are screaming, trying to run. Some manage to get away, at least for the moment. Some fight back, only to be beaten to their knees or bloodied into unconsciousness. We are torn in the opposite direction from Yvette.

The Nazis join then, a second wave of violence, their weapons raised. At first they are restrained, using their rifle butts as clubs, but soon, perhaps frustrated with those in the crowd who refuse to disperse—or who are trapped and cannot—they begin firing into the air. Volley after volley. There is the sharp retort of their rifles; there is smoke, crying, desperate wailing, pleas for help that won't come. I keep pulling on Jules, not sure which direction to take, not caring. Acrid smoke stings our eyes. The cacophony of shouting, screaming, shooting deafens us. We aren't fish, we are rats, desperate rats, caring for nothing and no one except to save ourselves—

And in a flash we are free, sprinting past soldiers too busy beating on our fellow manifestants to bother with us, two young kids, too frightened to fight them or defend anyone or do anything except run from the Champs-Élysées and down side streets and then alleys, sure we hear the jackboots behind us, drawing closer, the shouts in German to halt or be shot. We keep running. We have no choice. We slam into brick walls, we careen into others fleeing in the same direction, some howling with rage, some howling with pain, some bloodied and stumbling, some hurling stones behind them at an unseen enemy, some seizing us by the shoulder and spinning us around so they can vault past to a greater chance of escape for themselves.

Everything burns—my lungs, my eyes, my legs. My heart races and threatens to burst, but now it is Jules who won't let go of me when I try to slow down, when I plead with him to let me stop, just for a minute, just to be able to breathe, just so my heart won't explode. We see others ahead of us sliding to the cobblestone street. I fear they've been shot, except I haven't heard any guns for some time, for several blocks. But no, they are rolling under a stone slab of sidewalk into a narrow black space below, and then disappearing into the dark there, a sewer perhaps, but I don't have time to think it through before Jules is pulling me down with him to follow the others, scraping our elbows and knees, tearing our clothes, rolling under the stone, vanishing right there in the center of Paris into the unknown, into the underground where maybe we will be saved.

2

DEUX

The darkness swallows us whole. At the bottom is sewer water. I shove someone off me. Someone pushes back. I call for Jules and feel for him in the pitch-dark; he calls back to me faintly. "Here!" I shout, though there's no need to raise my voice, and when I do, the harsh echo hurts my head. The only sounds are the others moaning, splashing, speaking the names of their friends. In a minute, Jules's lips are next to my ear. "I'm here." I seize his hand and pull him to standing. "We have to keep moving," I say, though I don't know how or why I know this, or where in this absolute darkness we should go, when any step could send us down shafts to certain death, or any turn could open out into rooms full of Wehrmacht soldiers.

But we do move. And the others with us. Each with a hand on the shoulder of the one in front. I am leading the way, keeping my outstretched fingers on a damp wall, inching my feet forward to assure myself of solid ground, keeping to the edge of the shallow stream. And soon I realize that the darkness here isn't as absolute as it seemed at first. There, far ahead, is not black but a faint gray, so a light source of some kind, perhaps a torch, an opening to the world above and the last of the November daylight. I picture Yvette, bloodied, collapsed, frozen in the street on the Champs-Élysées. I see Charlotte, fighting back. Hear again the guns. Wonder where we are and what might be above us, what the light will show, what will be exposed.

I know about the caves, of course—the thousands of kilometers of sewers and caverns and tunnels that run deep under the streets of Paris, even deeper than the Metro in many places. There are underground lakes. The famous burial vaults where untold numbers of skeletons are stacked from years, decades, even centuries past when the city ran out of room for interring the dead aboveground and carted them down into the Catacombs instead. Many of the caves are left from limestone mining that has long since ended, leaving this, a subterranean Paris, with thousands of entrances, many in unexpected locations like the one we just scrambled down, literally right under our feet.

As we press on, we see a flickering electric light, then, drawing closer still, more lights at the edge of a cavern and a musty, dank smell coming from—what? A black underground field.

"Mushrooms," someone whispers. I turn to her voice and can just make out her features: a girl, perhaps Charlotte's age. It's hard to tell for sure. Her face is caked with mud, or perhaps blood.

Before any of the rest of us can speak, we see what appear to be three torches across the field, bobbing up and down, soon enough revealing the three men holding them, approaching us.

"Halt!" one of them shouts. They draw closer. One is holding a shotgun, the barrel bent forward over his arm, the stock tucked against his side. He locks the barrel into place with a loud metallic sound.

Jules pulls on my arm. "Run!" he whispers.

"Where?" I answer. "Our chances are better here."

"Or they will turn us over to the police or the Nazis," he says. He is trembling. Or perhaps I am the one trembling. There are four others with us, one of them the woman who recognized the mushrooms. They are holding on to one another like frightened children, inching away from the men, from the gun, which is still pointed at us.

I take a deep breath and a brave step forward. "Please," I say. "We need your help. We have stumbled here, escaping the Nazis."

None of the men speak at first, but the gunman finally nods and waves the barrel to signal a direction. Without another word, they lead the way and we follow, out of the widened cavern and back to narrow passageways where we can feel the walls on both sides. They stop suddenly. A wooden ladder anchored in stone rises up into darkness above. Next to it is a pulley with a wide bucket, half-filled with dirt-smeared mushrooms.

"Here," one of the men says. "Go quickly. And don't come back."

They leave us there, vanishing down a tunnel, and once again we're enveloped in darkness. We feel our way to the ladder. We climb, wondering how the world on the streets above us will have changed.

I am shaking when we emerge. I'm not like Charlotte. I have never disobeyed anyone before, certainly never run away from police or hidden in the underworld from Wehrmacht soldiers. We are in an alley, but I don't know where. It is night, and the streets are quiet, empty. Everyone has gone home. Or been arrested and detained. Or killed.

Jules is crying softly and shaking. I pull him into a hug until I feel his heart beating next to mine. We step apart and wander the unfamiliar streets as it starts to rain, trying to find out where we are. Twice we hear the screech of tires, and we dive into shadows, but nothing and no one passes. We cling to each other like frightened children, wanting nothing more than to be home and safe once again. And fearing that we may never be safe again.

Eventually we turn a corner and before us is the Seine, the banks swelling up with the downpour. From there, all the landmarks of Paris reveal themselves and we know where we are and where we need to go. We reach the moment where Jules turns away from me and I from him, and we head in our opposite directions. We used to live in the same apartment building, but after his father was taken, Jules and his mother had to move to another arrondissement to stay with his aunt Margaux. Though two or three kilometers away, I don't stop running until I am home, and I pray that Jules got safely home as well. I slip into the building, then climb the stairs, quietly, anxiously. Knowing Maman will be so worried and Papa will be furious.

Maman sweeps me into her arms the minute I step inside, crushing me against her. "Oh, look at how wet you are! Where have you been? Do you have any idea how upset I am with you?"

She says this—not giving me time to answer—but she doesn't seem upset. She seems happy as she wraps me in a towel, gives me a glass of water, and more water, and bread. I drink and eat, and only then does Maman try to speak to me to ask what happened.

I lie to her. "Jules and I only attended a wreath ceremony at the protest on the Champs-Élysées," I say. "For Armistice Day. We didn't know the police and the Wehrmacht would be there. We were on our bicycles riding past."

I tell her we left before the march and that I fell while I was riding and wasn't able to get home until late because the Nazis closed the streets. We heard about their attack on the marchers from others. We hid at a friend's. I don't tell her about Yvette being beaten into bloody unconsciousness, a rag doll tossed to the ground. Or about our wild sprint off the Champs-Élysées, the tumble into the underground, the mushroom men, the midnight race home in the rain.

"And Charlotte?" Maman asks. "Was she there? Did you see her? Is she all right?"

"Only briefly," I say. "I think it was her I saw. But I'm sure she's fine."

Maman nods. This is not the first time Charlotte has stayed out so late, or failed to come home at all. She always tells Maman that she is busy studying, sleeping over at a friend's apartment near the Sorbonne. Tonight, though, is different. Maman whispers a prayer for Charlotte's safety. I close my eyes and bow with her.

Afterward, Maman leads me to la salle de bain, fills a bath, and takes my mud-smeared clothes as I scrub my face, my hair, my skin until I feel I have shed a layer of who I had been, until I burn, until I am clean.

"Oh, what have you done to your hair, Nicolette?" she asks.

I tell her I'm sorry, that I should have asked for her permission. That I thought if my hair was shorter—short enough to hide under my cap—and if they thought I was a boy, they might let me race . . .

Maman shakes her head. "We'll have to think of something to tell Papa."

I look around the apartment, as if I'll discover him hiding somewhere. Only then do I think to ask where he is, though I'm afraid when I do that the next thing I hear will be his angry voice, shouting at me.

Maman clears her throat. "He was called to an emergency meeting at the Préfecture de Police."

"Emergency meeting?" I repeat it as a question.

"With the Wehrmacht," she says. "About the protest. There have been many arrests . . ." She trails off. I don't know what to say. What to think. So I am silent. Maman doesn't want to explain.

"I'll take care of these dirty things," she says, gathering my clothes. "You should hurry to bed."

School the next day is a blur. Everyone is talking about what happened, but I speak to no one, not even those who mention my hair. Everyone seems to stare. I am worried sick about Charlotte. I am worried sick about Yvette, who is not in school. Every time I am approached, I shake my head. My meaning is clear. Even the teachers do not scold me when I don't respond to questions. They can see in my face, perhaps, that I am only present in my body but not in my mind. In my mind I am seething, hating the Nazis and angry at the police as well, the ones on the streets with their bloody batons.

And what about Papa, who, like Charlotte, never came home last night? He wasn't out on the street with the Police Nationale. He doesn't wear a uniform. He wears a gray plaid suit, a waistcoat and suspenders, a proper overcoat, a black homburg. In the past, when Papa said anything about his job it was just to complain to Maman about his superiors, to grumble about budgets and scheduling and review boards and citizen complaints. Now I'm wondering if he could have known what was to happen yesterday. If he could have been involved in planning the police action with the Germans.

But how can I have these questions, these doubts, about Papa, who I have idolized all my life; who taught me all I know and love about cycling; who insisted I learn how to repair tires, true bike wheels, oil and clean chains, adjust derailleurs, replace brake pads, tighten cables on his beloved Favor, even though I am a girl; who has taken Jules and me countless times to the Vélodrome d'Hiver to see our cycling heroes, to watch the time trials and pursuits, and hours and hours of the six-day team races in which Papa himself once competed. It was for me, but also for him—even though I know he will be angry—that I cut my hair so short yesterday in the hope that I will be allowed to race someday, if the organizers think that I, too, am a boy.

As soon as school is out, Jules and I rendezvous. He attends the Lycée Rollin in Montmartre, in the shadow of Sacré-Cœur with its soaring towers and domed roof. I am at the boring, boxy

Jules-Ferry Lycée for girls, a few blocks away. We get an address for Yvette a short walk from our school and go to her apartment. Her mother answers the door. She looks older than a mother. Much older. Her hair is unwashed and hangs in her face, and she wears no makeup.

"We are Yvette's friends," I say. "We came to see her. Is she here? Is she all right?"

Her mother stares at us, her face blank, before she steps aside for us to enter and leads us down a short hallway. Yvette sits in a chair by a window, but the curtains are closed. On hearing us she looks up, but we can't see her face. Just the outline of her from what faint light leaks in from the shuttered window. Her head is heavily bandaged.

"Yvette. We saw what happened to you," Jules says. "I'm sorry we couldn't help."

She nods.

"How badly are you injured?" I ask. "How did you get away?"

She turns her head slightly to look in my direction, but I can't tell if her gaze actually finds me. She doesn't answer.

"What can we do to help you?" Jules asks. "You were very brave. We saw you try to stop the police from clubbing the others."

"They were talking about it in school," I say, though I don't know that to be true since I had conversations with no one all day. "Everyone was proud of you and worried about you."

Yvette seems to have her eyes closed now.

Finally, as we rise to take our leave, Yvette reaches for my arm and pulls me close to her. She whispers in my ear, "Fight back."

• • •

Jules and I speak very little at first, both of us lost in thought. We have to pass through two Wehrmacht checkpoints and show our identification papers—and make up lies about where we are going—on our way back to the Champs-Élysées to retrieve our hidden bicycles. Everything seems different overnight. The German soldiers, who were lackadaisical before, often just waving us through without bothering to even ask for our papers, now have their weapons drawn and trained on us, on everyone passing through the concrete barriers and coiled wire fencing. They study our identification. They ask questions in German or broken French and bark louder if we don't understand. We are nervous, ducking into the alley where we left the bikes, then walking them back to my arrondissement. Our thin racing tires, fine for smooth pavement on the wider boulevards, are no match for cobblestone and brick. There is a bloodstain on the sidewalk. Jules and I return the bikes to the storage shed in the courtyard of my apartment building—the lock is broken; it's easy to get in.

We promise to meet up after school tomorrow, and then go our separate ways.

I am so tired, it feels as though I am having to drag myself up the stairs to the apartment. Maman isn't home. Perhaps she's at the market or the boulangerie run by our upstairs neighbors, Madame and Monsieur Asher. Maman and Madame Asher are best friends. I stumble into the bedroom I share with Charlotte and am surprised and happy to find her, sprawled on her bed. She sits up suddenly when I open the door. Her long red hair is matted, her face streaked with dirt, her sweater torn.

"Did the Nazis do this?" I ask, quickly shutting the door and crossing the room to her. "Or the police?

Charlotte shakes her head. "No. Well, yes. Perhaps. Do you know what happened yesterday?"

"Of course," I say. "I was there, at the march. With Jules. I saw you in the crowd. Did you escape?"

She nods. "It was such chaos. We did what we could to help the others. Antoine was in a fight with two police officers. His friends helped him get away. We had to run when the soldiers attacked. Most escaped, but not all."

I tell her about Jules and me, about Yvette and running and the underground. I tell her Papa doesn't know. Yet. He was in meetings. He hasn't been home . . .

"Meetings?" she says.

I can't look at her when I answer. "With the Nazis."

Charlotte curses under her breath. She tries to change the subject. "At least no one was killed," she says. "None we know about, anyway. But dozens were arrested. We followed them to La Santé prison. A guard who is friendly to the cause told us this morning they were stripped, slapped, beaten. Made to stand out in the cold rain for much of the night. Some were lined up against a wall and the Nazis pretended they were to be executed by firing squad."

Horrified, I ask, "But you don't think Papa could have had anything to do with it?"

"You said he was in meetings," she responds, as if that's an answer.

But I desperately want her to reassure me. "Perhaps it was

Papa who stopped the executioners—convinced them to only frighten the protesters, to warn them . . ." My voice trails off.

"Perhaps," Charlotte says. "Or maybe the attack on the protest, the arrests, the mock executions, the beatings were his ideas. How are we to know?"

3

TROIS

Maman, Charlotte, and I go to the Ashers' apartment that evening to listen to General de Gaulle, broadcasting from London on the BBC. Papa is still at work, and Maman says we have time before he comes home. The Nazis have banned and confiscated all radios, or all they can find. The Ashers keep theirs hidden and only take it out at night, in a darkened room, with blankets nailed to the walls to hide the sound. Papa would be angry if he knew we were here, though he may already suspect what we've been doing these past months when we visit the Ashers. I get tired and bored sometimes, and always bring one of Papa's old cycling magazines. But Maman, Charlotte, and the Ashers hang on to every word from de Gaulle, who escaped France back in the spring only a few days—maybe only a few hours—before the Wehrmacht closed in: "Whatever may happen, the flame of French resistance must not go out; it *shall* not go out."

The Ashers, who are Jewish, are disheartened that America has not entered the war. Maman doesn't know what to think.

Charlotte is of course furious at anyone and everyone who won't join the fight. The only countries standing up to Hitler so far are Great Britain and Canada, and the voice we hear most often is the new British prime minister, Winston Churchill. The BBC carries his speeches from the Parliament, but my English is limited and I only understand a little of what he says.

Monsieur Asher translates: "We shall not flag or fail. We shall go on to the end. We shall fight in France and on the seas and oceans; we shall fight with growing confidence and growing strength in the air. We shall defend our island whatever the cost may be. We shall fight on beaches, landing grounds, in fields, in streets, and on the hills. We shall never surrender . . ."

We are back in our apartment when Papa arrives. He sees me right away—sees my hair, or what's left of it—before he even sits down in the living room. A single lamp has been left on, casting a dim light. "What have you done? Who gave permission for this?" he demands. Maman comes out of the kitchen but holds back as he glares at her, as if she must be responsible. It is hard to believe, with all that has happened—the protest, the police riot, the arrests, all of Paris in turmoil—that Papa only seems to care about this.

Charlotte steps in. "It's my fault," she says. "Nicolette wanted a bob. All the girls have them at her school. I'm sure it will grow back soon enough."

I'm not used to Charlotte trying to placate Papa. Usually she just argues with him, which only makes him more incensed. I have been afraid that she will confront him about his meeting with the Nazis, but she says nothing about that. I can tell he's thrown off. "Is this true?" he asks Maman. Charlotte rolls her eyes.

"It's not really so short as all that," Maman assures him, not actually answering his question.

Papa waves as if to dismiss the conversation but still stares at my hair and still shakes his head. I hate that I can't tell him about my plans with Jules to enter a junior amateur road race in two weeks—if it's not snowing by then. Thirty kilometers on a five-kilometer circuit around the Bois de Boulogne. Of course I will never be allowed if the organizers realize I am a girl. But with my short hair, dirt smudged on my cheeks, my cycling cap, and Papa's racing jersey, maybe it will work.

Papa never gets up from his chair, doesn't bother to switch off the light. Exhausted from his long day and night at the Police Nationale headquarters, he falls asleep there, as often happens. And as also often happens, Charlotte gets into bed with her clothes on, waits until Maman turns off the lights and closes their own bedroom door, and then Charlotte slips out from under the covers. She never tells me where she's going when she climbs out the window, but tonight I follow her, and from the balcony see her with Antoine down on the street. They kiss hello before disappearing into the shadows.

Maman wakes me early in the morning. Charlotte is back in bed, though I never heard her return. She pulls a pillow over her head and rolls toward the wall.

"You will go to the Ashers' boulangerie this morning before school," Maman tells me. "For work."

I protest that I haven't had breakfast, that I've only just woken up, that Charlotte should be sent instead.

"The Ashers will have something for you to eat," Maman says. "Papa and I have decided you need to become more productive, and I have convinced him to let you work at the boulangerie. You will help them until it's time for school, and some weekend mornings and afternoons, as you are needed. I will be down later."

Papa is sitting at the dining room table with his coffee and the German newspaper. "It will be good for you to keep busy, Nicolette," he says when he sees me. "So far, it is still legal for Jews to own their own businesses, but you must be careful and come home straight away at the first sign of any trouble with the Ashers."

Madame Asher greets me at the door of the boulangerie. Already there is a line, as everyone in the neighborhood has come for their morning baguettes. She hands me an apron with a sunflower pattern. "Will you help Monsieur Asher in the kitchen?" she asks, though she doesn't wait for an answer. She shoves a madeleine into my hand and gently turns me toward the back of the store. The smell of the boulangerie always makes me so happy—and hungry!

Monsieur Asher is a ghost, or at least he looks like one in the gloom of the back room. His face is white from flour—from, I suspect, his hands when he has to scratch his nose and cheeks and forgets where they have been. His arms are also covered in flour, and there are white handprints on his apron, everywhere. He directs me to pull the last batch of baguettes from the oven before they burn, while he finishes preparing the tarts, croissants, and pain au chocolat.

"I am so glad you are here today, Nicolette," he says. "So many customers! So many orders. I fear we will run out of flour, of all our ingredients."

"But you will get more?" I ask. "For next week?"

"That is the question," he says. "There is talk of rationing. I have not heard from any of our suppliers lately." He gestures toward the storeroom. "We're nearly empty. Of everything."

"Charlotte says the Nazis will take our food," I say. "For their army. To send back to Germany for their people. She says they will turn us into their slaves."

Monsieur Asher doesn't look at me when he responds. "It is best to not speak in this way. We must do our work, mind our business, do as we are told." He glances nervously at the door to the front of the store. Through the small window I see Madame Asher in conversation with a customer—one I recognize from the neighborhood. A woman who is Maman's age, though taller, elegant in her hat and gloves. Madame Asher has a grim look on her face and is shaking her head. Other customers are keeping their distance. Madame Asher raises her voice. I can hear her, but not what she's saying. The woman turns on her heel and marches out of the boulangerie. A few other customers follow.

One practically spits a word I hear all too clearly, even from the back room: "Juive!"

Jew.

Madame Asher brushes a sleeve over her forehead, then returns to the counter and waiting on customers. Monsieur Asher stands frozen. Unsure what to do, I fit the baguettes into a wide woven basket, on a cloth laid carefully at the bottom, and bring them out front.

Later, after the morning rush has finished and I am sweeping, I overhear the Ashers talking about the woman who came in. She accused Madame Asher of mixing sawdust with her flour. She said she wouldn't stand for it. She would find another boulangerie, and she would tell all her friends to avoid the Ashers'. Then she said, "But what could one expect from the Jews anyway?" It's good the woman is already gone, as I doubt I would have been able to hold my tongue if I'd heard what she said.

Charlotte is up when I get home from the boulangerie and I tell her what happened. I am worried that Papa will hear about it, too, and forbid me from returning. But instead of being angry at the woman, Charlotte criticizes me for standing by and doing nothing. "These French antisemites are as bad as the Germans," she snaps. "Worse. Perhaps the Germans can pretend they don't know any better, that they were raised to be this way. Some excuse. But the French—we can have no excuse. And there is no excuse for you to remain silent in the face of such hatred and bigotry."

I'm ashamed of myself but don't want to admit it. So I ask Charlotte why she is so angry all the time—at me, at Papa, at everything.

She turns it around on me, the way she always does. "Better you should be asking yourself, Nicolette: How can you *not* be angry all the time?"

I am taken aback. An icy silence descends over the room. I know she is right, but I refuse to tell her that. Plus I can be as stubborn as Charlotte in my own way—usually by withdrawing, as I do now. Instead of replying, I throw myself on my bed with a book, refusing to look at her or acknowledge the truth of what she said.

"Oh, Nicolette," Charlotte says with a sigh. "Here I've been criticizing you, but I forgot to congratulate you. My little sister, growing up so fast!"

"What do you mean?" I ask, genuinely curious, already forgetting my book.

"Why, your first job, of course," she says. "At the boulangerie."

"Ha," I say dismissively. "It's not as if I'm getting paid anything."

"Au contraire," Charlotte replies. "A job is a job. And there are child labor laws in France. At least I don't think the Germans have overturned them yet. Therefore, you could not have a job—paid or unpaid—if you were a child. Therefore, you must be a young woman now. Therefore, you can no longer be my *little* sister. Therefore—"

She has me laughing now at her absurd attempts at logic. Charlotte hugs me and I hug her back. I have never been able to stay mad at her for very long. She feathers my short hair through her fingers, then reaches for her brush so she can attack a nest of tangles that I somehow missed. Once the knots are gone, she grabs her scissors and says, "Now how about if I even things up a little for you in the back?"

Jules comes over the next evening. Papa meets him on the landing and they walk in together. Papa is asking Jules about his father, who was also Papa's longtime friend.

"And have you heard from him? A letter, perhaps? A notice from the Red Cross?"

Jules shakes his head and says, "No, monsieur, not one word from him or anyone else in his unit."

The stricken look on his face breaks my heart all over again. Any time the subject of Jules's father comes up, he is in despair. I think about how hopeful he was back in the spring, how hopeful we all were, when his father left to fight the Nazis. We were all so foolish back then. Our great army, two million strong, cut in half in the Blitzkrieg after one month of the great Battle of France. Those who weren't able to make it to the coast, to Dunkirk, and somehow survive, were captured in the east, and now languish like Jules's father in prisoner of war camps, hundreds of kilometers deep inside Germany. Jules and his mother and his aunt Margaux have been desperate to hear from him, to hear anything, to be assured that he is still alive, that he is not wounded or suffering, that there is a timetable for his safe return. Already there has been talk of the Nazis freeing those soldiers who have given up their arms. But so far, nothing.

Jules doesn't have to tell Papa any of this, of course. The look on his face says everything. It is not Papa's way to be reassuring, though, no matter how badly Jules or anyone else needs to hear it.

"The Nazis are reasonable people," Papa says. "Of course Herr Hitler can say some things that are inflammatory, even frightening, but one must distinguish between political talk and the actions a government takes. As they say, the trains now run on time in Germany. We have seen that the efficiency of the Wehrmacht—and I hate that it is true—did put to shame our French army, God help us. But fear not, young man. Your father will be released and sent home soon enough. You must be patient and accept that these things may take weeks or even months, as so much has happened so quickly. We do our part now in Paris, in all of France, to show that we will cooperate, of course. And we will be rewarded by the trust of the Nazis, who I have no doubt will withdraw most of their troops once they have established their defenses on the Atlantic, and secured their access to our ports, and once we have proven to them that we will be their most peaceful neighbor and nothing more."

He has accepted a glass of wine from Maman now and settled into his chair. Jules and I are standing in front of him like dutiful soldiers ourselves, waiting for his speech to end so we can be dismissed.

"In the meantime, we would be wise to learn from the Germans," Papa continues, oblivious to our impatience. "Discipline. National pride. An end to this open door policy for undesirables that is undermining the very fabric of our lives in France. We have been corrupted quite enough by the hordes that have infiltrated our great land. We have been too generous. We have ignored the dangers. Germany sees all this much more clearly than France and has taken the necessary steps to reclaim Germany for the German people. There have been far too many immigrants from Eastern Europe and North Africa coming here, thinking France owes them sanctuary."

He pauses to sip his wine. I sometimes wonder if he truly believes what he's saying about the Germans, or if he's trying to convince us—or, really, trying to convince himself.

He calls to Maman to refill his glass, and she's by his side immediately. It bothers Charlotte how much and how willingly Maman waits on Papa. "Why can't he do anything for himself once in a while?" she says. "It is not women's place to merely serve their men. Especially now, when so many of our men are in German prisons, and it's the women who are doing most of the work in factories and stores."

Maman protests that she does these things because she loves Papa, and because Papa works so hard at the police, keeping us, keeping all of Paris, safe. Charlotte just rolls her eyes.

Jules and I eventually make our escape when Maman calls Papa into the dining room. We go out on the balcony to plot our strategy for the upcoming cycling race, which we convince ourselves we're certain to win, though I've never been in a race before, and Jules has only been in two—and those were more like pretend races for little boys. There is also the problem of our bicycles—our *fathers'* bicycles—being just slightly too big for us, which means we can barely sit to ride, so we spend most of our time standing on the pedals. But having practiced on the roads and paths through the Bois de Boulogne, and with fathers who both raced back in their day, we're sure we're ready to set the cycling world on fire as the new champion tandem of Nicholas and Jules.

We have just settled ourselves, huddled together under a heavy horsehair blanket against the cold November night, when we hear Charlotte shouting. We hurry back inside and see her holding a sheaf of handwritten letters from Papa's briefcase.

"How can you have these?" she is demanding. "What are you doing with these—these lettres anonymes—these poison-pen letters? Is this your work now? Investigating slander? Anonymous neighbors turning on one another? Is this who we have become under the Nazis? Is this who *you* have become, Papa?"

Papa stands from the table and storms into the living room. He orders Charlotte to return what she has found, but she refuses. She pulls a letter from a folder and reads it out loud: "'Since you are cracking down on the Jews, and if your campaign is not just a vain word, then have a look at the kind of life led by the girl Marie Fournier, who calls herself an artist, now living in the French Quarter. This creature, for whom being Jewish is not enough, pursues the husbands of proper Frenchwomen. Also she makes derogatory statements—openly—against Vichy and against our German friends. And it is rumored that she consorts with communists. She should be investigated.'"

"Enough!" Papa shouts, seizing the papers from Charlotte, ripping them from her trembling hands. "This is official police business. Confidential. It is none of your concern."

"How could you?" Charlotte asks again, her face twisted with outrage.

He won't look at her, won't look at any of us, including Maman. Papa busies himself stuffing the papers back into his briefcase. Maman whispers to Jules that it would be best for him to go now. He touches my arm and then quickly leaves. Charlotte retreats to the bedroom. I hear her throwing clothes into her travel case—and sobbing. I remain frozen, unable to speak, unable to think, even as Charlotte emerges, hugs Maman and then me, and refuses to speak to Papa on her way out the door.

4

QUATRE

A week goes by and we hear nothing from Charlotte. I can barely sleep at night, sick with worry about her. Maman and Papa talk in low voices for hours in their bedroom, and though the sound carries, I can't make out the words. Papa leaves every morning at first light, often before I am up. He is angry all the time, but I don't know if it is because of the fight with Charlotte and her leaving us, or if it is the work he is having to do at the Police Nationale.

Maman continues to insist that I go down to help the Ashers at the boulangerie. Jules, too, has a job now—waiting in shopping lines at the boucheries for rich people who insist on having their allotment of meats but can't be bothered to spend the hours now required to cash in their ration tickets. When the weekend comes, I am up at dawn and busy at the boulangerie until the Ashers send me home at noon. I'm just walking through the door of our apartment building when Jules shows up on his father's bicycle. He is wearing his papa's oversized cycling gear and favorite Peugeot cap.

"Ready?" he asks, though it's obvious that I'm not.

"I'm sorry," I tell him. "It's just—I'm so tired. And we haven't trained for nearly two weeks. And—" I stop. Normally none of this would matter. I'd be running out the door and on my bike already.

"And what?" he asks, clearly disappointed.

"And my heart is no longer in racing," I realize. "With Charlotte gone. And Papa the way he is. And everything that has happened."

But Jules isn't ready to give up. "All the more reason for us to race," he says. "It's what they want, the Germans. To beat us down. To make us so tired that we no longer care. Please, Nicolette. We can do this together. We do this for my father. We do this for France!"

I have to laugh, though it's not really funny. Jules manages to smile, too, knowing how over the top his speech must sound. I let myself be convinced.

We ride carefully back to the Bois de Boulogne on the west bank of the Seine, taking a longer route on streets that are mostly paved, for the thin racing tires on the Favors, but still having to weave around potholes and cracks and cobblestone patches. No one questions me when I give the name Nicholas with my shorter hair tucked under my cap. There is much jostling for position at the front of the pack. Several cyclists and their bikes are shoved to the ground—and it's still fifteen minutes before race time.

More than enough time for police to come—a dozen uniformed officers mounted on horses—and announce that all public gatherings are suspended until further notice. By order of the Police Nationale.

The organizers are outraged. "But these are young people,"

one argues. "Junior amateurs." As if that should matter. He is clenching the entry fees in one hand and waving a clipboard with the other. I'm guessing he doesn't want to give back the money. The officer looks at him, looks down at the fistful of francs, looks at him again as if expecting a bribe. But he only repeats himself.

"All public gatherings are suspended—are banned—until further notice."

The organizer stuffs the francs into his pocket. "And when will that be?"

The officer shrugs. "Ask Herr Hitler."

The organizer turns to the peloton, waves his clipboard, announces that the entry fees are unfortunately nonrefundable, then he makes a quick exit, ducking behind the horses and the Police Nationale before anyone can dismount and give chase—or see what direction he takes so we might pursue him on our bicycles to demand our money.

Jules and I are still sitting on a curb, dejected, long after the other riders vanish. "At least we know you can pass as a boy," he finally says, breaking the silence.

A few days later, when I'm sweeping in the front of the boulangerie, I see the offensive woman from the week before, walking past on the boulevard. Monsieur Asher has gone out to the alley with the trash. Madame Asher is busy with a few late customers. My heart races.

I take a deep breath, step into the back of the boulangerie, and plunge the scoop into a barrel of flour. With Charlotte's criticism and echoes of the lettres anonymes she found in Papa's briefcase still ringing in my ears, I rush through the store and onto the sidewalk.

"Mademoiselle! Mademoiselle!" I shout. "S'il vous plaît!"

She turns. Stares at me with obvious disdain. Corrects me. "Madame."

"Excusez-moi," I say, all apologies and smiles. Then I throw the flour in her face. As she is choking, slapping herself to get it out of her mouth and nose and eyes, I hiss at her. "So you can see, no sawdust. Just flour."

Word gets back to the boulangerie almost quicker than I can return. Madame Asher drags me into the back, away from customers, though the store is practically empty. "What are you thinking? You have made things so much worse for us! We must keep our heads low, especially now with the Nazis here. You know they hate us Jews. Even French Jews. Even those like Monsieur Asher and me, who have always lived here."

"But she spoke that slander," I say. "And Charlotte said—"

But Madame Asher cuts me off. "There are worse things, Nicolette. So much worse."

I think she will say more, but her anger is already fading. She seems to become smaller all of a sudden. I apologize. It takes a moment to realize Madame Asher is crying again. Softly, silently. Even when Monsieur Asher comes to look for her.

"Here now," he says. "Here now. What is this?"

Madame Asher shakes her head. "Nicolette is upset that Charlotte has still not come home," she says, lying to cover up what I have done.

Monsieur Asher nods. "But I'm sure she will return soon," he says. "Of course everything will be smoothed over. Your father and Charlotte, they are people of strong opinion, of strong conviction. A little time apart, and then they will be sharing a glass of wine, and all will be right with the world."

I nod, even though I know as sure as I have ever known anything in my small life that our world will never again be all right. One look into Monsieur Asher's eyes and it is clear that he knows this as well. But we still speak the words people expect to hear, because what other choice do we have?

The next day, when the Ashers rise as early as they do—at four, despite the Nazi curfew, quietly slipping into the store to begin baking the day's bread—they find painted on the front door, *A warning: These Jew bakers use sawdust and piss in their flour.* They have painted over it by the time I come in to work. But people already know. A customer, an old lady who also lives in our building, whispers it to me. "You must be careful from now on, coming here," she says.

Maman comes into my bedroom that night when I am lying there in the dark, unable to sleep, my mind racing with the events of the past several days. I don't know if she has heard about what I did to the offensive woman. I hear the tramp, tramp, tramp of Wehrmacht jackboots marching in formation on the street outside, or at least I imagine that's what I hear. Because what would they be doing here at this time?

I pretend to be asleep. I am ashamed of what I have done. Or not ashamed exactly, but certainly regretful that I have caused problems for the Ashers. But I would throw flour on the woman over and over again. I know this.

Maman doesn't speak. She lies next to me on the bed and

holds me, but I can't tell if she thinks I need her to comfort me, or if she needs me to comfort her. I know she doesn't believe as Papa does, that the Nazis coming, the occupation, is good for France. Better the fascists than the communists, he is always saying. As if we have been under siege by the communists. And as if those would be the only choices anyway. She tells me Papa has been doing all he can to protect us, and to protect those targeted in the lettres anonymes. "As often as possible, after the investigations, he determines them to be unfounded," she says. "Even when there might be some truth."

"But not always," I say.

"Please, Nicolette. You must understand," Maman says. "Papa does what he can."

There was a time when I would have believed her. But now I'm not so sure.

We stop talking after that. I match my breath to Maman's and soon I think she is asleep. I fall asleep as well, but it is a troubled sleep, with troubled dreams of the occupation, of Jules and me again chased by the soldiers, only this time not able to disappear into the tunnels. We are exposed in the middle of the boulevard, their half-tracks and tanks and infantry closing in on us. I look for Jules, but he has gone, crushed beneath one of their vehicles. Blood everywhere.

The school term drags to an end as December turns Paris colder and colder, seemingly by the hour. Already there is rationing of coal, and already it is so cold in our apartment, in everyone's apartments, that you can see your own breath when you wake up in the mornings to dress, because you can't stay shivering under blankets forever. I race down to the boulangerie to warm myself next to the ovens, but the rest of the shop is nearly as cold as outside.

Two days before Christmas, official flyers appear all over the city, signed only by "The Military Commander of France." The announcement is brief. Meant as a warning.

> *The engineer Jacques Bonsergent, of Paris, received a death sentence by the German military tribunal for an act of violence toward a member of the German army. He was shot this morning.*

The true story spreads quickly, how a group of young Frenchmen, drunk after a wedding in the country, came out of the Gare Saint-Lazare and stumbled into a group of equally drunk German soldiers. Perhaps there was some shoving, some shouting, cursing. Most of the Frenchmen got away. Monsieur Bonsergent was detained. He refused to name any of his friends. It was a trivial offense, after all. But the Nazis decided to make an example out of him. He was taken away, accused, found guilty, and executed.

Everyone is outraged by the execution, the unfairness of it, the brutality. In the days and weeks that follow, many talk about revenge on the Nazis, but of course it is only just that, only talk. Soon the outrage fades. But not with everyone. Someone tears down the German street signs in our neighborhood one night, and on another night a confiscated Peugeot festooned with swastikas is set on fire outside a café frequented by Nazi soldiers after hours. Jules and I see the charred remains. We stand there and stare, transfixed, even as workers come with a truck to drag it away, and more workers come with whitewash to cover what the vandals have painted in bold red letters on a nearby wall: *VIVE LA RÉSISTANCE!*

5

CINQ

Jules hates Hitler. I hate him, too, but Jules in his hatred has studied Hitler and can quote him at any time. "He only lies," Jules says. "And he is proud of his lies. He has said, 'If you tell a big enough lie and tell it frequently enough, it will be believed.' So if he promises that Germany will set free their prisoners of war, people will believe it whether he does it or not. But look how long it has been, and my father remains a prisoner."

We are in my room, huddled under blankets. It is now January. A new year, but nothing about it feels new. We are still under the German occupation. Our lives are still not our own. Jules has had to wade through high drifts of snow to get here, and soon he will have to leave because of the nightly curfew. To be caught out on the street would mean trouble, perhaps even jail.

But we have big plans for tonight. Or, rather, small plans, but big to us, despite the terrible cold. The Nazis have continued covering the city with propaganda, and we have decided that it is our job to tear down as much of it as we can in our arrondissement. It will be our revenge—the start of our revenge. For Yvette and the protesters who were beaten. For the targets of the lettres anonymes. For the Ashers. For Monsieur Bonsergent. For Jules's father.

Half an hour after Jules leaves, I tiptoe out of my bedroom, expecting Maman to already be asleep, but no, she is sitting at the kitchen table.

I sit with her. "Are you all right?" I ask. "Are you thinking about Charlotte?"

She nods. Christmas has come and gone and still we haven't seen Charlotte since she left. "I worry about her. She can be reckless, and this is no time to be reckless." She pulls a folded piece of paper from her apron. "I received this today. From Charlotte. She is still in the city. Still with Antoine. She says to tell you she will visit soon." Maman sighs. "But only when she is sure Papa is away."

I put my arm around Maman and promise her, in the same way she has sought to reassure me, that everything will be all right, that surely Charlotte will come back home and make her peace with Papa, even though it's been almost two months. The things Maman has said to me, I now say to her. I tell her that surely things will return to normal in Paris, that some of what Papa says must be true: that the Nazis will have to go back to their own country eventually and leave us alone, and everyone will return to the city, and the war will end. Maman leans her head on my shoulder and lets me go on and on like this, making up fairy tale after fairy tale about what will be.

Jules returns at midnight. I am waiting, window cracked open, letting in a little of the freezing air to keep me from falling asleep. For some reason I have been thinking about happier times, our two families' cycling vacations in the hills of Alsace when Jules and I were much younger. Papa arranged everything, of course: the bicycles, the hostels, the route (not too hard, not too easy), the grand hotel in Strasbourg where we stayed at the end of that glorious week. Papa and Jules's father engineered seats for us on the back of their bicycles where we could pretend to be pedaling. Jules and I would throw our little heads back and shout, "Faster, Papa! Faster!" It made them all laugh so hard they had to stop cycling.

Jules and I are meeting two of his friends from the lycée, Rowland and Paul. Rowland has been furious about the occupation, of course, but also about those Parisians who fled but could not bring their dogs, so they turned them loose or poisoned them—either way, leaving them to die in the streets.

There are still many abandoned animals in Paris. Street crews with their pushcarts pick up the carcasses of the ones that have died. Where they are taken is anyone's guess. Perhaps they are simply dumped into the Seine. Rowland has been collecting the ones that still live and were left to starve. He has several of these dogs he is keeping in a neighbor's empty apartment in his building, on the ground floor so they can also run and do their business in the walled courtyard. Earlier today we collected what food we could to help him feed them, but they are always hungry.

The boys are waiting for us in a small park a few blocks away. Snow flurries dance around our faces. We slip furtively through the alleys, spring across open boulevards—as best we can in the snow and slush. But no one is out. Not even the Nazi patrols, at least not in our arrondissement.

Paul, who is the most serious, scowls when we approach. He and Rowland are stamping their feet to stay warm. "We've been waiting a long time," he says. "It is dangerous to be in one place like this."

Jules apologizes, even though this was the time we said we would meet them. Rowland is just anxious. We all are. But we have our work to do.

Keeping to the shadows, Paul leads us to the first poster, on a high cathedral wall. It is an image of Joan of Arc, surrounded by flames, her hands manacled but also folded in prayer, her eyes closed but her face turned heavenward. *Know your friends! Be suspicious of those who call themselves your allies. The British killed Joan of Arc!*

Paul slashes through it with his pocketknife. Again and again until it is shredded. We seize the hanging remnants and tear them away. Then on to the next poster, halfway down the block. And the next one after that. Some are the same: Joan of Arc, burning at the stake, and the indictment of the British. Some are mocking Winston Churchill, with a cartoon image of him, shorter, fatter, dog-faced, and an inscription that says he wants only to preserve the British Empire and that he has no love for France. We destroy those as well. In a mad frenzy we race down the street and over to the next block and more beyond, slashing, tearing, destroying, stomping, cursing.

We are interrupted by the sound of tires on slick pavement. Headlights flash a block away, coming in our direction. More headlights. A loudspeaker shouting in German, but we know the meaning. We are caught! And so we run.

Doors slam behind us. A thunder of boots. Whistles blasting

in the night. More shouts. Orders to halt. My heart is in my throat. I pray they won't shoot us. We keep sprinting. Then Rowland falls, sprawling onto a bare patch of street, yelling for us to stop, to help him, but we can't. We would all be caught. We must go on. I glance back, see him struggling to stand, but already a swarm of Nazis in their gray-green uniforms are on him. Jules, Paul, and I make our escape. The soldiers aren't chasing us any longer. We can't hear them, at least. The others protest—we have to keeping running—but I sneak back to see what has happened to Rowland. The soldiers are surrounding him, pushing him back and forth among them. They are laughing hard as he is terrorized. I can hear him crying, begging. A soldier lifts his weapon, points it at Rowland. Everything stops. Then Rowland grabs his pants. I think he has wet himself. The laughter starts up again and echoes through the neighborhood. Rowland sinks to the ground, sitting in his own piss, burying his face in his hands.

But one German steps forward, takes Rowland's elbows, and lifts him back to standing. He gives Rowland a rag to wipe his face. Rowland nods and squirms, then hands the German the rag, or tries to, but the soldier won't accept it. He raises his hands in a gesture to indicate this, that no, no, Rowland must keep it. Maybe Rowland thanks him. I can't hear what he says. I am deceived. I think for just this one minute that the Nazis aren't so bad. Just having their fun with a boy who has been up to a little mischief, but that's all. They have frightened him, yes, but perhaps they will even offer to give him a ride home. It has gotten quite late.

But what a fool I am to let my guard down, to think there can be any kindness from these Nazis. The one with the rag suddenly reaches forward and slaps Rowland hard across his face. Rowland staggers, and the soldier does it again, backhanded this time, and harder, on the other side of Rowland's face. Rowland clenches his fists but keeps his arms by his sides as the soldier slaps him yet again. I want to rush at them, bowl them over, rescue poor Rowland. But I don't move, don't make a sound, stay hidden half a block away.

The circle of soldiers parts then, and Rowland is shoved away. One of them has taken his identification card, though. I see him holding it up, waving it, as Rowland first stumbles, then begins walking, then running to get as far, far away from the soldiers as he can, though I'm thinking that nowhere can be far enough at this point to be safe anymore in Paris.

The next day I am helping Maman in the kitchen to prepare dinner, when Papa comes home from work. He is furious.

"You were destroying Nazi property? And your friends?" he demands. "What a stupid, foolish girl you are. Did you not think your little friend would give up your name and the others'? You are only fortunate that as your father I was able to address this at the central office, and it will hopefully go no further. But records are kept!"

He is yelling, so loud that Maman steps between us. She hates when he is angry, when he raises his voice, when he is disapproving—though usually it is of Charlotte. But now it is my turn.

"I'm so sorry, Papa," I say, though I only partially mean it. I'm sorry we were caught. Sorry he is in this rage. Sorry Maman is afraid of him sometimes, like now. Sorry Charlotte isn't here to stand up for me, to stand up to him. Sorry Jules and Paul and Rowland might not be protected as I am, by having a father who works for the Police Nationale.

"What of my friends?" I ask him, hoping beyond hope that he might be able to help them as well.

Papa waves the question away. "I have dealt with it. I have spoken with Jules's mother. And the parents of the other boys, Rowland and Paul. Rowland's papers have been returned. But he is on the watch list now. And he gave up all your names. So now Paul is also on the watch list."

"And me?" I ask. "And Jules?"

He shakes his head. "You are not. And in deference to Jules's father, I have managed to keep him off as well. For now. But this had better not happen again."

He calls Maman for his dinner. I am dismissed. There is no punishment—this time—except that I am ordered to never, ever again spend time with any of the boys. And that includes Jules. But I beg Papa, remind him that I have known Jules since we were little.

Papa sniffs and asks why I would want to spend my time with the likes of Jules anyway.

I take a step back. Papa has never said anything before about Jules. Not like this. Is it because his father is a prisoner of war? Or because Jules is a boy who likes boys? But in this moment, I don't care what Papa's answer might be.

"Jules is my friend," I say, looking him in the eye. "He will always be my friend."

• • •

In the coming days, the Nazis announce several new orders meant to restrict foreigners, especially Jewish ones. Sometimes these orders come directly from Hitler, sometimes through the French authorities. It doesn't matter—they are the same now. The harshest of these, for now, is that there can no longer be any employment for those not born of French parents. Only a few days after the edicts, we hear a BBC report that refugees and unemployed foreigners are being rounded up throughout occupied France and sent to detention camps.

The Ashers have been in France for generations, so they are safe. But Monsieur Asher is still skeptical about the future. "They will come for all the Jews," he says, shaking his head. Maman says surely not—and especially not those who have been good French citizens.

"Oh, they will start with the immigrants," Monsieur Asher says. "The ones from Germany, Poland, all the rest. But they will come after us as well. It is only a matter of time."

Madame Asher tells him to hush such talk. "Look at what the Nazis have done so far," she says. "They ordered the curfew. Changed street signs to German. Hung their propaganda posters. Started the rationing. All to be expected in wartime. So not so many changes really."

Monsieur Asher looks around, as if to make sure no one else can hear him, though it is just the four of us sitting in their quiet room with the illicit radio. Lately I have been listening much more intently to the news from London and to the Ashers' concerns.

"The Germans have taken the homes of many Jews," Monsieur Asher says. "From the minute they arrived, their officers knew which homes, which addresses. And everyone believes it is only a matter of time before the synagogue is shut down. And the street signs they are changing? Not only the names into German. Any name that sounds Jewish to them, they have renamed."

"But what can we do?" Madame Asher asks. "It is too late to leave."

Monsieur Asher shakes his head again. "It was always too late to leave. And already those who left are returning. Have you not noticed?"

But of course we have all noticed.

A yellow sign is pasted in the window of the Ashers' boulangerie the next week. It's there when I slip in to help them in the morning. *Juif*, it says. Meaning "Owned by Jews." Monsieur Asher just shrugs when I ask him about it. Madame Asher scowls. "These signs are all over," she says. "How efficient are these Germans, yes? One must be impressed." She pauses. "Is this your father's work as well?"

As soon as the words come out of her mouth, she quickly apologizes. "Forgive me," Madame Asher says. "I should not have said that."

I can only nod, because I have been wondering the same thing: Could this be Papa's work at the Police Nationale? I want to insist that it isn't possible. He would never do such a thing. Especially knowing how close Maman and Madame Asher have always been. But suddenly I am not sure.

"There is good news," Monsieur Asher says, oddly cheerful today. "Some of the Catholic businesses, they are putting the signs in their windows as well. In solidarity."

“They will have trouble,” Madame Asher says, shaking her head. But I can tell she likes hearing this.

“There are also reports that the yellow signs will keep the Germans out,” Monsieur Asher says. “Of course they would never shop in stores owned by us Jews. Ha! Even though we lose, we win. Right, Nicolette?” He elbows me as if we’re conspirators. I smile and nod. Happy that he’s making the best of this, but still discouraged and worried myself.

I leave the shop early that afternoon to ride my own bicycle to the Latin Quarter to find Jules, who I haven’t seen since the night we destroyed the propaganda posters. I miss him, though it hasn’t been that long. At home, without Charlotte anymore, I have been lonely. Also, Paris has become so quiet since the occupation. Quiet and dark. In most neighborhoods, the curfew has also meant electricity must be turned off. And few automobiles are out on the streets since the Germans ordered most of them surrendered for “purchase” by the authorities. Lines of cars were left at the vélodrome, with their owners walking away with little more than a slip of paper, the promise of a payment that most are certain will never come. So the narrow streets are quieter for all these reasons, made even darker by the crowded upstairs apartments that shade the shops and sidewalks and streets below. And darker still when the sun goes down because there are no headlights at night. And no streetlights, except on strategic corners where the Wehrmacht patrols hold fixed positions, and anyone passing must provide their identification and justification to be allowed to go through.

Jules’s aunt Margaux is asleep in her bedroom when I get

there. Jules says we have to whisper to not wake her because she works at a café frequented by Wehrmacht officers, which is why it is allowed to stay open so late and why she sleeps during the day.

We let ourselves out on the small balcony to talk. "My father said he was coming to see your mother about Rowland and the Germans," I tell Jules. "Rowland gave them our names."

He nods. "Oui. He didn't stay very long. There were two policemen with him, but he made them wait outside. He told me I needed to be very, very careful in what I do from now on. Who I'm with. How I behave."

Jules is no longer looking at me. He studies the tops of his shoes. Gazes over my head at something on the wall. He is keeping something from me. I know there is more.

"What else, Jules?" I ask.

Jules shrugs. "He gave me a fistful of francs and said I was to stay away from you. Or things would get very bad the next time he saw me." He pulls the money out to show me.

I snatch it from him, furious. "You will do no such thing. We will use this for supplies. For more work for the Resistance. Yes? Only we'll be more careful this time."

Jules smiles. "Of course," he says. "I was going to suggest the same thing."

And so that's what we do.

6

SIX

Later that afternoon, I am stopped at a checkpoint as I'm leaving the Latin Quarter, heading toward home. There is a line of bicycles, some pedestrians. I have been lost in thought about Jules and my father and what Jules told me about their encounter. The more I think about it, the angrier I get. Jules has been my closest friend my whole life. Our fathers were best friends. How could Papa do such a thing as try to buy off Jules?

The checkpoint line is barely moving, and I shake myself out of my reverie to see why. At the front are two young women, perhaps a few years older than Charlotte. They are talking to the young Wehrmacht soldiers. At first I think nothing of this, but then I hear the high trill of their laughter, a false laugh. I can't believe what I'm seeing and hearing. These women—these *French* women—cannot be flirting with German soldiers, not even a year into the occupation, with a million French soldiers still in prisoner of war camps, thousands killed, our fellow Parisians arrested or thrown out of their homes or forced to identify their businesses as owned by Jews—presumably so that "proper" Parisians will shop instead at Aryan shops.

But no. The young women—in their shiny shoes, carefully rolled socks, pleated skirts, floral-print blouses, trailing scarves, fashionable coats, and berets—are indeed flirting with the soldiers. It is warmer this afternoon than it's been in weeks. Even a little sun has managed its way through the heavy clouds that have hung over Paris since the start of the new year. The streets are mostly free of snow—for the moment. I inch forward, going around the line, to get closer so I can hear what they're saying. One of the soldiers speaks French and seems to be doing the talking for the others.

One of the women touches his sleeve. She runs the tips of her fingers over what may be his officer's stripes on the shoulder. The other soldiers elbow one another and say something to him in German. He translates for the women, tells them his friends think that they are much lovelier than the girls and women from their village back in Germany. There is more laughter, more touching, more translating, more compliments, questions about when they might see the women again, and might they meet at a café not far from there, perhaps this evening? Perhaps another night if tonight isn't possible?

The others in line are looking away, pretending this isn't happening. But like me, they must be eager to get somewhere else. Anywhere else.

I want to say something, tell them to stop flirting with the enemy. But I am invisible to them, to the Wehrmacht soldiers, to the others in line, and I find that I can't speak. I am a fourteen-year-old girl, dressed in trousers and suspenders and my father's old blue-and-white striped jersey.

So I don't speak. I bump the front tire of my Rollfast into the women's bicycles instead. The flirting stops as they turn to stare at me. I bump them again, deliberately but silently. I pull out my identification and wave it at the soldiers. They, too, have stopped their conversation with the girls. I keep bumping their bikes, pushing them ahead. The Germans tell me to halt as they pull the other bicycles forward. They shove my papers back at me and wave me on, but before they can turn their attention to the women again, the women, too, are pedaling away, though not without glancing behind and smiling at the handsome Nazis. I want to vomit. But the others who have been waiting—much longer than me—are relieved, because for whatever reason, at least the line is moving now and they are able to get through.

A block away from the checkpoint into our arrondissement I see something that surprises me so much I nearly crash my bicycle into a fruit stand. There on the opposite side of the street, pushing a baby stroller down the sidewalk, is Charlotte!

She sees me, too, standing awkwardly on my half-fallen bike, one leg of my trousers caught in the chain. She starts to step out into the street, but then looks down at the stroller. Checking on the baby inside? But whose baby?

I manage to drag myself and the bicycle across the street to where Charlotte is able to rescue me from the chain. I feel so stupid and embarrassed. She actually laughs, though.

"You have grease all over your trousers now," she says. "And on me as well. Look." She shows me her hands, now smeared with black. She wipes them on the bottom of my pants.

"Charlotte!" I say, but she just laughs again and says, "They were already stained."

I lean my bicycle against a low wall and sit next to her—and the stroller. I try to peek inside, under the blanket, but she stops me.

"Asleep?" I ask, the first of a hundred questions.

"In a manner of speaking," she says. "Not awake, anyway."

"Can I see?"

She glances furtively up and down the street, sees no one coming, and then nods. "Only pull down the blanket a little," she says.

I do. There's no baby. Naturally. But stacks of paper, arranged, I suppose, to look something like the outline of an infant. I lift a sheet, which is as thin as tissue. There is nothing on it. Puzzled, I look back at Charlotte.

"Papillon," she says. "Butterfly paper."

"For flyers?" I guess, though it isn't hard to figure out.

She nods again. "Oui. You can breathe word of this to no one. Not even Maman. And certainly not Papa. Do you understand?"

"Of course," I say, annoyed. "I'm not a child, you know."

"I must go," she says. "It is dangerous to invite attention."

"But right now it is only paper. Papillon," I say.

"They will know," she says, once again looking up and down the street. She straightens herself suddenly. Three Wehrmacht officers are rounding the corner, heading our way, so she grabs her stroller and begins pushing it in the opposite direction.

"Wait, Charlotte!" I say, following her with my bicycle. "Where are you staying? I want to see you. I miss you. I want to help."

She hesitates, blurts out an address, then hurries off, though trying to appear nonchalant, in a hurry, but not *really*. She doesn't look back.

• • •

It takes all my strength not to scream at Papa when he comes home that night—for what he said to Jules. Instead I hide away in my room, refusing to come out when Maman calls me to dinner, refusing even to open the door to her.

The next afternoon after school, I ring up from the lobby at Charlotte's address, a small, run-down apartment building that smells of cat urine and old cheese. I wait. I ring again. Finally there is a heavy tread on the stairs that wind down around a lift that doesn't seem to work. No one gets off or on, in any event.

It is a young woman. Her arm is in a sling and she walks with a limp. She asks my name. I tell her and add that I am Charlotte's sister. I hear the loud music from a phonograph before we step inside, and right away I see why it is turned up so high: to hide the sounds of a small hand-crank printing press churning out flyers—anti-German, anti-armistice, pro-Resistance—on the papillon paper I saw yesterday in the stroller.

Charlotte is the one turning the crank. Antoine stacks the flyers in neat piles, careful that he doesn't smear the ink. Charlotte mouths a hello. Antoine pauses to kiss my cheeks and say, "Bonjour, Nicolette." He apologizes that he can't stay to talk. Before, when he would visit our house, before the Germans, he would always make time for me, as long as Papa wasn't home. He would tease me about being a tomboy—an American expression he picked up from the movies. He would quiz me about world affairs he was certain we should be learning in school. Once, he even took me for a ride on his motorcycle. It was only around the block, and he never went higher than second gear, but I was still thrilled. He even let me wear his leather motorcycle jacket, though it was enormous on me. But today, once Charlotte finishes, he crams the flyers inside a canvas pouch, slings the pouch over his shoulder, and leaves straightaway.

"Antoine has to get back to his work," Charlotte says. "And there is little time for him to distribute the flyers. Everyone has a job. He has to be at the drop sites at precisely the right time. We cannot afford to arouse suspicion."

There is another knock on the door. The other woman, whose name is Annette, places the printing press in the stroller, covers it with the same baby blanket, and wheels it into the hall. I never see who has come to collect it.

I tell Charlotte again that I want to help, but she immediately says no. "I shouldn't have invited you here in the first place," she says. "It's too dangerous for you. Too dangerous for us if too many know what we are doing, and where. I don't know what I was thinking."

"But we have already been involved," I remind her. "Jules and I. We were at the march. And I have been going out at night. Climbing from the balcony—as you used to do."

Charlotte is surprised. "You knew?"

"Yes," I say. "And now I meet Jules and our friends out on the streets. We have destroyed the Nazis' propaganda posters."

I don't tell her that we only did it once—and that we were caught. She studies my face as if seeing me for the first time. "Did you know they have ordered the Sorbonne closed?" she asks. "I cannot go back to university even if I want to. So now this—the Resistance—this is what I do. But you would have to stay in your school, do you understand? Everything would have to remain as normal for you and Jules." She gestures at my clothes. "You would need to dress properly, like a good French schoolgirl, and not like a bicycle mechanic. You would need to be able to pass as innocent at all times, even if you were out in the night, after curfew. You would have to pretend to be a girl sneaking off to see a boy."

I nod. Of course. I will do whatever is necessary.

Annette hands us both a coffee. Charlotte clinks my mug with hers and says, "Salut."

Two days later, Jules and I get the signal—a woman in a red hat standing in the dirty snow on the corner across the street from the lycée. I recognize Annette right away but say nothing. When I am sure she is looking my way, I reach up to adjust my beret, which is the return signal, and she leaves. Jules and I meet halfway between our schools as usual and walk together toward our homes.

"Tonight we begin," I say as we part ways.

Jules bites his lip and nods.

At midnight I climb out my window onto the balcony, careful not to disturb the cages of baby chicks and baby rabbits Maman has had built just this week in anticipation of the food shortages that Charlotte had convinced her are coming.

I leave my heavy Rollfast and instead take Papa's Favor and pedal furiously across the city, convinced that I can outrace anyone who might try to catch me, until I find a certain small, secluded park not far from Charlotte and Antoine and Annette's apartment. Jules is already there and has already retrieved the thick stack of flyers left for us in the hollow trunk of a tree. We barely speak, barely breathe as we immediately set ourselves to work with brushes and paste, racing from wall to wall, filling every dry inch of space we can find on buildings, doors, columns, street signs. It is still freezing out. Soon we can't feel our fingers, but we press on, our breaths ragged, clouds of condensation forming around our numbed faces every time we exhale. When we hear, or think we hear, footsteps, the squealing of tires, engines revving off in the distance, we duck into whatever alley or doorway is nearest, or we just run. I don't know why Charlotte insisted I dress like a good French girl. All the scarves and berets and ribbons in France won't protect me if I'm caught. Plus it's not practical for riding Papa's racing bike. But orders are orders.

After three nervous hours, finally finished, or close enough, we litter the empty streets with the remaining flyers in hopes that pedestrians will pick them up and read them in the morning. I take a different way back to my apartment, jealous that Jules's arrondissement is much closer than mine. I'm relieved when I finally get home—and frozen, and exhausted, and proud of the work we've just done for the Resistance. It seems I have only just snuck back in and gone to bed when Maman is in my bedroom, shaking me back awake.

I sleepwalk through the morning working at the boulangerie before heading to the lycée. But despite my weariness, I am excited seeing people on the street with our flyers. I glance around to make sure there are no police and no soldiers, and pick one up myself. It is hard keeping our work a secret. Hard staying awake during classes. Hard being afraid every time I see a Wehrmacht soldier, every time there is a knock on the door, every time Jules is late, every time I hear a noise that shouldn't be.

But still, every afternoon after that, for the next month, even through the next heavy snow in early February, I look for Annette after school, or Charlotte, or a woman I don't know, wearing a red hat, standing on the corner across the street from my lycée, giving me another signal, summoning Jules and me for another long night of work for the Resistance.

7

SEPT

Now I live in two worlds. In one world, the visible world, there are Maman and Papa, and much of the rest of Paris, complaisant—accepting of the Nazi occupation and all that has come with it. But so far at least there have been only sporadic shortages of food. Even the Ashers found suppliers so that they can continue operating the boulangerie uninterrupted most weeks. There has continued to be rationing of coal as well. That has perhaps been the worst of it. How cold we often are. Officially, according to Papa, there is a nationwide shortage—everyone is sacrificing—but Charlotte says the Nazis are loading it onto trains and trucks and other transports and taking it back over the border to their Fatherland.

I mention this to Papa once I'm speaking to him again—Charlotte says I must at least pretend to get along with him, to avoid suspicion—but he scoffs at such ideas. He says once the British sign their own armistice, as our president Pétain did last summer, life can return to normal. There will be no more need for the Wehrmacht to occupy France or continue bombing Britain. Certainly they won't take our coal. They will return across the Rhine, he says, repeating himself for the hundredth time, as if that will make it true. What is left, Papa says, will be a new Europe, under German control, defined by order and prosperity, and things will settle down.

But then there is the other world, mostly invisible: the world of the Resistance. Jules and I throw ourselves fully—or at least nocturnally—into the clandestine work of pasting these flyers all over the arrondissement. No matter that the Nazis tear them down the day after they go up. People still see them in the mornings. And of course another night, another round of new flyers, informing our fellow Parisians about the latest developments in the Battle of Britain, the fighting in North Africa, the Americans sending supplies to England and elsewhere, even though they still have yet to declare war themselves.

One afternoon, while we're waiting for Charlotte, Annette tells us how she was injured.

"I intervened on behalf of some neighbors," she says, speaking softly. "The parents of two small children were accused of being communists. The children tried to follow as their parents were dragged from their apartment. I only meant to go help the children, find other family members who could care for them. I suppose I should have known what would happen, but we were all so naive back then. The soldiers said nothing. One twisted my arm and slammed me into a wall. Another kicked me over and over in my side, breaking ribs, then stomping on my ankle with his jackboot. They threw me over the railing and left with the parents."

Jules and I are horrified. Annette is silent for a moment, and

Jules reaches over to gently put his hand on her arm. Annette looks down at it, then lays her other hand on top of his and pats it, as though Jules is the one who needs to be comforted.

"It is true, the parents were communists," Annette continues, her voice even softer now, so quiet Jules and I have to lean in to hear her—as if she is afraid of more Nazis just outside the door. "Like many in the trade unions. Even I went to some meetings. I am no doubt on a list somewhere. But a small fish. The Gestapo has their sights on too many others to come after me. So far."

"The Gestapo?" I ask. I haven't heard this word before.

"The Nazis' secret police," Charlotte says. She and Antoine have just come in. "They are in Paris now. It is one thing to be taken by our French police. Or by Wehrmacht soldiers. There might not even be an arrest. Only an interrogation, a warning."

"A beating," Jules whispers.

"Oui," Charlotte says, glancing at Annette. "A beating. Even a bad one. But not death. Not torture. Those are the specialties of the Gestapo. And we fear they are only getting started, only finding their way to pressure the Police Nationale to adopt the Gestapo tactics."

I wonder how Charlotte knows so much, and I do not. We are only four years apart, but she has always been this way, to Papa's eternal chagrin. It is her choice of friends, of course. The intellectuals. The ones who rebel. The ones who would remake society with what she says are true French values, and not just those to which the rest of us—Papa especially—give only lip service. *Liberté, egalité, fraternité*. Our French motto. Charlotte says it has true revolutionary meaning, which we needed to reclaim even before the Nazis came. And now that they are here, the demand for action, for the emergence, or the reemergence, of a true France and true French values is even stronger.

I listen in rapt attention when she speaks in this way, though she is always cautious enough to close the windows to the balcony so her voice doesn't carry. And one never knows, as Antoine keeps reminding her, keeps reminding all of us, who will be listening, and who will take what they hear and turn us into the authorities. Papa's Police Nationale, or the dreaded Gestapo.

It is only a matter of time, Antoine says, until there is no difference in who is more brutal to their prisoners. "Both will use torture," he says. "The French police are learning quickly from the Nazis. Or perhaps they have always known."

Meanwhile, the war goes on with the Nazis' bombing of London; the desert war in North Africa; the continuing imprisonment of a million of our French soldiers; the rumors about the concentration camps in Germany and Poland filling with Jews, criminals, homosexuals, Romani, communists, the homeless and disabled, anyone who dares speak ill of Hitler and his Third Reich. We all are asking the same questions: Can Britain survive, alone now against the Nazis? Will the Americans join the fight? Will the people of France rise up against the occupation?

But Charlotte and Annette and Antoine and their shadowy compatriots have not given up. Their spirit will never die, and neither will mine or Jules's. There is too much work to do—distributing yet another new flyer that explains how best to conduct oneself during the occupation:

Even if you speak German, if a soldier addresses you in his language, act confused. Keep walking.

If he speaks French, ignore him as well.

If he tries to strike up a conversation in a café, let him know that nothing he has to say is of the slightest interest.

If a shop owner has a sign in his window saying he speaks German, go to another store. He may have all the German business he wants. He does not deserve the French.

Don't complain about the nine o'clock curfew. It is a reminder that when you get home you can hear de Gaulle on English radio and get news of the war and the world.

Outward, act indifferent to the Germans but hold on to your rage in your heart. Keep fighting.

There is still snow as February rolls into March, but not as much. For most of the past month I have had to stop riding my bicycle, which means it takes me longer to meet Jules at night, so tonight, as soon as I hear Papa and Maman close their door, I slide open my window and slip out onto the balcony, thankful that Maman keeps it clear of snow, lowering myself into the courtyard. The street is empty and dark; the electricity is out again.

Several times on the way I have to leap into shadows, down tight alleys, away from the sounds of Nazi boots. They must never sleep, these Nazis.

I hear Jules before I see him. "Nicolette. Here."

"Do you have everything already?" I ask quietly.

"Of course. And I have something else," Jules says. He holds up a small contraption: a mousetrap. Actually several mousetraps.

And in his bag he shows me a few small tin containers, all filled with water.

I'm annoyed. "What are we going to do with those? We have serious work to do."

He explains that the mousetraps hold a can with water on one end, a stack of papillon on the other. We place them on the edge of buildings above the busiest streets. Poke a small hole in the containers and leave them. The water drips out, slowly, slowly, then, when we are long gone, when the weight of the can will no longer hold, the spring-loaded mousetrap snaps shut, sending the empty can tumbling away and shooting the flyers into the air, where they will rain down on the street below like confetti, showering everyone, even any German soldiers.

I am speechless. It is a brilliant invention. A brilliant plan. Except for one thing.

"But if we put them out now, they will have long since gone off before morning," I say. "Street sweepers will have cleaned them up before anyone can see them."

He smiles. "So we wait until five o'clock when the curfew ends to set them off. Just in time for when everyone is going to work and the streets are at their busiest."

"But if we wait that long, it will be impossible for us to sneak back home without getting caught," I say.

Now he frowns. "That's not a problem for me. But you should go now. I'll stay up and set the mousetraps. It's okay."

I don't like this part of the plan. I don't like the thought of Jules having to do everything by himself. But I can't see any other way, at least not tonight. I say I'll wait up with him for a few hours, anyway, so he won't be facing the night alone. We ease our way through the winding alleys and narrow streets in the Latin Quarter until we reach a busy boulevard where cafés and nightclubs are still open with special permission from the Nazi command—like the one where Jules's aunt Margaux works her late-night shifts.

"Here," Jules says, pointing to a four-story building of shops and apartments. We climb the ladder, duck behind a low wall to escape the cold wind, and wrap ourselves as tightly as we can in our coats and hats and scarves. We don't speak for a while. There is piano music from somewhere below. The sounds of what I take to be Nazi laughter. A French woman's voice, singing. German voices, many of them, also raised in song, one of their beer-drinking songs, no doubt. The occasional vehicle passes on the street. Boots echo. A glass breaks. There is more Nazi laughter.

After a time, somehow, deep in the freezing night, I fall asleep.

I sleep too long, despite the bitter cold. It is dawn when I awake, and Jules has left. I panic and pray that no one has noticed I'm not home. I quickly descend to the street. Curfew has ended and the sidewalks are busy. There is a shout, and everyone looks up as papillon flyers rain down from what must be the first of Jules's contraptions. People snatch the leaves out of the air—so many, so quickly that no flyers seem to make it to the ground.

I follow the street, watching people read and laugh and shout the best lines. A block away, another mousetrap goes off, sending more flyers sailing over the edge of the parapet on another tall apartment building. More leaves cascading down, more excited Parisians looking up and grabbing and reading. Two Wehrmacht soldiers in civilian clothes are stumbling down the sidewalk but stop to pick up a flyer. Clearly they don't read French because I see them squint, converse in their language, ask questions of passersby—who pointedly ignore them, following instructions on the flyers!

Yet another block farther, a full Wehrmacht patrol is marching in the middle of the street, in tight formation, goose-stepping, their bootfalls echoing off the building walls. People are moving out of the way as a third explosion of flyers suddenly fills the sky and falls like more light rain this time on the soldiers. Some must know French because they immediately go into a rage, tearing up the papillon, turning it into true confetti, pointing to the rooftop, some even raising their guns. Their commander barks orders, and several of the soldiers dash into the building and up the stairs, presumably to arrest the degenerate who would do such a thing.

I am laughing myself when Jules materializes next to me on the street, breathing heavily. The soldiers who have remained on the ground glare at us. They glare at the others who join in with our laughter. They yell at us in German, but everyone ignores them, just as it says to do on the flyers. It is a good morning in Paris, for once. Like fresh snow on Christmas Day.

Maman is worried sick when I finally get home, so tired all I want to do is crawl in my bed and sleep. "I was at Charlotte's," I say, before Maman can get a word out herself. Papa has long since gone to work, and we're alone in the apartment. "I found her. I went out last night, after you and Papa were in bed, but I got caught by the curfew. I didn't want to tell you because I was afraid Papa wouldn't allow me to see her."

What can Maman say to that except to ask a hundred questions about Charlotte, whom she has been so desperately missing? I tell Maman everything I think she wants to hear about how Charlotte is doing: happy; planning to go back to university in the fall, if they reopen the Sorbonne by then; still with Antoine, who has kept his job as a machinist; living in the Latin Quarter with the artists and performers and freethinkers. The last part she doesn't like, I can tell. She frowns but is nonetheless relieved to finally have word about Charlotte, whom I also assure Maman will come to visit soon, though Charlotte hasn't said any such thing. But what's one more little lie if it makes Maman feel better?

At school, everyone is talking about the flyers, the way they showered people on the street and drowned the Wehrmacht patrol. They're also talking about the retribution the Nazis have taken, dragging in anyone for interrogation who so much as gives them a look on the street. They have sworn to find out who is behind the mousetraps and the flyers, but since only Jules and I know, we feel we are safe.

But we are soon reminded safety in occupied Paris is an illusion. That afternoon as we are filling in Charlotte on what we've done, Jules explaining how the traps work and how they'll give the Resistance a chance to set them and get away, Antoine bursts into the room, not bothering with secret knocks or passwords.

"We have to leave here immediately," he says. "We have just

gotten word that Gestapo agents are searching door to door, only a few blocks over."

Charlotte springs into action, grabbing our arms. "Come with me," she says. Jules and I follow, our hearts pounding, but Antoine stops me as I'm heading for the door. He hugs me tightly.

"We are counting on you to carry the torch," he whispers. "Should anything happen to us. You and Jules will continue to fight. Oui?"

I can only nod as he smiles and shoves me gently toward the door. As I stumble out of the little apartment, Charlotte hugs me, too. "I will be in touch when things are calmer. But I fear it's only going to become worse."

"For the Resistance?" I ask.

She shakes her head. "For everyone, once the Germans' true plans for France are revealed."

Jules stands quietly, as always, waiting. But I need to know. "What true plans?"

Charlotte is chewing on her lip again. "France will become a giant work camp. We will exist for our labor. For our food. For our resources. Also for our geography. I have told you this before: Hitler wants to create a Fortress Europe. The French coastline will be the first line of defense against England and the Americans and anyone else who thinks to challenge the Reich."

"Then we won't stop," I say. "No matter what."

Charlotte nods in approval. "Don't come here again. We'll no longer be here. We would have had to move again soon anyway, even if the Gestapo wasn't searching for us. I'll contact you when I can."

So Jules and I go. But there is a sudden stabbing feeling in my heart as we descend the metal stairs. I don't understand it at first, and only later come to realize it is a premonition that something might happen to Charlotte, that this *is* all too real, and dangerous, and that any time I see her, even this time, could be the last.

8

HUIT

We begin recruiting right away—just days later—to form our own Resistance cell. Perhaps we're not the only ones. There are whispered conversations all over, the kind where students who are speaking in such animated fashion with one another get suddenly silent when someone else tries to join in. The classmates with the darker expressions—and it bothers us that there aren't very many—are the ones we want, the ones quietly complaining about the occupation, sharing information from the British radio, quoting General de Gaulle. I begin with Yvette, who tells me she will join before I can even finish asking.

"I have been waiting for this," she says.

"For me to ask?" I say.

Yvette nods. "I thought it might be you. Or Jules. Or a few others I've been watching, considering. You came to see me when I was hurt. Most here at school avoided me after the demonstration."

Yvette directs me to two other girls she knows a little, both of whom have lost their fathers to the war. We insist they don't use real names; instead we give them code names—Zuzu and Simone. I introduce them to Jules at a café where we meet after school.

Simone tells us her father is dead, killed at Dunkirk, and that her mother has been working three jobs since to provide for their family. Zuzu's father, like Jules's, is a prisoner of war in Germany. She and her family have recently gotten word through the Red Cross that her father is alive and well.

Yvette shares her story next. "My father was a leader in his union, but now they have disbanded, gone silent, of course. Because of the occupation. But questions are being asked. There are spies. Collaborators. My parents worry that as our old neighbors return, some of them will report on anyone who has been involved in the trade unions or with the communists. My father tells us to prepare us for whatever may happen. But I don't believe in just sitting and waiting. I think it is time for action."

There is a long moment when the girls look at us expectantly. Jules and I lean in close to them at the small sidewalk table where we have been nursing our coffees, and we tell them our plan, or just enough of it that we'll be able to gauge by their reactions whether they will be with us.

"You should know that our first time, we were careless, and we were caught," Jules says. "It was just after the new year. Perhaps the authorities, they still had the Christmas spirit. We were let go with warnings."

"But now there are no warnings," I say, looking at Yvette, who nods knowingly. "Now it is much more serious, the work we are doing. The work *you'll* be doing."

Their eyes widen with excitement as we recount more of what

we have been up to—the vandalism, the flyers, the mousetraps, leaving out any direct mention of Charlotte and Annette and Antoine, of course. They assure us that they want to join and that they will do anything—*anything*—to hurt the Nazis.

Jules and I meet up again the next day after school. Monsieur and Madame Asher have started closing the boulangerie most afternoons as supplies run low, so I have this time to recruit members.

"Our old friends Rowland and Paul have already showed us they can't be trusted, so we'll need to find others," Jules says as we trudge through the wet streets. It is April now, but still cold, no sign of spring. The grim weather, always overcast, continues to reflect the pall that has taken over the spirit of Paris.

Jules has three other boys from his lycée who want to join us. He swears that we can trust them. They, too, all have family stories that confirm their hatred for the Nazis and the occupation. We're already too large a group to meet in public, so Jules gives them directions to a hidden area in one of the parks surrounding Montmartre. Jules is a great one for nicknames and calls the boys the Three Stooges, after the characters in American movies. He also gives them code names: Jean Pierre, Frederic, and Ángel. Simone, Zuzu, and Yvette he refers to as Les Triplés—the Triplets.

"What about us?" I ask on our way to meet the Stooges. "Do we have nicknames as well?"

There seem to be Wehrmacht soldiers everywhere today on the streets. One can hardly walk a single city block without being stopped with the command to show identification. Even when the order is in German, everyone knows what it means.

"I will call us Les Parents," Jules says. We both laugh at the absurdity.

"It's perfect," I say. I elbow him. "Papa."

"Maman," he replies, throwing his arm around my shoulders. It always surprises me to be reminded that he is taller than I am. I always feel that I am the larger presence, that Jules is more like my shadow. But he has grown bolder, stronger, larger himself through the winter as we've thrown ourselves deeper into this work.

We find the Stooges nestled between boulders that shield us from the prying eyes of spies and Wehrmacht soldiers and anyone who has no business knowing our business. "We need a mimeograph," I say. "That's the first thing for printing, making copies of flyers, a newsletter, if that's what we want to do." We haven't seen or heard from Charlotte and Antoine in three weeks, and it's clear that we will have to go fully our own way. But that also means we have to come up with our own means of production.

Jules is taking a German language class at school, as are two of the Three Stooges, and they think their professor might be sympathetic to our cause. Professor Pajot has already said things—criticism of Hitler, the occupation, President Pétain, and the armistice—that have the students talking, some saying he is foolish to expose himself in such a way, others defending him, praising him for standing up, and urging everyone to do their part for a free France.

"I will see if he might allow us access to one of the school's mimeographs and paper and a typewriter," Jules says. "Perhaps in the evenings or weekends, when no one is around."

So it is decided.

It is also decided that we will be vandals in the meantime, destroying or defacing as many of the German street signs as we think we can get away with, working in smaller groups of two or three. One of the Stooges, Jean Pierre, reminds us to paint or write or scratch the cross of Lorraine everywhere we can, as it is the symbol of de Gaulle and the Resistance.

The other two Stooges, Ángel and Frederic, seem to be taking their cues from Jean Pierre. "I once scratched it into the side of a German truck!" brags Frederic.

"And I have scratched it a dozen times onto the walls at the lycée." Ángel grins. "Only small. But still . . ."

We agree on this as well, and then one by one we leave, each in a different direction, careful to make sure we aren't observed and aren't followed.

That night, after Papa and Maman have gone to bed, I slip out the window to meet Jules, Yvette, and Jean Pierre. I quickly climb down into the courtyard, retrieve my bicycle, and race across the arrondissement, my panniers stuffed with paint and brushes, some of Papa's tools, a long knife. I am ready to do battle with the Nazis.

Yvette is fearless. With a boost from Jean Pierre, she scampers up poles and hangs with one hand while she paints over German signs with the other, splashing herself and us down on the street in the process. We whisper-shout at her to be more careful, that it will be hard to hide the paint splatter on our clothes. But she doesn't flinch. Nothing will distract her from her work. Not even the squeal of tires a few streets away, though we're begging her to climb down so we can hide, just in case the vehicle comes our way, tearing around the corner and on top of us before we can do anything about it. But that doesn't happen. Our luck is good tonight.

Vive la France! we paint on walls, on doors, everywhere we can find. *Vive de Gaulle!* With Papa's tools we take down signs, pile them on my bicycle, push it to a canal, and dump everything in. Or we reverse the sign directions. Or we paint over the directions with crosses of Lorraine.

We don't stop until deep into the night when we run out of paint and we're so tired we can barely stand upright. Jules and I salute Yvette and Jean Pierre, call them good soldiers, tell them to hide the clothes they're wearing and put them on next time we meet. It will be their Resistance uniform, and we will do the same with ours. They say they can't wait to do it again. We can't, either.

There is good news at Jules's lycée later that week. Professor Pajot has said he will help us. Well, not exactly that. Jules approached him, began his careful pitch, but the professor cut him off. "Please," he said. "I cannot hear any more. Already I have spoken out too openly in your classes. I will only tell you this: On Saturdays, I and a few other teachers come to the school to prepare for the coming week. If someone were to find a certain door into the building unlocked, one perhaps in the alley, there would be nothing to stop that person from entering, from slipping quietly to the second floor and finding a mimeograph machine in a corner room also left unlocked. If he were to work quickly, this person might have time to type a flyer, run off copies, and leave with those copies—being careful not to leave any evidence—without anyone finding out what has been done."

Jules says Professor Pajot turned away abruptly and walked off without another word, leaving Jules to wonder whether he had just been offered the use of the school machine, or if Professor Pajot had had a change of heart and was setting us up for arrest. "But I don't believe it can be that," Jules says. "He would not betray us. Not from what we have heard about him. There are so many rumors. They can't all be true. But some of them surely are."

"What rumors?" I ask.

"Guns," Jules whispers. "Smuggling. The Resistance. British spies. All sorts."

It sounds too cloak-and-dagger to me, even after all the secretive work we've been doing.

"It is best that we not speculate," I say. "And that we do not repeat any of the rumors. But it does sound as though we can trust him."

"So Saturday it begins?" Jules asks.

My heart is pounding already. "Yes," I say. "Saturday it begins."

9

NEUF

I help the Ashers at the boulangerie every morning the following week. In the afternoons after school, when they close the shop, I meet with Jules for planning and reconnaissance. I tell Maman that I have been struggling with math and so must stay late at the lycée for extra tutoring.

Too anxious to just sit and wait for Saturday, I slip out at night twice that week to rendezvous with Jules or the Stooges or Yvette and Zuzu and Simone. We make sure to mix up who will work with whom each time. Already too many of us know too much that could put the others in jeopardy in the event of a capture. We have heard more frightening tales of harsh interrogations and torture at the hands of the police and the Gestapo. It is no longer the case that the Nazis will humiliate someone they catch and take their identification, as they did with Rowland months ago. Now they would surely beat them right there openly on the street. Or much worse. And they would not let them go, no matter how young they are.

I wake up early on Saturday, hoping to avoid seeing Maman and Papa. Papa is gone, but Maman is sitting alone at the small kitchen table drinking her morning coffee, or what is called coffee, anyway—made from finely ground acorns and chickpeas. It is all we can get anymore.

"Bonjour, Maman," I greet her, trying to sound like my normal self, though I'm anxious to be on my way to the lycée to meet Jules.

"Bonjour, Nicolette," Maman says. She offers me some of the new "café national," but I turn up my nose. Even the smell of it makes me nauseous. I can tell she wants me to sit with her, to keep her company. Lately, she has seemed lonely—with Charlotte gone, with me so often away, with Papa angry and distant. But I can't stay.

"I have to hurry to the boulangerie," I tell her, giving her a hug. "I promised Madame Asher I would be early, and I'm already late." For a moment, I wish more than anything that I could sit with her here at the little table, that Charlotte would stumble out of the bedroom as well, rubbing her sleepy eyes. That Maman would have fresh baguettes and butter and jam for us, and our bowls of hot chocolate that she used to always fix on cold weekend mornings.

Maman sighs. Waves me off. "Be sure to eat something there," she says as I hurry out the door.

I assure her I will, but moments later I am on Papa's bike, racing across Paris to meet Jules. With the streets so empty of automobiles, there is little to keep me from flying free down the open thoroughfares. In twenty minutes I am there, cutting down a side street, tucking the bike behind a row of overflowing ash cans. I wait only a few minutes more before Jules materializes out of the morning shadows, his face half-hidden by an enormous scarf. He looks as anxious as I've felt all morning and doesn't even bother to greet me. He only says, "Hurry, before someone comes."

The door from the alley is unlocked, just as Professor Pajot said it would be, and we duck inside. Everything else is also as he said it would be. Jules is the better typist, but I am a much better speller. Together, working quickly, nervously, we are able to produce a flyer, though we manage to jam up the mimeograph machine several times in the process, each time throwing us into a panic that we won't be able to fix the damage, and that we'll be caught, and that Professor Pajot, busy with his own work somewhere else in the building, will be found out. But we succeed in the end.

Most of our first flyer is taken up with a report about a dozen young men, suspected communists and trade unionists, who were recently detained and brutally beaten in secret rooms—not by the Nazis, but by our own Police Nationale. Yvette provided us with the details, which she'd gotten from her father through his trade union contacts. The police wanted to know who was responsible for the flyers everyone had been talking about. One of them was in a coma. One lost his teeth. Several had broken limbs, skull fractures, deep lacerations that were left untreated. The young men kept saying they didn't know anything about the flyers, about anti-Nazi propaganda, about anything. The police kept saying they didn't believe them, but finally had to let them go.

Our headline is straightforward: "Where Are Our Patriots? German Brutality Infects French Police."

"Success!" Jules practically shouts as we're gathering the

hundreds of thin sheets. I clamp my hand over his mouth, certain that I hear footsteps in the hall outside the copy room. I switch off the light and we cower behind the machine as the footsteps draw closer, closer, until they're just outside the door—and then continue on, fainter, until they fade to nothing. We tiptoe out, careful to bring with us any evidence that we've ever been here.

We meet the others, by ones and twos, at cafés, at parks, prearranged rendezvous sites, to distribute the stacks of flyers. One of the Stooges, Ángel, is late, so we have to wait. A faux coffee. Another. We are anxious sitting here, exposed, at a cold sidewalk table with what seems to be half the Wehrmacht soldiers in Paris strolling by, some in uniform, some in street clothes, but all a threat because at any moment they could stop and demand we show them our identifications and the contents of our panniers. And then we will be doomed. But our luck holds, and Ángel finally shows. We've been here too long already, so I suggest we walk our bicycles down the sidewalk—him and me—while Jules rides off in the other direction.

A block away I speak. "You put us in danger when you are late," I say. "We need to be able to trust you."

"You don't understand," Ángel says. "My parents have lost their jobs. Because we moved from Spain, they cannot work here. The new law says that you must have been born to French parents to have a job here. All who are immigrants are being found out, their jobs taken away."

"What will you do?" I ask, my anger gone, now just worried for him.

"Sell what we can," he says. "Find jobs that will pay cash.

Hope no one reports us. I won't be able to attend the lycée any longer. I will have to find ways to make money as well."

"So you're finished with us, then?"

He looks startled when I say this. "Of course not!" he says. "I will work harder, that's all. Now give me the flyers. I have my bicycle. I can still do my part. I hate the Nazis. I hate all fascists. We left Spain because of the fascists. I will do what I can to fight them here. There is nowhere else to go."

I know what he says is true. France has been a place of refuge for so many countries, people fleeing persecution. The Jews from all over. Soviets. Poles. Romani. Moroccans. Tunisians, Algerians. Spaniards.

And now they are all without jobs. Leaving me to wonder—leaving everyone to wonder—what will come next?

Maman makes a rabbit stew for dinner that night from one of the hares from the balcony. Papa is unusually talkative as we sit down to eat, though the subject matter is dark.

"There have been assassination attempts against the Nazis," he says. "South of Paris. And ambushes on Wehrmacht patrols."

"What's going to happen?" Maman asks as she serves us bowls of stew.

Papa scowls. "The Germans have given orders that the Police Nationale are to turn over a dozen prisoners, those suspected of subversive activities. They will issue a warning to the public—that these men will be executed if there are any more attacks against the Wehrmacht, whether officers or enlisted men."

I nearly choke on my bite of stew. "What sort of subversive actions?" I ask.

Papa shrugs, lowers his face to his bowl of stew, and takes a spoonful. "More attacks, of course. But also stolen weapons. Sabotage. This sort of thing. Also there will be more subversives sent to the labor camps, and punishment for those who deface the Germans' signs or are caught distributing anti-German flyers."

I'll write it down later for our next flyer.

Maman and I hear it confirmed on the radio with the Ashers a few nights later, though the news has become difficult to follow. The Nazis have begun jamming the signals coming across the English Channel. But enough gets through that we are stunned into awful silence. The Nazis arrested a dozen members of the Resistance, people publishing underground newspapers like *La France Continue* and *Resistance*. Several of them were executed at our own French prisons. The rest have been sent to labor camps. The Nazis are making no secret about what they are doing. The risks to us all grow greater every day.

Maman and the Ashers talk frequently about how life has become more and more difficult for everyone in Paris. At times, the Ashers don't have enough flour and sugar to even bother opening the boulangerie at all. They search the city for suppliers and supplies when their regulars run out, which is increasingly often. Income is down—for the Ashers, for many of the Jewish people in the city, for most of us in Paris.

"Perhaps we should leave the city," Madame Asher says again one night as we huddle under blankets, having given up on trying to tune into the London radio because of all the interference.

"And where would we go?" Monsieur Asher responds. "In every direction are the Germans."

"The Pyrenees," Madame Asher says. "Into Spain. To Portugal. To find a ship to America. Others have done it."

"That was months ago when they were able to do so," Monsieur Asher says, looking at his hands as if he might find traces of flour there in the lines and cracks. "And even then, the Americans turned away one ship after another of refugees. They weren't allowed into South America, either. Where is safe for us Jews?"

Maman squeezes my hand, hard. She is angry, but like me doesn't know what to say, what to do, how to help, how to change anything. Meanwhile, Papa sits alone at his desk in our apartment, smoking his pipe, perhaps reading through more stacks of lettres anonymes, and making lists. Maman assures me yet again that he is only just trying to stay in the good graces of his superiors for our survival, who in turn will do anything to stay in the good graces of the Nazis, even if it means turning against their friends, their neighbors, those of us who would resist.

Madame Asher says she has heard even more Jews have been thrown out of their homes in several arrondissements. "It is only a matter of time before we lose our boulangerie, before all Jewish businesses are shut down. Not just those yellow signs."

She is crying now, silent tears of despair. Maman lets go of my hand to reach for her friend. Monsieur Asher shuts off the radio, ending the futility and the static for this evening, and he takes it into the next room to remove the secret panel behind which he makes it disappear until another night, until we try again.

The first Saturday in May, just when we're expecting the relief of spring, the weather takes yet another brutal turn to freezing.

Jules and I have to practically skate our way down the icy roads to the lycée. We make shadows of ourselves as we ease down empty hallways, duck inside a classroom to let a cleaning woman pass, and wait until we're sure we are still undetected, and then proceed to the office.

Jules is soon typing furiously—about Resistance attacks on Vichy ships, and about the Maquis, guerrillas out in the country, living on the land, the ones attacking Nazi patrols in bold actions, then vanishing once again into the forests, as if they themselves were the very rocks and trees of the French countryside. Suddenly we hear an outer door opening, and he freezes. I shut off the small lamp we're using. Footsteps cross the reception room floor. The knob turns and the door opens. A dark figure stands over us, backlit by faint light from the hall filtering in. Jules's hands are still literally poised over the typewriter keys.

I back away to the far wall. Jules lifts his hands, rises, and joins me. It is as if we are anticipating the firing squad.

The figure turns on our lamp, redirects the bulb to illuminate us. It is a woman, perhaps one of the professors at the school, judging by her formal dress. She bends to read what Jules has been typing—still having not spoken to us. A glance our way, no more than that, then she sits, removes the paper from the typewriter carriage, and replaces it with a blank sheet. She retypes what Jules has written, scans it, hands it to us.

"You must check your spelling," she says. "Always remember to proofread your work."

Then she leaves. We have been holding our breaths the whole time. I am dizzy and slump to the floor. Jules collapses into the chair. But we can't afford to break down like this for long, no matter how hard our hearts are beating. And so, minutes later, we are running the hand press so furiously that the heated metal threatens to burn our fingers. We stop for nothing until our schoolbags are full of papillon flyers, then we flee the building before the professor can reconsider her decision to help us rather than to turn us in, or before anyone else comes around.

10

DIX

The harsh winter continues well into May. At night we still huddle beneath blankets. I try to read under candlelight, but at times my fingers are too cold, too numb to turn the pages of the books for school. It is the same for Maman as she tries to sew. Papa still wears his overcoat, his gloves, his hat as he sits in the evenings in his chair, still drinking his wine, smoking his pipe, studying his papers from work, seldom speaking to Maman or me. I know I have become a disappointment to him, but I'm not entirely sure why. I've kept my Resistance activities hidden from him and Maman both.

Every few nights, Maman and I continue to make up excuses to visit the Ashers. I go to the bakery as often as I can to stay warm in the back of the shop, near the ovens—when the Ashers are able to scrape enough coal together from their various suppliers, usually at considerable cost. Most of the news is terrible. The Battle of Britain, which started with the Nazis' first bombing raids in September, is still going on. The BBC reports on successes, too, of course, as much as possible—Nazi bombers shot down from the sky, crashing into the English Channel.

Brave schoolchildren risking their lives to save others during the bombardments. And reports on the Allies: the Canadians, the New Zealanders, the Australians, even the Indians and South Africans who have joined the British in the war against the Germans and Italians in North Africa.

But where are the Americans? Every day we ask ourselves why they haven't joined the fight. The world is on fire. Hitler grows stronger by the hour. He is a vampire, draining France of our resources. Not just our coal and our fuel, but, increasingly, despite what Papa said for so long, our food, our livestock, our men, the prisoners of war, like Jules's father, forced to labor for Hitler's evil war on the free world. And there are even darker stories, too. And worries that Hitler has allied himself not just with Mussolini and the fascist government in Italy but Imperial Japan as well, the Emperor Hirohito, and their own plans to conquer the East while Hitler takes the West.

I wonder more and more how our pathetic little Resistance efforts can matter in the face of this onslaught. Few of the adults will stand and fight. Few will resist, or even speak out. I think about the Maquis, attacking the Germans not with typewriters and mimeographs but with guns and bombs—and I fantasize about joining them.

I wish Charlotte were here to share with me her passion, her commitment to the cause, her refusal to accept defeat. But I continue to worry about her as well. What can it mean that I haven't heard from her in nearly two months? I pray for her. I pray for warm days. I pray for the strength, for the will, to keep going, to be like Charlotte in my heart. To never give up.

• • •

Some days and nights now, it is as if all of Paris has gone into hibernation. Icy winds blasting the empty streets make riding my bicycle impossible. Even with gloves inside mittens, my fingers freeze. My cheeks are chapped and red, the skin dried and cracked, even my short hair is in frozen tangles. Plus there are so many rules for bicycle riders. The Wehrmacht or our own police will detain us if we violate them: both hands on the handlebars at all times, no second rider, no stealing a ride by holding on to a passing bus or trolley, no riding side by side with a friend, but only in single file. And of course the registrations, the yellow licenses we are now required to purchase and display.

I sleep so little at night because of the cold apartment that sometimes I crawl in bed with Maman like I did when I was little, until Papa, who hates to be awakened, senses my presence and orders me back to my own frigid room. Jules and I force ourselves out to meet with the others, to destroy the Germans' street signs, deface their posters, and, once, puncture the tires on a Kübelwagen left unguarded, worried the whole time that someone might hear our ragged, frozen breath. We hide down the block afterward and watch as three drunk soldiers, still in their uniforms, stumble out of a bar. They don't even seem to notice as they drive off, the rims cutting through the flattened rubber and a loud grating noise following them down the street.

But mostly I stay home, under blankets, in the kitchen with Maman and what small heat we have from the stove. Papa works later and later at the Police Nationale office, and I wonder if it is because of orders from the Nazis, or if the police headquarters are still kept warm while the rest of Paris freezes so deep into what is supposed to be spring.

• • •

Zuzu and Simone grab me at school one day, wanting to know if I've heard. "There was another round of executions," Zuzu says. "More university students caught printing and distributing an underground newspaper. Like us!"

I have to tell her to lower her voice, plus it's not good for us to be seen talking to one another too often—something else I've warned them about in the past. But they're too upset.

"One of them was my cousin," Zuzu says, her face red, her eyes welling up with tears. Simone wraps her arms around Zuzu.

"I'm so sorry," I tell her, but the words sound hollow, I know.

"They say only a handful were actually involved in the production," Simone says. "The others were merely guilty by association."

We find out the rest later. Some were guillotined. Some were hanged. Some were killed by firing squad. The Nazis spread the word with their own flyers all over the city. The haunted faces of the dead are left up for days. They warn that it is a crime, punishable by the same fate, to tear them down.

Zuzu waits for me the next day after school. She is standing alone in a recess near the corner of the lycée. She seems smaller somehow, and as she speaks, she seems to retreat inside herself, as if it might be possible to disappear altogether.

"Bonjour, Zuzu," I say, trying to sound upbeat, though it's clear something is wrong. But of course, she has just learned of the murder of her cousin. How could anything possibly be right?

"Je suis désolée, Nicolette," she says. "I'm sorry." She glances behind me furtively, but no one is paying us any mind.

"Pourquoi?" I ask.

"I can't continue," she says. "I'm too afraid."

"Because of your cousin?"

She nods.

"But, Zuzu," I say, "surely you want to avenge his death. We can do that. We *will* do that. I promise. For your cousin and all the others."

"With our pointless little papillon flyers?" she says. She speaks in short sentences, as if she's struggling to breathe, gasping between each shallow breath. "Even the flyers would cost us our lives. They cost my cousin his life. His name was Emile. He was three years older than me. Every holiday we were at their home. My aunt, her heart is broken. Now she speaks to no one. Not even my mother."

She shakes her head emphatically, then pushes past me. Tells me she has to go. Asks me to please not try to contact her, even here at school, even in passing.

The rest of us are frightened as well, and sad that Zuzu has pulled out. But we are also furious, determined to have some measure of revenge—for the executions of the university students, of Zuzu's cousin. For the loss of Zuzu to her understandable fears. So one night not long after, we throw bricks through the window of a café where we spy several haricots verts and their vulgaires drinking and eating and singing their nauseating German oompah songs.

For a moment, as we race away down the street, ducking into alleys, turning the city into our maze through which no one can follow, we find ourselves laughing and dancing, not minding the danger, or perhaps acting so foolishly *because* of the danger, and perhaps because the endless winter that held Paris in its grip for so long has finally given way to something like spring, and we can at least pretend there is hope going forward.

The Stooges take their leave, melting into the shadows, all of them grinning from ear to ear, pleased with our handiwork.

Jules insists on walking me home, even though he will have a much longer journey back to his aunt's apartment. He can be so gallant like that. We don't speak, but as is often the case, we don't have to. I know, when he is quiet, he is often thinking about his father, worrying, wondering. These are the moments when I leave him alone, but only for so long. Then I throw my arm over his shoulder and make him sing with me—"J'attendrai" and "La mer" and "Parlez-moi d'amour," popular songs, songs Maman used to sing to me in the kitchen, songs Jules and I have been singing together since we were little. We even stop in the deserted street and dance, though Jules wants to lead and so do I, so we end up stepping on each other's feet, tripping, falling, laughing. It is foolish. The Nazis are still out. They still own the city, or are convinced that they do. We are in violation of the curfew. But for those few moments we do not feel the night chill of the occupation. For those few moments at least we are free.

I wake early one morning later that week to hear Maman and Papa arguing in the kitchen. I am surprised. Maman never contradicts Papa. She will often go against his wishes, of course—the rabbits, the chickens, our regular evening visits to the Ashers—but these things are unspoken, unacknowledged. Now, though, for perhaps the first time, it is different.

Papa says firmly, "It is not done."

Maman, in a deeper voice than I've heard her use in the past, responds: "But it *can* be done." What she says is not a question.

I slip down the hall and peek through a crack in the door, though I am shivering from the cold.

"They are Jews," Papa says, but once again Maman replies immediately: "They are our dear friends."

"*Your* friends," Papa corrects her, but Maman will have none of it.

"Before the occupation, before the Germans, they were your friends as well," she says. "And we must help them."

"I could lose my position," Papa says, though I can sense in his voice that he is weakening in his argument. I still don't know what they're arguing about, other than that it has something to do with the Ashers and them being Jews. But they already have the sign in the front of their store identifying them as Jews, and many customers are already staying away.

The silence that follows between Maman and Papa feels louder than their voices. I wait for one of them to break it, but there is nothing. I quietly retreat to my room, still shivering.

Maman explains everything to me later. "There is a new edict forbidding Jewish ownership or management of any business, no matter how small. No Jews may even hold any profession. No doctors, lawyers. Non-Jews can apply to take over the businesses, however. All businesses must have what the Nazis call Aryan managers."

I ask the obvious: "So the Ashers must give up the boulangerie?"

Maman nods. "I have told Papa that I would like him to use his influence to have the authorities transfer the Ashers' ownership to us. He is thinking this over."

"But what would happen to the Ashers?" I ask.

Maman says we would be managers of the boulangerie in name only, but I don't know what that means.

"It means, though, officially, legally, the shop would belong to us, in truth, the Ashers would still do all the baking, and they would keep the income to pay their rent and their bills and their expenses. You and I would have to help even more, of course. We would have to manage the front of the boulangerie, meet with the customers, handle all the money and the ration cards."

"And the Ashers?"

Maman looks down. I can see she is upset but trying to make the best of the situation. "They would have to remain in the back of the boulangerie, hidden as much as possible. They would be our—" She pauses. "We would pretend, I mean, that they would be our employees."

"And Papa, you think he will agree to this? He will make this happen?"

Maman nods again, but she doesn't look up.

"But this is the best solution," I say to cheer her up. "We will only be pretending."

"Yes," Maman says, trying to change her expression to something more hopeful. "But then what will come next for the Ashers? For anyone who is a Jew in Paris?"

I can tell she fears the answer. I fear the answer, too.

11

ONZE

Over the last month of school, as what had once been a frozen May finally warms into June, I spend even more of my time at the boulangerie. Now Maman is the one who goes in the early mornings and runs the shop until I am out of school. Our Resistance cell can only meet in impromptu conversations on the sidewalks if I am to be involved. Otherwise, Jules has taken charge. I race home on my bicycle and push Maman out the door of the boulangerie, then I don my apron and greet the afternoon customers picking up the last of our baguettes, or, if they're lucky, any remaining pastries, though there are few the Ashers are still able to make to begin with, as the supplies continue to dwindle.

When we close the shop, I help the Ashers in the back, cleaning up for the day. In the past, they would talk nonstop, break into song, laugh with each other, ask me questions about my day, my classes, my friends, rumors on the streets, any word from Charlotte. Now they say little. There is a distance between us. I know they appreciate what Maman has done for them—and what Papa did to make the arrangement, however reluctantly—and they always thank me for my help and try to give me a few francs, which I steadfastly refuse, and so Monsieur Asher tucks them into my coat pocket anyway when I'm not looking. But there is a sadness, a heaviness about them that wasn't there before, or that I hadn't noticed.

I know they, too, are worried about what will come next, as we continue to hear stories of mass detentions of political prisoners, homosexuals, Romani, priests, teachers, intellectuals, Jews—in Poland, in Germany, even here in France, at places the Germans call Konzentrationslager.

The newly formed French secret police—the Brigades spéciales—began their work back in February, when it was announced that they had infiltrated and broken up a major Resistance network operating in Paris, the most extensive so far, intellectuals and academics at the Musée de l'Homme. Two dozen were arrested and imprisoned. Since then there have been tribunals. Executions.

As chilling as it is knowing about the Brigades spéciales and their spies, their rats, the traitors among us—their mouchards—now we are hearing about yet another organization, Carlingue, that is even worse. People are calling it the French Gestapo, specializing in torture, in summary executions. I hear all about this at dinner one night from Papa, who says he is disgusted with what has become of the police establishment.

"The Police Nationale, we pledged from the beginning to work with the Germans," he says. "And we have held up our end of the agreement. We even cooperated in forming the Brigades spéciales, though a case could be made that the work they do should instead be under the auspices of the military. But these criminals running the Carlingue! They belong inside a prison themselves. The whole lot of them. They are an embarrassment to true police."

Papa goes on for a while as Maman and I listen in silence. Eventually he trails off, then stands abruptly and walks out to the balcony with the chickens and the rabbits, staring alone into the dark Paris night.

I slip off to meet Jules after Maman and Papa are in bed. "We must be more careful," I tell him as we huddle together in a doorway out of the night wind. I go over and over in my mind all I know about the Stooges and Les Triplés. How can we be certain they won't give us up if they are ever captured by the Brigades spéciales or by the dreaded Carlingue?

But of course, no one can know these things. No one can know how they will react if caught, if threatened and beaten and tortured.

"I think it is the opposite," Jules says. "I think we must be bolder. Every time the Brigades spéciales succeeds in taking down the Resistance, the Resistance must strike back even harder. And we should find out what we can about this new French Gestapo, the Carlingue. Where are they doing their evil work, and is there some way to stop them? We must be visible, or our actions must be. And yes, there is great risk. But what does it matter?"

I shake my head. "It matters. It is not only those in the Resistance who suffer. The Nazis or our own police will retaliate against the families. No matter how innocent."

But Jules won't hear what I'm saying. "There is only the

struggle," he says, sounding more and more like Charlotte all the time.

A part of me agrees with him. He is already without his father, who I know he is starting to believe will never come home. It must be this despair that drives Jules to say these things, to sound this way, to not acknowledge that as committed as he is to the cause, as committed as we both are, there is also fear, terror in our bones over what might become of us if we are ever caught.

14 June 1941 is the one-year anniversary of the Nazi occupation and of the death of the great French surgeon Thierry de Martel, who took his own life rather than see the Nazi swastika flag flying from the Eiffel Tower. We mark the occasion with a special flyer, our last of the school year.

Near the end of the month, a freak summer storm sweeps over the city, black skies blocking the sun for days on end, swollen clouds dumping countless liters of rainwater into the Seine, flooding the streets, shutting down arrondissements, stranding what few cars are left in the city. It feels like the end of the world. Or it would, if we hadn't already seen the end of the world last year when the Nazis marched in and took over all our lives.

But gradually, the rains stop, the waters recede, the streets dry, the dead are buried. The occupation continues.

One Wednesday afternoon in July, the boulangerie's line snakes down the block despite the heat. But we've already run out of flour, so there will be no more baking this week, and I have to announce it to those waiting. Most turn away, dejected but understanding. A few curse loudly—at me for being the bearer of bad news, at the Ashers, at the Nazis. This has become the life of many, perhaps of most: waiting in lines, disappointment, hunger, boredom. So many have turned to the black market, making it impossible to keep up on the counterfeit ration tickets.

Jules is still working for wealthy families as a waiter—not serving in a restaurant, but standing in line at the queue for the horse butcher's. It is only a few blocks from the boulangerie, and when I can, I slip away to bring him a burnt baguette that would be thrown away or cheese with only a little mold. He tells me this is how the occupiers truly control the citizens of Paris: through deprivation, through the demands on our time, through the interminable lines. And still he waits. His family needs the money.

When I find him today, he has just finished his purchase and slips me a small cut of meat he has had separately wrapped. "My employers won't miss it," he assures me. I try to convince him to take it home to his own family, but he insists I keep it. All I have for him in return is more burnt bread, but he tells me it's fine.

I bring the meat not home with me but back to the boulangerie, where it's my turn to insist that the Ashers should be the ones to take it. For all they have done for me. For the gifts of bread and pastries and those francs Monsieur Asher keeps slipping into my pocket. Madame Asher hugs me for a long time. When she lets go, her eyes are rimmed with tears. Surely it can't be because I brought them the meat from Jules. But perhaps so. There is so little kindness left in the world.

It is the last time I will ever see the Ashers alive.

• • •

I am jolted from my sleep that night by the heavy sound of jackboots on the stairs. I stumble into the living room, where Maman is rushing across the room, terrified.

"Que se passe-t-il, Maman?" I ask her. "What's going on?"

"The Ashers!" she says. "We must warn them." She throws open the door, but it's too late. The Nazis have already swept past our floor. Papa catches up to us on the landing and forces us back inside the apartment. He slams the door behind us and locks it.

The jackboots continue up the stairs. A German voice barks orders. We hear fists pound on the Ashers' door on the floor above ours. There is a crash, a splintering sound from what must be the soldiers kicking their way inside. Maman collapses, buries her face in her hands. I start for the door again, but Papa moves quickly to stop me.

We are forced to sit and listen to them storming above us, tearing apart the Ashers' apartment, hunting for them. In a moment there is banging on another door as though it's being ripped from its hinges. The Nazis must have figured out where the Ashers are hiding. Or maybe another neighbor gave them away, cracking open the door to their own apartment and pointing before retreating to a coward's safety. Either way, we hear the soldiers' hobnailed boots thundering into an apartment next to the Ashers' that's supposed to be empty.

I am frozen, desperate to do something, praying that somehow the soldiers don't find the Ashers. Hoping the Ashers have vanished like an impossible magic trick.

Then we hear a gunshot. A second gunshot.

Maman wails. I tear away from Papa and this time manage to

fling open our door and race up the stairway. At the end of the Ashers' hall, I stop, nearly vomiting at the sight.

The Nazis have dragged two bodies out of the second apartment that has been empty since the occupation. The Ashers. They throw Monsieur's body facedown next to Madame's. One of the soldiers, who is older, like Papa, stands apart from the others, grim-faced. Another soldier bends to retrieve a small, short-barreled gun, a Ruby pistol, from next to Madame Asher's body. Like one Papa owns. He says, "Andenken"—*souvenir*—and laughs, and the rest join in. They tease the grim soldier, who only stares at the ceiling, not at the other men, not at the Ashers. Then they shrug, step over the bodies, and leave the mess for someone else to clean up, as if it is nothing, because two dead Jews—no big deal.

They march past me without a word, as if I'm not even there, their jackboots leaving a trail of bloody prints on the polished wood floor. I go to the Ashers and kneel next to them. Madame Asher's arm is thrust out from her side, as if she might be reaching for something. I take her hand in mine. She is still warm, but there is no pulse.

I am beside myself with grief. I can't think of what to do. Maman eventually comes upstairs and settles in next to me. Doors open and then quickly close, but no one on the floor, no one else in the building, comes out to join us. We are the only ones to bear witness. Papa, or someone, calls the Police Nationale and they come, hours later, to take the bodies.

Madame Asher had explained to me before that when Jewish people die, there are rituals that must be followed. The body must be buried as soon as possible. There can be no cremation, but rather a natural return to the earth. And after the funeral, the friends and family, fellow Jews, come for seven days to sit shiva, to mourn. But who among the Jews of Paris is left to do any of this? I ask Maman if we might be the ones. If Papa will allow us to bury Madame and Monsieur Asher and to sit shiva, even though we are not of the faith. She has no answers for me.

Once they take the bodies, no one will tell us where they've gone. Not even Papa, with all his connections, can find out, though I wonder how hard he tries. Jules and I slip into the Ashers' apartment two nights later to retrieve the radio, but it's not there. Maybe that's why the Nazis came. Maybe someone in the building found out about the Ashers' radio and turned them in. Everything has been destroyed: pictures, furniture, clothes broken and torn and tossed into piles. Anything of value taken, of course. One thing that is left: Swastikas carved into every wall. And *Juden*. And *Heil Hitler*.

Maman will no longer speak to Papa. It feels colder in the house than it did in the worst nights of winter. Papa rarely moves from his chair unless he is at work. He is worried that there might be backlash, because of our family's association with the Ashers. But nothing comes of it. I bring Papa a tray with his meals, which I prepare in the kitchen. I return for the tray when he is finished. I bring him tobacco for his pipe. Matches. His German newspaper. His briefcase when he brings his work home. I am his servant. And I grow to resent him even more than before, worse even than Charlotte. Like Maman. We blame him—perhaps unfairly, but these are unfair times—for the deaths of Madame and Monsieur Asher.

I can still feel Madame Asher's hand in mine—warm at first.

Then a terrible awareness that her fingers are turning pale, then white, the skin translucent, all the warmth gone. I have waking nightmares of Madame Asher on the floor, her hair wet and matted, her dress torn, one arm jutting out from her side, the trail of blood.

Maman and I do our best at the boulangerie, but we are novices at baking, and none of our breads turn out right. It isn't clear to either of us why we even bother any more. We are haunted every day by the ghosts of Madame and Monsieur Asher. People are angry. They refuse to give their ration cards for burnt baguettes, or undercooked loaves, or tasteless confections, not that we have the ingredients for much.

Within a month, because of our ineptitude, because I am too busy with school, because our hearts are broken, Maman gives up. Papa makes the arrangements to transfer ownership of the boulangerie once again, and soon there is a new Aryan manager.

"We should never have been involved," Papa says in disgust after he turns over the keys. He has said nothing about the Ashers, about the Nazis who came, about what has become of us all that this horror could be allowed to happen. Maman sinks deep into her despair. She stays in her room. Papa stays in his chair.

Some nights, when I'm able to coax her out, I sit with Maman on the balcony, with what remain of our chickens and rabbits in their cages. We watch the sun set. We stay there until it's too dark to see each other, until we are only disembodied voices in those rare moments when one of us speaks.

It is here that Maman tells me what I already know: that she was the one who gave the Ashers the gun, Papa's Ruby pistol, that they must have used, or tried to use, to defend themselves. Or perhaps, knowing what was to come, they took their own lives. "Perhaps if they had gone quietly," Maman says. "Perhaps if I hadn't given them the gun. Perhaps they would still be alive."

We are silent again for a while. And then she whispers, "I will never forgive the Nazis. And I will never forgive myself."

12

DOUZE

In August, at a Metro stop near the Gare du Nord, a partisan slips behind a Nazi officer stepping off the train, raises his pistol, and fires two shots, executing him in the middle of the afternoon, the first such killing in daylight. No one sees anything, though there are dozens present when it happens. The assassin—people are already using his code name, Fabien—walks away. In the days that follow, the Nazis, furious, retaliate once again by murdering a dozen hostages whom they claim are also with the Resistance. They pledge to kill a dozen more the next time, and even more after that.

Everyone in school is talking about it, but still there are too few who are truly outraged and willing to join us in the fight against the Nazis. At night, Jules and I continue to meet with the Stooges and Yvette and Simone, continue to unleash what chaos we can in the streets, anything to cause difficulty and frustration for the occupiers. Anything to avenge the Ashers. People know it is the young who are behind most of the mischief, the Resistance, such as it is in the city. They even have a name for us now: Bébés Terroristes.

Jules and I print and distribute more flyers reporting the atrocities, exhorting Parisians to follow suit, in the spirit of Fabien, and fight back. We share hopeful reports that the Nazis, who invaded the Soviet Union in June, have been unable to defeat Stalin's defenses at Moscow, that Hitler's initiative is already bogging down deep inside enemy land, that the heavy bombing of Britain, which ended back in May, still has not resumed. We make no mention of the horrible loss of Soviet life, of setbacks to the British in the deserts of North Africa, of American transport ships sunk in the North Atlantic, of the million homes and tens of thousands of lives that were lost in the Blitz before Hitler turned his attention—and his troops and his weapons—to the Soviets.

In September, the authorities open an exhibition, "Le Juif et la France," that is meant to "prove" the corrupt influence of Jews over the army, cinema, the economy, literature, virtually every aspect of French life. Thousands line up to see it. We tear down as many posters as we can. Frederic paints a caricature of a greasy-haired Hitler with his tiny mustache outside the exhibition hall. Beneath it he scrawls, *La tête de chou et la France*—the cabbage head in France.

A few nights later, I climb out as usual to meet with Jules and the others. The Stooges have boxes of nails, and our plan is to find unguarded German vehicles outside the nightclubs and the cabarets, and jam the nails into their balding tires.

As I descend the trellis to the street, a low voice calls to me from the shadows.

"Charlotte!" I cry out, too loudly, and I throw myself toward her and land in her arms. "Where have you been?" I'm so excited that I can't stop myself from babbling. "I was so worried. Are you all right? Have you been in Paris all this time? Maman has asked me about you so many times and I haven't known what to say. I reassure her, of course. I even make some things up—that, yes, today I saw Charlotte and she is well and she sends her love and—"

Charlotte stops me. "I'm fine. I'm fine. And yes, I've been here in Paris the whole time, but we've had to be discreet. I'm sorry you were worried. I've missed you all so much."

She squeezes me to her again, tight enough that I can barely breathe. "I'm so sorry about the Ashers," she says. "I wish I could have come to see you then. I wish we could have done something to save them."

We are both crying now. "But why don't you come home now?" I ask her, once I can speak. "Is it not safe yet?"

Charlotte hesitates. "Things have happened," she says. "Antoine has been injured, but our friends have managed to get him out of the city. I'm leaving tonight to join them. But I had to see you first to let you know."

My heart sinks. "How badly is he hurt?"

She doesn't answer. Just takes my hand and says, "We can't talk here."

And with that we go, running from shadow to shadow, not stopping when we reach wider streets where we risk exposure. Charlotte glances quickly and sprints, and I follow, my breath ragged, my lungs burning, my legs aching, but still we continue, out of the arrondissement, into a park and behind a line of trees where everything is in blessed darkness. Charlotte leads me down a narrow trail to a small grotto, pulls a flashlight from her pocket, and crawls inside. I have no choice but to follow.

She stops suddenly inside the narrow space. Feels her way carefully along the wall, then climbs down a hidden ladder even deeper underground to a small room barely large enough for us both to stand. There are planks jammed into the cave wall. Charlotte removes them. Inside are a dozen guns. German Lugers. Rifles. A metal box that she opens. Ammunition. Another box. Wooden, with German markings. Hand grenades.

Charlotte shoves a paper into my hand. "I have drawn a map. Memorize it, then destroy it. Don't come here again, unless . . ." She pauses. "Unless you don't hear from me again. And then only if things get desperate for you. But the minute you take up weapons against the Nazis, you must know that you are unlikely to survive."

I swallow hard. "Is that what happened to Antoine?"

Charlotte shakes her head. "We ambushed a German truck, but only with our fists and clubs. They must have been drinking, so we were able to surprise them. But one had his bayonet and stabbed Antoine in his abdomen. It was so hard to stop the bleeding." She spits on the ground. "But he will be okay. We carried him to a friend, a surgeon who does work for us, and he was able to save Antoine. We took what we could carry from the truck, these boxes of weapons, and brought them here. We're going to join the Maquis once he is healed. I will come back when I can, but it won't be safe for some time. You are the only one in Paris who knows where the weapons are hidden. We will try to come back for them, but that may not be possible."

"What can you do with the Maquis?" I ask, reluctant to let her go. "You are so few, and the Nazi are an army. And our own government sends agents and police against you, against all of us."

Charlotte's voice is firm. "Every patrol we attack, every weapon we steal, every bridge or bunker we can destroy, every message intercepted—the Nazis have to devote their time, their men, their resources to defend or rebuild, or to chase after us. What we can divert from their war effort, all of that is a victory."

We follow shadows back home. Charlotte hugs me one last time. "We will fight," she whispers. "And we will defeat them." She presses her hand over my heart. "And I will always be here with you."

Then she vanishes into what remains of the night.

Months go by, and I hear nothing from Charlotte, nothing about Antoine. Once, on a crowded street in the Latin Quarter, after visiting with Jules at his aunt's, I think I see Annette, but either it isn't her or she doesn't want to be recognized. She limps away from me before I can cross the street, desperate for news of Charlotte, thinking perhaps Annette will know something, anything. I keep the weapons a secret from everyone, even Jules, for fear they might insist on using them.

The Resistance is active in the night again and again. We become more brazen, and even venture out at times during the evenings before curfew. We are chased often, but it becomes almost laughably easy to elude the Nazi patrols or the police. There are so many places to hide—by simply melting into a street crowd or jumping on the Metro. The streets of Paris are a labyrinth, and no map will help the Nazis learn every alley, every byway, especially those too narrow for their heavy vehicles. We have no trouble disappearing into the sewers and tunnels and quarries, the parks thick with cover, the banks of the Seine, the balconies and eaves. The mansard roofs atop so many of the buildings in Paris are perfect avenues for our escapes with their long, flat crowns that allow us to race easily from one to another. The Stooges, Yvette, and Simone have been recruiting, so our numbers are now in the dozens, and we hear about other Resistance networks around the city. There are more attacks—bricks, stones, even homemade bombs thrown at Nazi patrols.

For a brief time, we convince ourselves that we are invincible. We may be so sleep-deprived that we are always in trouble at school for falling asleep during our classes. We may have grown distant from our families, living these secret lives. But we are fighting the good fight, and we let ourselves think we are triumphant with our small acts of vandalism.

Yet as autumn dies off, leaves disintegrating from the chestnuts and elms, café awnings helplessly flapping in the stiffening winds, another feeling washes over me when I am not busy planning and running and causing whatever chaos we think will infuriate the occupiers and perhaps move us one step closer to ending the occupation. When I am alone at night in bed, when my breathing slows and my mind no longer races and the exhilaration is gone, I have an awful sense that we are all being drawn in the other direction—not a noble and heroic climb to freedom, to liberation, but an inexorable slide into something so much worse than we can ever imagine.

• • •

The bitter cold returns, and we retreat as much as we can from the world outside. It gets harder and harder once again to force myself from under my nest of blankets and out into the night to meet Jules and the others. Sometimes I just can't do it. Sometimes they're the ones who don't show up. There are recriminations, arguments, angry words. But forgiveness also. We all understand.

In December, the Japanese destroy the Americans' Pacific fleet in a massive sneak attack at Pearl Harbor. Britain and the US declare war on Japan. Germany declares war on America. The Americans are neutral no longer.

In January, the Soviets mount a counteroffensive against the Germans, but that is the only good news. February, March, April: Britain loses Singapore to the Japanese. The Americans retreat from the Philippines. Japan conquers Burma. The entire world is now at war. And the Allies, so far, appear to be losing.

In May, Jews in all of France are ordered to wear the yellow Star of David.

In June, the Nazis burn the Czech village of Lidice to the ground in reprisal for the assassination of a high-ranking German official. All men and boys in the village are executed. All women and girls are sent to concentration camps.

In July, Police Nationale arrest nearly fifteen thousand Jews, all who are left in and around Paris. They are held for weeks in the vélodrome, where Papa used to take me to the cycling races. Four thousand of those arrested are children. They are deported by train, in cattle cars, to a concentration camp, Auschwitz, deep in occupied Poland.

One evening I ask Maman if she still wishes she hadn't given the Ashers Papa's gun to defend themselves. Maman is quiet for so long, the two of us sitting together in the glow of the lamp, all but lost from each other in deepening shadows. But then she says, "I should have done more for the Ashers. So much more. I should have helped them get away. I should have helped them to their freedom. It will always be to my shame, to my dishonor, that I didn't do more."

In this way, another year passes—another year of the occupation, of rationing, of deprivation. A year of Maman sitting silently for hours by the window, as if waiting past all reason for the return of Madame Asher. A year of Papa in his threadbare suits dragging himself to the Police Nationale, then, twelve hours later, dragging himself back home to his chair, his pipe, his glass after glass after glass of wine, to sleep. A year of me sneaking out and continuing to keep my hair cut short, like Charlotte did for me. A year of the three of us barely speaking. A year with no word from Charlotte.

One day late in October, Jules is sitting in his German language class, waiting for Professor Pajot to arrive. A few students are whispering among themselves, but suddenly turn quiet. The principal enters the room and walks slowly to the lectern. He makes sure to meet the students' eyes, even though his are red and watery. "Your German professor," he says, his voice hoarse, "has been executed by the army that occupies our city."

For the longest time, the students sit in stunned silence, unable to move, to speak, to react, even to cry. Jules is the first to act. He stands, leaves the classroom, and never returns. He walks the three kilometers to the girls' lycée and is sitting on a wall outside, waiting for me to emerge into the waning sunlight later that afternoon to tell me what has happened. Tears well up behind my eyes, but I refuse to release them. Jules is the same. We are soldiers of the Resistance, as was Professor Pajot. We walk together in silence, struggling with our emotions, until it occurs to me that we might also be in danger. And in that moment, I blurt out to Jules the secret I've been keeping from him all this time, since the night Charlotte brought me to the underground, the last time I saw her.

"Jules," I say, lowering my voice to a whisper, though we are far enough away from passersby that no one can possibly hear. "There is something I have to tell you." I'm not sure why I'm divulging this now. But what if we are in danger? What if we need to defend ourselves? What if Professor Pajot has given the Nazis our names? Papa might be able to protect me again, but what protection would there be for Jules?

"Qu'est-ce que c'est?" he asks, or demands. "What is it?"

"I know where there are weapons," I tell him.

Jules is incredulous. "Weapons? But how? Where? Why have you not told me this before?"

He knew about Charlotte and Antoine leaving Paris, of course, and joining the Maquis. I had told him those things. "Charlotte swore me to secrecy," I say. "She was going to come back for them if she could. And she promised she would visit me then. But it's been so long . . ." I trail off, not sure how to finish, as if giving voice to dark thoughts might make them true. "And perhaps now we are the ones who need them."

"Will you show me?" he asks.

A part of me is still reluctant. A part of me already wishes I hadn't said anything about the weapons to Jules. But I can't say no to him now. And perhaps there's another part of me, a part I'm not ready or able to admit, that wants to have the weapons in my hands as well.

That night we retrace the route I memorized from Charlotte's map. Deep in the bowels of Paris, so far underground that it seems possible the known world could be gone, obliterated by war, whenever we return. Jules lifts each of the weapons one by one, studies them with his sharp student engineer's mind to figure out how they work: the PO8 Lugers, the Karabiners 98k, the M24 Stielhandgranates. The Lugers and the Karabiners are all loaded, with extra boxes of ammunition. The hand grenades are live. Jules wraps them back up in burlap, tucks them in their box, and shoves the box deep into shadows in a shaft in the cavern wall.

"In an emergency," I say. "Just in case. If they do come for us. If we have time."

He nods. "Just in case." The way he says it makes me uneasy, makes me wish once again that I had kept the weapons and their location a secret. But I have never been able to hide anything from Jules—not forever. Not even this. Especially this.

I am supposed to meet Jules again a few days later, but he doesn't show. We need to discuss what to do about the loss of our access to Professor Pajot's mimeograph and typewriter. It is the same the day after that. I go to his aunt Margaux's apartment. The first time I knock, but no one answers. The second time, after two more days, the door is left open and the apartment is empty. I am sick with worry, and fear the worst: that the Carlingue has taken him. That they will find me next. I panic at the sound of footfalls on the stairway in the apartment building. I am convinced that I am followed everywhere I go. I'm desperate to talk to someone, anyone, but I can't tell Maman what's going on, and Charlotte is gone. I even consider Papa, who has grown morose, who seems bowed under the weight of his job, who I even heard one evening curse to Maman about the Nazis and the occupation. But how can I trust him?

Another week goes by, and still only silence from Jules. I try and try to convince myself that we are safe, that there is a good explanation for what has become of him. I go yet again to his aunt's old apartment building. I knock on neighbors' doors, but none of them know anything.

I call a meeting with Yvette and Simone and the Stooges, who say they have heard nothing from Jules, either. We are all silent for a few moments, each wrapped in our own worried thoughts.

Until Ángel breaks the silence. "We must carry on," he says. "There is much to do. More guerrilla actions. We need to come up with new ideas for publishing our flyers. New sources for information about the war."

Frederic, who has been doodling a new configuration of his Hitler graffiti, nods in agreement.

Ángel says his parents have friends in the community of Spanish Republican refugees. These friends have friends. Who have a radio. Who monitor the BBC. Who can provide us with the latest news. Since the Ashers died, we have been behind in what we can find out, second- or thirdhand, about the war, about the ongoing Nazi atrocities, about the Resistance. If we can only find another mimeograph, another typewriter, more papillon.

The others throw out the names of teachers who might be sympathetic to the cause, but in the end, none sound very promising.

It has been Jules all along who has had the best ideas, who has given us our sense of direction, who has been our planner, and I miss him more than ever.

A few nights later, we steal a German Kübelwagen and roll it into the Seine. Hundreds of Parisians flock to the riverbank to see the back end jutting out of the shallow water. It is a party, with singing and wine, and soon even a trio of musicians show up with their instruments while some of the onlookers dance there on the bank of the Seine until the gendarmes arrive to chase everyone away. Followed by the Wehrmacht, who vow to execute ten more hostages in retaliation. But French officials at the Police Nationale respectfully suggest that the fault may have been elsewhere. An accident, of course. An innocent mistake. Someone—but never mind who—must have forgotten to apply the emergency brake. Left the vehicle in neutral. It rolled down the bank and into the river. These things happen.

Papa, of all people, is the one who tells Maman and me this, and he even laughs about the Germans and how gullible they can be. Of course, he has no idea that I am one of those responsible, and I can only imagine his outrage if he were to ever find out. But for now, it makes me happy for the three of us to be sharing something like this, for Papa to show his sense of humor, for Maman to smile. It's been longer than I can remember since we laughed together.

13

TREIZE

A week later, as the third winter of the occupation approaches, I am just leaving school when I see him: Jules! Sitting alone on the same low wall as before, waiting for me! But his drawn face tells me something awful has happened. I sit carefully beside him, try to smile, and say, "Bonjour, Jules." He tries to smile as well, but fails; it is painful to see. At first we sit in silence.

Then he digs into a pocket on the side of his bag and pulls out a crumpled letter. He hands it to me. "We received this," he says. "A few weeks ago, from the Red Cross. It was smuggled out of the prison camp in Germany. I couldn't tell you before. I couldn't speak of it. And then we were evicted from the apartment. There has been no money. So that as well."

I start to read but can't finish.

J'ai le regret de vous informer . . .

I regret to inform you . . .

"He has been dead for six months," Jules says matter-of-factly. "We are only now finding this out."

I feel tears on my cheeks. I cannot imagine what grief Jules suffers. Even the grief of Maman for the Ashers, and my own grief as well, must be only a fraction of what it is to lose your father, to know that he died without his family, alone.

Soon, without thinking about it, we are walking, aimlessly. I put my arm around Jules's shoulders and he lets me keep it there. I have a moment of déjà vu, wishing as I've so often wished: for us both to be on bikes, pedaling furiously through the streets of Paris once again, our Peugeot caps jammed tight on our heads, our faces bright pink from the rushing wind, the roads opening up before us as if we could ride on them clear out of the city and into the open countryside, away from the Nazis, away from the occupation, away from all this grief and loss and pain—

We turn a corner in real life and find ourselves suddenly at a checkpoint between arrondissements. I pull out my identification card. Jules has to dig through his schoolbag.

Two soldiers block the narrow opening between heavy concrete barriers. One takes my identification, glances at it, and hands it back. The other scrutinizes Jules's, staring at his book bag.

"What is inside?" the German asks. He points, as if Jules might not know what he's talking about.

Jules looks at the bag, then back at the soldier, and, without missing a beat, says in German, "Handgranaten."

The soldier's jaw drops.

I frantically scan the street to see where we can run, where we might have a chance of escape, but there is nowhere, no time. They're too close. They would shoot us before we took two steps. I look at Jules, my heart pounding, sweat pouring off my brow, but his face is blank, impassive.

And then the soldiers burst out laughing. "Handgranaten!"

they bark. "Handgranaten!" They can't stop themselves. One doubles over and the other follows. They wave us through the checkpoint. I follow Jules's lead and walk slowly, deliberately, trying not to show any trace of panic.

But of course, it must have been a joke, I tell myself. But of course. Even I was fooled.

Only it's not a joke. Since he had to move, and since he quit the lycée, and since the news of his father's death, Jules has been exploring the caves under the city. He has retrieved half a dozen of Charlotte's hand grenades. And he wants us to use them.

Two days later, we gather with the others in a park not far from school, hidden by a thick stand of horse chestnut trees, each of them pruned bottom to top so they look like big green boxes pressed up against one another in the current fashion. No one can see us from the road, but just in case, we squeeze together between oversized boulders, where Jules demonstrates the proper way to detonate a hand grenade.

"Seize the pull cord at the bottom of the hollow wooden handle," he explains as we watch him pretend. "Then yank down hard to ignite the TNT loaded into the head of the grenade. You'll have five seconds to throw it at the target before it explodes."

Simone counts slowly to five, out loud. "Un, deux, trois, quatre, cinq."

Frederic says a quiet "Boom." We laugh nervously.

"We will divide up," Jules says. "Three teams. Two hand grenades each. Choose your targets for maximum effect."

"Meaning what, exactly?" Jean Pierre asks. "Rolling a

Kübelwagen into the Seine is one thing. Or a brick through a plate glass. But this . . ."

"You will have to follow your own conscience," Jules says. "But whatever you do, be sure you know your escape route beforehand. There will be confusion after the explosion. People will run away from it, and then they'll return to see what has happened, what damage or injuries. That would be the time to throw the second grenade, if you're still close enough, and still think you can escape afterward."

"How do you know about this?" Ángel asks Jules. I'm surprised as well. I haven't heard Jules speak in this way before.

Jules shrugs. "It is only common sense," he says.

Jean Pierre speaks again. "I can't do this. Not to hurt anyone."

Yvette scoffs. "Even a Nazi? Even after what they've done to us?"

"As I said before, follow your conscience," Jules says. "If you can damage a vehicle, a shop, a bar where the occupiers have gathered, even if no one is injured, you have made them fearful of what could have happened and about what might happen the next time."

Jules and Yvette are a team. I am with Jean Pierre. Simone and Ángel and Frederic will work together. We decide to leave the others they have recruited out of it. For now. And the remaining hand grenades that are still hidden underground, Jules says he has bigger plans for those.

Jules and I climb on our bikes, the first time we've ridden together in months. "Follow me," he says, and I do, not bothering to ask where we're going. My heart is just happy at this reminder of who we once were. At an intersection, we wait for what traffic still exists on the street—two German trucks followed by thick clouds of black exhaust, a dog-pulled cart, a squat Peugeot. Then we cycle on, north across the Seine in the shadow of the Eiffel Tower, into the 16th arrondissement. At first I think we're going to the Trocadéro Gardens, that Jules wants to race, but we coast past the garden, angling toward the Arc de Triomphe. We turn, and then turn again, and soon we're heading in the opposite direction, south on a narrow, one-way street.

"There," Jules says as we pass by a row of gray, nondescript stone-block buildings. The one Jules singles out has a black door, black shutters, and long, vertical, door-length windows, all of them barred.

We're two blocks away, turning off the narrow street, rue Lauriston, before I ask, "What was that place?"

"Our next target," he says. "The Carlingue headquarters. Where they take their prisoners." He doesn't say what is done to them there. He doesn't have to.

"How do you know this, Jules? It's just a building. There are no signs. No guards."

We are passing the Eiffel Tower again, crossing the Seine onto the open avenue. A cold November wind skips over the water and makes me shiver. Or maybe it's something else.

"My aunt Margaux," he says. "The criminals who are in charge of the Carlingue, they are regulars at her café. She hears things."

We ride for a while in silence. But there is another question I have to ask: "If we attack this Carlingue building, won't the prisoners be hurt as well?"

"Perhaps, yes. But those who are captured and brought there—they are as good as dead already," Jules answers.

It is a terrible thing for him to say, no matter if it's true. Overnight, it seems, Jules has become a different person from the boy I've always known. He is still himself, still my dearest friend, still the keeper of all my secrets, just as I am the keeper of his. But since he learned about his father's death, he has become harder. Angrier. Resolved to see this fight through, no matter what it takes, to the end.

I climb out of my window that night and down the trellis from the balcony. Maman and Papa have long since gone to bed. No one is around to see or hear as I pull open the door to the storage shed tucked in a corner of the courtyard and wheel out Papa's Favor. It takes half an hour of furious cycling to rendezvous with Jean Pierre. He's on foot but already there and steps out of shadows when I arrive, following me into an alley so I can hide my bike. "Are you ready for this?" I ask him. He only shrugs. I can tell he's nervous, sweating, though the night is cold. We make our silent way a few blocks over to a wide, noisy street in the Latin Quarter, lit up with garish lights, unlike so much of the rest of Paris. Here there are half a dozen bars and nightclubs, a favorite of the Germans. From a nearby rooftop, hidden behind a double chimney, we can just see down to the sidewalks, where men in civilian clothes are sprawled in chairs at outdoor tables. We can tell at a glance that they are off-duty soldiers. Or some of the increasingly common German tourists, sent to Paris from other postings, like the Soviet front, for what they are calling their rest and relaxation.

Jean Pierre spots a sleek black Citroën, not far from the sidewalk tables, and takes aim with a grenade.

But he freezes. "I can't," he whispers. "What if I miss? What if it's too big, the explosion? What if someone is hurt?"

I tell him to throw it even farther, then. "Don't even aim for the men or the Citroën," I say. "Remember what Jules said. No matter what you hit, they'll at least be frightened."

But he still can't do it. I don't want to do it, either, but I think about Jules, about how disappointed he will be if we fail to act. I think about his father. I think about the Ashers.

I seize the hand grenade from Jean Pierre. Pull the cord at the bottom of the hollow wooden handle. Yank down hard to ignite the TNT loaded into the head of the grenade. Hurl it as far as I can, past the Citroën. Count un, deux, trois as it flies through the air and lands on the sidewalk and bounces, as if I've aimed it precisely there, into a sewer grate.

The explosion lifts the sidewalk, shatters the windshield on the Citroën, destroys the glass front of the nearest café, and sends the soldiers diving for cover. A geyser erupts from underground, shooting a fountain of water five meters into the air, raining down on the street below. People are shouting. Someone is blowing a police whistle. More soldiers pour out of the bars and nightclubs, their weapons drawn, scouring the streets, the alleys, the rooftops. I quickly scramble away from the chimneys and onto the fire escape off the rooftop, Jean Pierre right behind me.

I catch him before he drops from the hanging end of the ladder to the alley a couple meters below. At first we are racing together, our hearts pounding through our chests from the fear and excitement. But then I remember it's always wisest to split up, so at the next corner I call out, "To your right!" And off he goes.

It takes me a minute to get my bearings, to remember where I need to go to retrieve my bike. I hear the sound of boots, an army of boots, echoing through the streets behind me. More whistles. Now the grinding of gears, the blaring of horns, the screaming of tires.

I throw myself onto the bike, and when I do, something hard slams into my thigh. I know right away what it is—the second hand grenade. We forgot to detonate it. Jean Pierre gave it to me. I yank the cord on this one, too, throw it as far as I can into the alley behind me, and start pedaling while it's in the air. The shock wave from the blast nearly knocks me off Papa's Favor, but I manage to stay upright, ears ringing, adrenaline rushing through me. I sprint down an open boulevard, tearing madly off into the Paris night.

I'm not sure where I am; I only vaguely know that I'm heading south and west. I shove down the panic and tell myself to breathe. That I'll soon enough see landmarks, soon enough know where I am, soon enough outrun the sounds of the Nazis in pursuit.

But suddenly a black van with dark windows careens out of an alley and pulls behind me, bright headlamps reaching out, enveloping me as if I could be caught by the light itself. The van draws close enough to force me off the road, making me swerve to avoid being hit. I turn down a side street, to get away, but hear the van behind me screeching to a stop, then backing up, then following me again. I'm still standing on the pedals, picking up speed, darting through an intersection, tight around a corner, throwing the derailleur into higher gears, cutting down another alley, another empty street, through another intersection, this time just barely avoiding a collision with two Wehrmacht soldiers who appear from out of the night—as surprised to see me, and the chase, as I am to see them.

I don't stop. I can't stop. I don't see the van any longer, don't hear the whine of the engine, but no matter. I keep going, now onto a wider boulevard with smooth pavement and few hills, where I continue through the gears until I am at the highest one and flying and free from the chase and forcing myself to think, think, think: *What now?*

As I'm plotting my next move, the van comes out of nowhere and clips my rear wheel, sending me vaulting over the handlebars, flying for real, then landing hard, scraped and bruised before I can roll to a stop. I am dazed. Taste blood in my mouth. Feel blood on my hands where I broke the fall. The black van appears next to me. I am seized by men in dark clothes. They shove a rag into my bloody mouth, bind my arms behind my back, fling open the double doors, lift me in, and throw me to the floor. When the doors slam shut behind me, it is pitch-black and silent and I am no more.

BOOK TWO

NATZWEILER-STRUTHOF

1942

14

QUATORZE

Time stops. A windowless room. A chair. A light bulb hanging on a frayed cord from the ceiling. Shadows like bloodstains on the walls. I don't know how long they make me wait. Fifteen minutes could be three hours, could be my last fifteen minutes, could be my last three hours. I am desperate for water, can no longer swallow. My tongue feels swollen and I have an irrational fear that it will continue to swell and block my throat and I won't be able to breathe, and already it is difficult to draw a full breath. I am no longer gagged. No longer bound. I take shallow sips of stale air. My panic rises. I obsess about Papa's bicycle. Did they leave it in the street when I was taken? Will it be stolen, or will someone kind find it and keep it for me until I can come back and claim it? Papa will be so angry if I lost his Favor. But how will he even know?

A day passes? I have to relieve myself, so finally in desperation I squat in the corner. There is no choice. The stench worsens as the hours pass, maybe into days, into nights. I lie on the floor because there is nowhere else. It is cold, but I sweat. I remove my sweater and use it for a pillow. I realize I am crying but no tears are coming from my eyes because I am so dehydrated. I sit, I draw my knees up to my chest, I press my face to my knees, I hug my legs, I pray, I quiver with rage, I sink deeper into despair, try to make myself invisible. I hear the scrape of a key in the lock, the door opening, heavy footsteps, but I don't look up until one of them grabs me by the hair and jerks my head back and slaps me hard across my face.

This is how it begins.

It is days later. I am in a black transport again. No windows. No light. One of my eyes is swollen shut. Some of my teeth feel loose. I have lost feeling in my arm. I fear I have broken ribs. There is sharp pain every time I take a breath. I push myself up from the floor where I have been lying against other prisoners' shoes. I blindly scoot forward so I sit with my back pressed against something hard, but I still wince every time there is a bump in the road and metal hammers my bruised flesh. I can make out the shapes of the other prisoners but cannot tell if they are beaten and broken in the same way as I have been. Someone coughs. Someone else slumps to the floor. There is a gurgling sound, a rasping, a painful moan, then silence. The others lean forward. There is a laying on of hands, as if this may heal the fallen man. Someone says, "He is dead, dear God, he is dead."

I try to pray again, for this man, for myself, for my family, but I cannot remember the words. Already I am beyond prayers. I have betrayed everyone, given up all their names: Jean Pierre, Ángel, Frederic, Yvette, Simone, even Zuzu. I have even given them Jules. I told them Papa's name, begged them to call him at the Police Nationale. They wrote everything down. The more I pleaded, the more they laughed.

I am wracked with guilt. I tell myself I confessed to nothing, really. Code names—except for Jules and Yvette. Harmless pranks with my friends. Distributing flyers. Defacing signs. Breaking windows. Slashing tires. Much of what we did. I said there was just the one grenade. We found it but didn't know what it was. We only meant to throw it away. They continued beating me—with open hands, then with fists, then a belt.

I am so tired. I cannot remember when I last slept, when I last ate. When I last saw Maman and Papa—and Jules. Have they taken Jules as well? Is he even alive? I have to believe that Jean Pierre got away, that he warned the others, that they, too, have escaped. I tell myself this. I can't let myself consider the other possibility. But I can't keep the dark thoughts away, either. Because even if they escaped, I gave their names. The dry weeping begins again. I must be making noise. Someone tells me to stop. Other voices, male voices, chastise that one. "He is just a boy. Leave him alone."

I realize then that I am the only girl in the black transport, but they think I'm a boy. Perhaps this has all been a mistake. Perhaps when we get there, wherever we are going, they will straighten everything out, they will send me home. They will speak to Papa. Things will be made right. No need to apologize. These things happen. I'm sorry for what I did. I won't do it again. *Merci, messieurs. Merci.*

It is night when we arrive, but I can tell by the swaying of the transport that we've been traveling for some time on mountain roads. We're stopped before a massive double gate of wood and wire that appears suddenly out of the thick forest. Someone mutters that we are in the Vosges Mountains, Alsace-Lorraine, the easternmost French province, now annexed by the Germans. Where I went with Jules and our families that time on the bicycle tour, where we chanted, *Faster, Papa, faster!*

We are pulled roughly from the back of the van, thrown to the ground, ordered to stand, beaten with clubs for moving too slowly, for stumbling in line. There are uniformed Nazi SS guards. In fractured French, dripping with German accent, they command us forward into a low building, the disinfestation building, command us to strip. I try to explain: "But, monsieur, monsieur, there has been a mistake. I am not a boy. My papers. You can see." This brings a club hard between my shoulder blades, and I go down to my knees, gasping for breath, still struggling to breathe when I'm yanked back to my feet. Already the others have taken off their clothes, and the clothes have been shoved in a barrel, and the barrel has been rolled outside and set on fire. I avert my gaze as the men are herded through a door into another room thick with steam. The door slams behind them. There is the roar of high-pressure showers, intense heat from scalding water that I can feel even through the wall. My captors shout at one another as they pore over my papers. I remember enough German from school to follow what they're saying:

A mistake. Yes. A mistake. But how can this be? What will we do with her? Transport will have to be arranged—to Ravensbrück. The women's prison. But for only one? This will take time. She will be treated like the others until then.

I'm ordered again to strip and this time I have no choice. My clothes are taken to be burned like the others'. Not by the guards but by other prisoners, Poles and Slovenes judging from their voices, who are there to do the guards' bidding. The guards call them kapos. I cover myself with my arms, my hands. There is nothing else. The door to the showers is opened. A kapo shoves me inside. There is a horrible smell of burnt flesh, but how can that be? I gag, I vomit, though I have had no food in days. It is only dry heaving and bile. I'm on my knees. The powerful streams from cannons of water bend me over even farther until my forehead is pressed to the concrete floor. I cover my mouth, my nose. Force myself to stand. It ends. I'm lost in a thick fog that remains. All the men have already gone—through yet another door. I see it now. It opens and I don't wait to be beaten again; I cover myself, stay close to the wall, peer around the doorway. The smell, the horrible smell, remains.

The small herd of new prisoners is lined up again as kapos in filthy striped uniforms shave them. The barbers leave streaks of blood on scalps. And below. One of the new prisoners complains. He is beaten to the floor by one of the SS guards. A kapo finishes the job by kicking the downed man hard in the ribs. He is left there, blood coming from his mouth and nose, as the rest of the prisoners are given their own striped uniforms, torn and threadbare and stained. There is a pile of wooden clogs, and the prisoners race to find a pair that might fit. Most do not look at me, still standing naked just behind the door frame, but some do, and their eyes widen. They shake their heads sadly.

One of the SS guards gestures to me, demanding the kapo shave me just like the others. I can tell from the look on the kapo's face that he finds it distasteful. He does his work quickly while I stand, humiliated. The barber takes greater care with the razor but still nicks my ear as he shaves my head, and blood stains my own striped jacket. The uniform is much too big, so I roll up the legs and the sleeves. I can barely keep the clogs on my feet because they are so large. Another kapo hands me two rags, which I understand are to be tucked around my feet inside the clogs.

Then I'm shoved toward the door, ordered through to whatever terrible dark world lies beyond.

Minutes later, I am walking in a long single-file line, while vicious dogs, German shepherds—Deutsche Schäferhunde—bark, lunge, strain against leashes that threaten to snap, releasing them to attack. Already they're so close I can feel the slobber from their frothing mouths, the heat from their raging faces despite the bitter November air. German voices shout at the dogs, at the line of prisoners, at me when I stumble and fall into the man in front of me and we both hit the ground hard. Someone seizes me, shakes me as though I'm a rag doll, throws me to my feet, and kicks me forward.

There's enough moon that between blinding sweeps of searchlights from guard towers I can see the terraced landscape inside the fences. We pass a gallows, entering a wide courtyard where four bodies have been left to rot in the dirt and grass. We march along rows of white buildings with caged or boarded windows, cross through more fencing thick with coiled razor wire, and finally stop at a building at the top of the mountain, perched on the final terrace. The letters *NN* are painted over the door in crude script.

Kapos fling open the door, herd us inside, slam it shut, and leave us standing there in the black night, fumbling our way to wooden shelves that run the length of the building in four tiers on either side. There are thin straw mats, thin sticks of men lying on them, ghosts of who they might have once been, easily shoved to the side to make room for the new inmates, and for me, no longer a girl in the dark, no longer anything except another prisoner curling up in exhaustion, trying to ignore the biting fleas, the moaning figures all around, the stench of urine and feces, the rotting odor of diseased flesh. I fall asleep despite everything, fall into chaotic dreams that, no matter how troubling, still aren't as frightening as everything I've seen, everything that's been done to me, when awake.

It is dark yet when sirens scream at the hundreds of us crammed into the squalid bunks. I'm swept into a rough line on the floor and immediately marched out in my ill-fitting uniform and thin jacket and wooden clogs. I've lost my striped hat to cover my now-bald head. I step out of line and dash back to find it, knowing without being told that without it I will be victim to another beating. All the others have theirs and I panic with the fear that I won't be able to find mine, that it will prove impossible in the still-dark of whatever time it is. I dive back onto the bunks and flail around until miraculously I feel it, or someone's, but no time to worry about that. I jam it on and jump back to the shuffling line, and as I emerge from the barracks I imitate the others: head bent forward, eyes trained down at my feet, hands clasped behind my back. I can still see the stark landscape of the Natzweiler prison, carved into the side of the mountain like a giant gash, a festering wound, all the trees cut down inside the five-meter fence that marks the perimeter—and the mountainside barren outside as well, as far as I can make out in the harsh searchlights that cut through the night.

We descend the terraces between the rows of barracks we passed just a few hours before going the other way. They look different to me now that I know what's inside—how many wasted bodies are crammed into each, forced outside by their own shouting, cursing kapos to join the stream of prisoners pouring down the mountain prison to a vast courtyard where they instinctively or by training organize themselves into frozen formation. I take my place among them, try to make myself invisible. We're ordered to stand, to not move. We do as we're told. Kapos with lists of names bark them out. If someone fails to answer it starts over again, and again. An hour passes in this way, tired legs trembling, empty stomach rumbling, bowels demanding release. I am so frightened that I hardly notice when I lose control of my own bladder. So tired that I have to fight the urge to lie down in the wet dirt, give up to this bone-deep fatigue, escape back into sleep from this relentless waking nightmare.

Guards circle a man near me. He has dropped to his knees and is struggling to stand. They beat him with their clubs, systematically, as if they're bored doing it, despite his cries, his bleating from the pain. The kapos start the roll call over yet again. They come to my name and number. They pause. Check their roster. Consult one another. Call again. I answer. They continue. They finally get through the list, but no one gives further orders, so still we stand in the dark, shivering in the predawn mountain air. And we wait. And we wait. Guards with German shepherds return to the beaten man. The dogs attack, tearing at his flesh. But the man doesn't react—he must be dead. The guards call off the dogs, seeming disappointed, as though there is no sport in defiling a dead man. Two prisoners appear with a cloth stretcher. They lift the body, arrange limp arms and legs just so, and carry him away from the courtyard, farther down the terraced prison yard toward the entrance to the camp, to the building where those of us brought here in the black transport entered the night before.

The horror of it all is too much for me to comprehend. I squeeze my eyes shut, press my fists over my ears, hard and harder until my temples throb, until I can feel blood welling up behind my eyes. And still I want to block out everything. And still it gets through.

Kapos blow shrill notes on their whistles. We're forced back up the mountain, back through the fencing and the razor wire, back to the wooden NN barracks where other kapos dump watery stew into metal cups, toss out scraps of stale bread. I'm elbowed out of the way by others, shoved to the rear, uncertain about what I should do, worried that I might be hurt if I try to fight my way forward for my share of the food. Eventually I get there—the prisoners know better than to return for a second serving—and I'm grateful that there is still some left. Until I fish through the gruel and see what appear to be insects and maggots swimming in my cup. I drop it to the floor and half a dozen prisoners dive past me to scoop up the spill, grabbing what they can with desperate fingers, sponging the soup up with their tunics and wringing it out into their mouths. I hold on to the bread, but my mouth is too dry to chew it enough so that I can swallow. I try and try. There is another line for water: kapos dispensing to another swarm. I join them this time and work myself as close to the front as I can, ducking under the larger men, though none have much bulk. I can feel their rib cages, each and every one, as I press through with the metal cup I managed to retrieve. I get mine. I cry with relief when the water fills my mouth. I shove in the husk of bread, chew and swallow, miss it the minute it's gone because there is no more and I foolishly lost my stew and already I understand that you eat what you're given here, no matter how revolting, or you starve.

Moments after the kapos take away the empty stew pots and water barrels and the metal cups and the baskets for the week-old bread, a voice asks, "You are also from Paris, yes?"

I nod at the young man. I think he is Charlotte's age, though it's hard to be sure because of his deeply bruised face and the encrusted blood that has dried coming out of his ears and down his cheeks.

"I am Denis," he says. "I was brought last night, too. The man who died on the black transport, he was my friend."

"Nicolette," I say in return, voice cracking. "I'm sorry about your friend." The words sound empty, but I don't know what else to say.

Denis shrugs. "We knew what we were doing, that there would be risks. But even hearing the stories of what happened to others, there was no way to fully understand the lengths to which the Nazis would go—the brutality—until it was too late. And now we are here, who knows for how long? Who knows if we will ever leave?"

"I heard the guards say it was a mistake, them sending me here," I tell him. "I will be sent to a prison called Ravensbrück instead, a women's prison, whenever they can make the arrangements. But my father, he is with the Police Nationale. I told them this in the interrogation, but they must not have contacted him yet. I'm sure I would have been released, or at least not sent away from Paris."

I don't know why I tell Denis this. He looks skeptical but doesn't say anything that might kill my faint hope.

I want to ask him what will happen now, but of course he just came at the same time as me, so how can he know anything? Yet he seems to know a great deal already. I ask anyway.

"This is a work camp," he says. "The other prisoners have told me that later this morning we will be taken out, perhaps to one of the sub camps, perhaps to one of the granite quarries in the Vosges Mountains nearby, to cut and haul stone."

Denis sounds like the tour guide who led the bicycle trip through the Vosges my family took what seems like a lifetime ago. I tell him this. He laughs.

"And NN?" I ask him. "What does this mean?"

"It's for the German expression *Nacht und Nebel,*" he answers. "Night and Fog."

"But what is that?"

"To break the spirit of our friends, our families, the Nazis have begun this program of Nacht und Nebel. If you are taken prisoner and executed and your family knows this, you are a martyr to the cause, an inspiration for others to join the Resistance. But if they capture you in secret, if no one knows what has become of you, what you may have told the Nazis or the secret police about your fellow members of the Resistance, what tortures you may be forced to endure, or worse, then they believe—Hitler believes—it will break the spirit of those left behind, those left not knowing. So, Night and Fog. Nacht und Nebel."

"And why are we here in this barracks, separate from the others?" I ask, panic rising.

We hear boots on the gravel outside, marching to the barracks door.

"Others in the camp come from Poland, from Austria, from Germany, from all over. Here in the NN, we are all from the Resistance, in France, the Low Countries, Scandinavia. Here they can devote themselves to breaking our bodies and our spirits as well. They say no one leaves the NN barracks alive."

And with those words, that faint hope I have been holding—that Papa will find out where I am, that he will use his influence to bring me home—grows even fainter, until it's just a flicker, or perhaps not even that. An ember, burning itself out.

15

QUINZE

An hour later, instead of being assigned to work crews, we are made to march yet again, this time all the way down to the lowest terrace of Natzweiler-Struthof. I find myself standing once more in a sea of prisoners who at first glance all look alike—gaunt, stooped, lethargic, beaten and shaved and skeletal in hanging rags, some with wooden clogs that still hold up, others with pieces of wood or simply strips of fabric bound under and around their sore and blistered feet. On closer inspection, there are some, a few like Denis, who still have flesh filling out their faces, their arms and legs and torsos, who still have a shape that is human.

A guard barks orders, first in German, then in French, for us to face the gallows: "Anyone who looks away, anyone who averts their gaze, anyone who cries out, who weeps, who protests, who mutters so much as a word, a syllable under his breath, will be punished, may suffer the same punishment as this vermin who will now be executed as all prisoners watch."

Another prisoner mutters to Denis and me, "If they want him to suffer, to strangle slowly, the rope will be short. It they want it to be over quickly, mercifully, a longer rope is preferred. The neck will snap. Not as immediate as the guillotine, of course, but not so bad."

The dispassionate way he says this freezes the blood in my veins.

Uniformed guards half carry, half drag the condemned man up the wooden steps, drop him to the platform as they prepare the noose, lowering it just so, to just the right height, in just the right position. The executioner waits, hand on the lever, which I can see will release the trapdoor. The condemned man is lifted to a kneeling position, facing the audience of prisoners. When his head drops forward, a guard slaps him and yanks him back upright so his face, a swollen mass of bruised and bleeding flesh, can be seen. I study the face, because if I look away there is the trouble that has been promised, but also because there is something familiar about it. I can't fight the terrible feeling that I may know this poor man from somewhere.

But I still haven't figured it out when a contingent of officers marches down the hill in their crisp SS uniforms with their knee-high boots polished to a brilliant sheen, their jodhpurs, their tight jackets, their ridiculous rows of medals and commendations, their riding crops, though there are no horses I have seen anywhere, their hats cocked on their heads at jaunty angles, as if they are walking into a café in Paris and not onto a gallows to hang a man.

The first among them is the Kommandant, a young man, perhaps in his mid-thirties, with a rectangular head, a dour expression, a hint of mustache, eyebrows that threaten to meet and join at the bridge of his nose, separated by a deep cleft that could have been left by the blade of an axe: Hauptsturmführer Josef Kramer.

He stands before the condemned man as if the prisoner isn't even there, as if his execution isn't imminent, as if the Hauptsturmführer is here to give a speech much as one would address a group of businessmen at a formal luncheon to honor one of their own.

"The rules of Natzweiler-Struthof are simple," he intones, in a voice that carries in the thin mountain air. "The first thing to remember: Arbeit macht frei."

He pauses. "Work makes one free."

It does not seem that he is being ironic, despite the vast coils of razor wire, the armed guard towers, the snarling dogs, the menacing guards, the grim kapos, the stench of burnt flesh that still permeates the camp.

He continues. "Anyone who is found guilty of agitating in the camp, who meets without permission with others, who is heard discussing forbidden subjects will be hanged."

He doesn't say what these forbidden subjects might be, and I understand that he is being deliberately vague. I understand that the man about to be hanged has been found guilty of this "crime of agitation." My hands are shaking and I can't seem to stop them. I press them against my thighs, hard, dig my fingernails into the flesh, as if that will be enough to keep me from screaming and running, as every new horror in Natzweiler somehow eclipses the one before.

Hauptsturmführer Kramer steps to one side. Guards reach down to lift the man to his feet, but he shrugs them off, attempts to stand on his own, as if through that one act he will show the world that he retains his dignity. But he is too weak, and his legs won't hold. They crumple, knees buckling as he slumps to the platform again. One of the guards kicks him, but he barely registers a response. He stares out at the crowd of prisoners. He stares at me, I'm sure of it, and I see in that moment, in his eyes, what I haven't been able to fully recognize until now.

The condemned man is Antoine.

Charlotte's Antoine.

This time it is my knees that threaten to buckle, me who is too weak, me whose legs won't hold. Yet I manage to stay standing. And as much as I want to look away, I don't—not from fear of the guards or the kapos, but because I refuse to let Antoine die alone. Maybe it was an illusion, the certainty that he was looking straight at me. But maybe it was the truth. And if he looks again, he will find me here with him, in my eyes, in my heart. I am his witness. I am present for him in his last moment. Here for Charlotte.

He is raised up. The noose is fitted around his neck. The rope, I can see, is long. I pray he will not suffer, pray that death is quick. The executioner pulls his lever. The trapdoor opens. Antoine falls. I watch. I absorb everything, every detail, the way a wooden clog drops from one of his feet, the way the foot twitches and then stops. The thin gruel I was fed this morning rises in my throat, what little of it I managed to keep down. I want to vomit it out. I want to scream and run, but there's no escape from any of this, from Antoine's agonizing death, from the straining sound of the rope pulled taut. The sun burns now in my eyes as I continue to face east. The scream is trapped in my throat with the bile, and my heart aches in a way I've only felt once before, for the Ashers, except this time in a way that I am afraid will never stop.

The Hauptsturmführer descends from the platform, turning away from Antoine. I feel something burning inside me and realize it is hatred. I watch as Hauptsturmführer Kramer and his men make their slow march up the mountain to the officers' dining hall, leaving me and the other prisoners to stare at Antoine's lifeless body until we are given orders for what happens next in these lives that are no longer our own. Antoine will be left hanging as a reminder to us. Until nothing remains.

Eventually I am led to a work building known as Block 6, spared for the day from a dusty ride with most of the NN prisoners to the granite quarry, thrown in instead with the elderly and the infirm—French, Dutch, Norwegian. The sign at the entrance says *Weberei*—weaving mill. A kapo shoves me onto a bench set before a wide table, one of a dozen that run the length of the block. The older man beside me is surprised when he realizes I am a girl but says nothing, busies himself with the work: a pile of rubber and canvas strips that must be sliced into thin bands by pressing them against small, sharp blades set into the tabletops, then twisted into braids. I imitate what he is doing, what the others crowded on the benches in Block 6 are doing, under the watchful gaze of the Polish kapos, who stand near the door, muttering to one another in a language I don't know, smoking hand-rolled cigarettes that smell less like tobacco and more like dried grass. I am still grateful for the smoke that wafts over the room, as it partially masks the rotting stench of open, suppurating wounds on the faces and arms and hands that surround me.

At first the work, which requires my focus, helps to dull the images I cannot fully escape of Antoine's gaze; of Antoine beaten, tortured, unable to stand; of Antoine dead, left hanging on the gallows.

"You must be more careful," the old man whispers, but his voice is so soft I have to ask him to repeat himself, to be sure I heard him correctly. He steals a glance at the kapos, but they are still busy in conversation, except for one who scurries to the end of a table to slap a prisoner repeatedly on his head for some perceived infraction and shouts at the victim in Polish.

"You must be more careful," the old man says again. I see that he is not in fact so old as I first thought. He is just emaciated, as are most of the others. "You have been speaking to one of the new ones, in the NN barracks," he adds. "I have seen this. In the morning."

"Yes," I say. "His name is Denis. We are both from Paris."

"He may be harmless, of course," the old man says. "But it's best to be cautious here. This Denis—he has been observed speaking to others in the barracks who we suspect to be mouchards."

"Spies?" I ask.

"Oui. Seeking information. Insinuating themselves. Trading information for favors. Mouchards. Sneaks."

"And you also suspect Denis?"

He shrugs. "Everyone is trying to survive here. They do what they are drawn to do. Each man is different in this way. For some, they can endure very little. Others may be able to hold out much longer. But always there are limits that reveal themselves—sooner or later. A price for every soul. So always, especially in here, you must be careful who you trust."

"But how do you know? How do you know he is a mouchard?" I ask the old man who is not so old. "How do I know I can trust *you*? How do you know you can trust me?"

He doesn't answer directly. He only says, "Now you understand," and then lapses into silence. His fingers are bleeding from the work. I look down at my own hands and see that I am bleeding, too—a little at first, but as the hours go by, soft skin puckers into blisters, blisters burst and weep, skin peels off, and blood stains the braids. I find it harder to avoid contact with the blades, harder to twist the braids into proper strands, harder to keep my head up, to keep my mind off my rumbling stomach and my parched tongue, to keep from begging the kapos for water. Others around me begin to slump forward. The kapos are suddenly busy slapping and hitting and shouting their Polish curses. The worst is not knowing when this will end—that this is only the first day of the life I now live.

Much later, judging by the deepening shadows of the late fall afternoon, I think to ask the man what all this is for: the cutting, the braiding.

He seems to find this amusing. The corners of his dried, chapped mouth turn up slightly and he coughs. "I am told they are to be combined into thick pads to protect ships from the sides of stone piers. For the German navy. For the war."

Later, on the prisoner line back to the NN barracks, we talk in quiet whispers when it seems like the guards aren't watching.

He tells me his name is Henri Perrin. That he is a music teacher in Lyon. He *was* a music teacher in Lyon.

"In Paris, have they heard of this man, the head of our Gestapo, Klaus Barbie?" he asks.

I shake my head.

"His nickname is the Butcher of Lyon, and for good reason. Most of those in the Resistance who have been taken prisoner there, they never leave Klaus Barbie's dungeon alive. I suppose you could say that despite all of this"—he sweeps his arm in an arc, gesturing at all that surrounds us—"we are the fortunate ones."

He sighs. "Well, the good news is there will be more watery stew," he says. "More stale bread!" He laughs. "It is a simple diet for us country folk. It is why we are so healthy!"

I don't know how he can have any humor, but it makes me feel better. For a moment. And then I blurt out what I can no longer keep to myself.

"I knew him," I say. "The boy who was hanged. He was my sister's boyfriend. I think he may have seen me. Do you think that's possible?"

"Would that have been a good thing?" Henri asks. "Or might it have been better for him not to know you are here?"

I don't have an answer, not that he seems to be expecting one. I think he wants to say something that will give me comfort, yet he does not want to lie to me. But before I can reply, a man in front of us staggers. Henri and I each grab an arm and hold him up, help him struggle the rest of the way to the barracks, guide him through the crush of bodies to the steaming vats of stew. At first I hold on to his metal cup once it's filled, but the poor man snatches it out of my hands and gulps it quickly down, as though afraid I will keep his meager portion for myself. Henri helps the man to the edge of a bunk, where he collapses, gripping the crust of bread tightly in his fist. Though lying awkwardly on his side, the man buries his face in the mug to lick the sides. Stabs at the bottom with arthritic fingers. I don't know how he can chew the bread. He will have to return to the line for his ration of water, but I can't concern myself with him any further. I am too hungry and I have my own food to protect and to eat. I don't look at it this time. I can't look. I bring the cup to my lips. I steel myself. I eat. I drink. I chew. I gag. I swallow anyway. I despair that as awful as it is, it is too quickly gone. My hunger is unabated. My thirst still rages. I want desperately to force myself back in line for more food, for more water, but Henri has warned me that I will be beaten if the kapos see. And other prisoners, if they think they've been deprived, or if they think someone else has gotten more than his share, will exact their own revenge.

Across the barracks I see the young man from this morning, Denis, speaking softly, perhaps conspiratorially, with two other prisoners. He seemed so nice, so friendly. How am I supposed to know if he can be trusted? How am I supposed to know if anyone can be?

Henri takes my elbow, interrupting my thoughts. "We may sit outside for a few minutes," he says. He leads the way and we join dozens of prisoners sprawled in the dirt on the cold ground just beyond the barracks steps. The fence, the coils of razor wire, rise five meters high between us and the rest of the prison, but beyond that, far beyond, past the other barracks, the outer fence, the guard towers, the fields, the pine forest, are streaks of red and yellow and orange, all that remain of the sunset. Henri hums. Three other Frenchmen sitting nearby join him. It is a song vaguely familiar to me, but I'm not sure where I've heard it before, or if I ever really knew it. No one sings the words, if there are words.

I ask Henri, and he gives me a sly smile. "Surely they know this in Paris, too," he whispers. "'La complainte du partisan.' We would likely be executed just for singing the lyrics, no?"

I remember it now, remember Yvette singing it one night as we ran through the city, committing what we convinced ourselves was necessary mayhem for the Resistance.

In the stillness of the gloaming, when Henri and the others lapse into tired silence, I find myself wondering what has become of Yvette. Could she have been captured as well, after I gave up her name and the names of the others? Might she have been sent to the women's camp, to Ravensbrück, and when I am transferred there, could we be reunited? The thought lifts my spirits despite my guilt, but it is a strange hope, and I quickly squash it, because of course I want Yvette to have escaped capture, to have avoided the fate of Antoine. Of me. Better that I am in Ravensbrück without any of my friends—or here at Natzweiler—than for them to have been taken by the Nazis.

As the stars come out, claiming the night sky, my mind continues to wander to thoughts of Antoine. I force myself to picture him not in death, on the gallows, but how he was before, how rugged, how dashing on his motorcycle, Antoine with Charlotte on the seat behind him, her arms wrapped around his waist as they ride off down the street in front of our Paris apartment, while Maman and I watch them go, and I dream of doing that with a boy someday when I am older, and perhaps Maman dreams of a time when she did that with Papa, or with some other boy she used to know.

16

SEIZE

I sleep in the NN barracks on a narrow section of bunk partitioned off by a blanket the kapos nailed to the underside of the row of bunks above. The kapos—those Poles and Slovenes who are supposed to have been active in the Resistance in their own countries, but whose stories everyone doubts—are next door, in a spacious compartment just inside the barracks entrance. Spacious, at least, compared with the rest of us. There are no other concessions for me. One of the kapos—the other inmates call him Ivan the Terrible—makes comments to me in a low voice that sounds lewd, even if I don't know what he's saying; another kapo, the one who insisted on the partition, speaks to him sharply and keeps an eye on him, especially if I am nearby.

Morning after morning, I am rousted from my bunk in the dark, long before dawn, forced to stand in formation with the other prisoners for roll call, frustrated and then angry if someone fails to answer when his number is called, which means standing longer, starting over again, suffering through the dogs, the clubs, the beatings, the cries for help that no one can answer or else he will be next. Invalids fall and cannot rise. Sometimes they are left on the ground—for hours, even for days. Eventually the kapos order two prisoners to retrieve a stretcher, to pick up the body sprawled in the dirt—usually, but not always, dead. The prisoners, the stretcher, the body disappear down the steep terraces, toward the entrance to the camp, but I don't know where beyond that.

There is food, also usually but not always. The same watery stew, the same stale loaves of brown bread that the kapos apportion based on who is in favor and who isn't. Ivan the Terrible punishes me for not returning his attentions. I may get a handful of crumbs. I may get nothing. The other kapo, an older man, gives me extra on some days to make up for it, but not enough extra that the other prisoners notice.

As the first interminable week turns into the second, Henri explains to me how the camp works, how most of the NN prisoners are sent daily to the sub camps surrounding Natzweiler where they work in mines, just as Denis said—laboring twelve hours or more, with no breaks for food, only occasionally water. When they come back—those who do return, fewer every week, it seems—they are covered in red dust, dragging themselves on trembling legs, their hands bleeding, sometimes unable to open or close their fingers into fists, or hold on to their food cups. Henri says it is Hitler himself who demands the pink marble that can only be found here for his buildings and monuments and statues, and there is increasing pressure for the Natzweiler prisoners to carve more and more out of the Vosges for shipping back to Nuremberg, Berlin, Munich. We hear the trains sometimes at night when the wind carries their mournful sounds back to the camp.

I continue to accompany Henri and the invalids to the

Weberei, where I do what I can to help those who struggle to stand, to walk, to negotiate the uneven stone steps. Because we aren't sent to the mines, we are considered the lucky ones, but most of the men in Block 6 are as bad off as, or worse than, the miners. Trudging through an overnight snowfall, one man, more skeletal than the rest, moves at an excruciatingly slow pace, as if in a trance. Perhaps he is. Eyes glazed over, gaze fixed on nothing. At roll call he sways, shivering, and I am certain that the slightest breeze will knock him down. I don't remember seeing him back at the barracks for the meager breakfast. He lags farther and farther behind as we make our way to Block 6. A kapo approaches, raises his club but lowers it back to his side. He shoves the stick figure, but again, miraculously, the skeleton doesn't fall. But it is only a matter of time. Everyone sees it. Henri backtracks to help.

I hear someone mutter the word *Muselmann*. I have heard it before. Later I ask Henri. "Nazi slang," he explains. "The SS guards—and now the prisoners—they use it to describe those who are too starved, too exhausted, too ill to go on. The Muselmänner are those who have given up, who are already dead, though they continue to live. Though they have very little time left. They no longer bother to drink, to eat."

The man is listless at the workbench. His hands motionless, his jaw open, his dried tongue protruding over blackened teeth. Once again, the kapos don't bother to beat him with their clubs, don't slap him as they have done repeatedly to anyone working too slowly or nodding in sleep. But they can't ignore him forever. The Hauptsturmführer's words hang heavy—and heavily ironic—over the camp. *Arbeit macht frei*. Because work does make you free—if you equate death with freedom. Finally, late in the afternoon, the kapos pull the skeletal man from the bench and lay him on the dirty wood floor.

"You and you," one barks, pointing to Henri and to me. Henri has done this before. He goes for the stretcher in a corner of the block, returns with it, sets it on the floor next to the dying man, whose breath comes in shallow tremors. Together we lift him onto the stretcher. He weighs nothing. I could have picked him up myself, the way I would a child. We carry him out of Block 6 and make our way carefully to the next terrace below. But his limbs, twitching, won't stay in place, keep falling off the stretcher. Each time we have to set it down, lift his arm or his leg back onto the canvas.

Henri gives me instructions. "You are in the back, so higher as we go down the steps. You must hold your end lower so he doesn't slide. You can see, his skull keeps bumping into my back. It is difficult to walk this way. Painful for him."

"I'm not sure he's still alive," I say.

Henri doesn't respond. The body twitches again, a spasm. An arm and a leg both pitch over the side. The stretcher tilts and the man falls to the ground. I think I hear a groan. A prisoner work crew is marched past. SS guards laugh at our predicament. One takes pity, points to a wheelbarrow leaning against the barracks nearby, tells us, first in German, then in broken French, that we can use it instead of the stretcher. The journey is much easier after that. I push the man in the wheelbarrow; Henri leads the way. I still don't know where we're going. I follow. Past the gallows, where another prisoner has taken the place of Antoine. It's been two weeks since his execution. What's left of him, what flesh the crows haven't yet stripped from bone, still hangs there. I glance, then look away. Focus on my footing, on avoiding the raised edges of the stone steps, on keeping up with Henri.

But something awakens inside me and I force myself to look back, to give my full attention to the dead man, to take in everything: his stricken face, his ragged clothes, the horror of it all. I tell myself I will remember him, just as I will always remember Antoine. If the rest of the world forgets, I will remember. Their lives mattered. Their deaths must matter, too.

Henri must sense this, because he waits patiently until I turn. Then we continue with the wheelbarrow, into a cellar beneath the disinfestation building, under the boiler room. Henri tells me to stop. He feels for a pulse on the man we are carrying and shakes his head. He whispers a hurried prayer. I bow my head and try to pray with him, but nothing comes of it. We wheel the body down a steep ramp. Nothing is locked here. The door swings open to reveal a stack of bodies, skeletal cadavers. Perhaps a dozen. I cry out, sickened, unprepared—as if anyone could prepare for such a thing. The cry echoes as if it came from someone else across the room, or as if there are two of me. Bile again rises in my throat. The stench is overwhelming. The image yet another nightmare come to life. The dead have all been stripped of their striped caps and jackets and trousers. They are a pile of loose flesh and bone. Henri nods but doesn't speak. We leave the body there with the others. Henri and I push the wheelbarrow out of the cellar and close the door behind us.

I'm short of breath, climbing the steps back to the Weberei. In just a brief time at Natzweiler I have lost weight, can feel my rib cage, struggle to banish incessant thoughts of food as my stomach aches from the acute emptiness. My lips are chapped and peeling. I dream of lakes and streams, rivers, waterfalls. Stare at the sky, wishing the gray tinge to faint clouds will turn darker, will fill and swell and explode into merciful rain.

Henri struggles up the terraces as well. I had thought him to be healthy, perhaps because I've compared him to the invalids in Block 6. But now he is wheezing from the effort of carrying the Muselmann down the mountain. I take his elbow to guide him along the path. He spits up blood. When he is done, he wipes his face on the sleeve of his striped jacket. The kapos let us back inside the block, and Henri sits heavily on the bench. I take my seat beside him, nodding to the other prisoners. Few speak—to me, to Henri, to one another. They try to make themselves invisible. No one wants to draw the kapos' attention. They fight to keep their heads up, their fingers busy with the work. They hide their injuries, disguise their sores. Occasionally request permission to relieve themselves in a bucket kept in the corner.

Some of them don't make it and soil themselves, or leave puddles or worse on the floor. This enrages the kapos, and they descend with their clubs. Twice today I see men, helpless, unable to defend themselves, unable to move, beaten into bloody unconsciousness. Both times, Henri keeps a firm hand on my shoulder when I start to rise, to protest. I sit back in shame and stare down at the fabric, at my calloused fingers, at the fixed blades jutting up from the table before me. I wish I could pry loose one of the fixed blades. I wish I could stop the horror.

I have been in Natzweiler for three weeks. Or have I lost count already of the days and nights? Time has no meaning. It creeps forward at an interminably slow pace, and what follows one hour is the same as what I already endured, and what follows that will be even more of the same, and I will be starved for food, desperate for water, starved for news of my family and my friends and my home, and I will be haunted by the image of Antoine, murdered; by the bodies in the cellar; by the brutality of the kapos and the guards; by the lost souls who stumble with Henri and me down the steps to Block 6. My fingers ache. My hands cramp. My back goes in and out of painful spasms from the hours hunched over the work, from helping the old ones pick up and empty the bucket a dozen times each day.

Henri does what he can to lift my spirits. To lift the spirits of others as well. He leads us in song, still the music teacher he was in Lyon. "Music is the purest expression of joy," he tells me. "It is impossible to feel low when there is a song in your heart."

"But what if you can't hold a tune, Henri?" asks his friend Albert one night as we stand outside at twilight, the ground too wet with snow for us to sit, though everyone is bone-tired, especially those who have been working at the quarries. But the kapos won't let us stay in the barracks for this half hour, after the meal, and there's nowhere else to go.

Henri claps a hand on Albert's shoulder. "Yes, well, as I said, as long as you have a song in your *heart*." And then he breaks into another tune, dragging Albert and a handful of others—and me, whispering the words—along with him.

When all is quiet, only the faintest of colors still tinting the western sky, Henri tells me this is the time of day when he misses his wife and daughter the most. "This would be the time I am coming home from the lycée. My little Celeste always runs out to greet me. She always has questions. So many questions. She has been saving them up for me. 'Is it true, Papa, that Mozart composed "Twinkle, Twinkle, Little Star" when he was only three? Is it true, Papa, that we breathe the same air that Napoleon once breathed?' I must answer her, even if I have to make something up, or she won't let me inside the house."

He has a faraway look when he speaks of his family, and I know he has left me then, but I don't mind. If I could transport myself through memories to my own home and Maman and Papa and Charlotte back in Paris, I would do it, too.

Later that night I try. I fix my mind on Jules, push past the guilt and fears that he has been killed, and instead imagine him free, Jules and the others—Les Triplés, the Stooges—in the countryside with the Maquis, with Charlotte, with the other guerrillas, attacking Nazi patrols, blowing up bridges, bombing installations, wreaking havoc, tying the occupiers in knots from which they can't escape, forcing them to devote more and more troops in failed campaigns to catch my friends and their fellow Maquis as the Resistance grows stronger there and also in the city, where dozens, hundreds, thousands surely have risen to take my place. I have done my part. I will do whatever I can in this prison to continue the fight. I will stand tall. I will never stop singing "La Marseillaise" in my heart. And "La complainte du partisan." I will believe. I must believe. It is the only way. I will survive. I will never become like the old ones, never lose my soul to the Nazis, never be taken away to the cellar, never, never, never, never, never give up.

It is another fairy tale, but no matter. I say my prayers—something I rarely did at home: for Maman, for Papa, for

Charlotte, for Jules. I pray for forgiveness. I pray for all the friends whose names I gave the Nazis. I pray that they're safe. At last I sleep.

Soon too many prisoners are turning up too feeble to work in the quarries and at the other workstations in the camp. The food is rotten, the water tainted, there's not enough of either, and we all grow weaker. The kapos are ordered to increase rations. Productivity is everything to the Nazis. Arbeit macht frei.

When prisoners first begin working in the quarries, they look much as they did back home, before arrest and torture. But quickly, because of the grinding work, the accidents, the strained muscles, the starvation, the illness, the beatings, they fade. Many die there. Those who survive, but who have stopped being useful, end up working in the Weberei or a handful of other jobs in the camp. But they are usually so broken by then that it's only a matter of time before they, too, end up in the stack of bodies in the cellar of the disinfestation building.

I can see Henri growing weaker. He has protected me, but I know he is ill, that he cannot hold on for much longer. When Denis has tried to talk to me back at the barracks, I have done all I can to avoid him. He has retained too much of the flesh on his cheeks, too much of his color. Anyone who is like this, I have learned not to trust. The healthy ones. That's how I think of them, though of course even those such as Denis, who I suspect have been receiving extra rations, are slowly but surely losing their inner light.

When the stench of sickness gets too bad, the kapos flood the barracks with light, force all the prisoners out of their bunks, force us to strip and bundle our soiled trousers and jackets and carry them down the mountain to the disinfestation building, where all the clothes are dumped into boiling cauldrons and all the naked prisoners are inspected and shaved again and then herded once more back into the scalding showers. Afterward, wet clothes are retrieved, are wrung out and pulled on despite the damp and the bitter cold of winter night in the Vosges. I cover myself through it all with the wet uniform, but I, too, have become emaciated like the others, can feel the bones starting to protrude—my hips, my ribs, my spine. My hands seem translucent. Perhaps I'm becoming truly invisible.

We are forced back up the mountain, shivering through the deepening snows under the threat of the kapos' clubs while the SS guards watch and laugh in their towers and the attack dogs bite at our heels to hurry us along through the middle of the night. Exhaustion will be compounded by the interrupted sleep and the misery of the cold uniforms.

A wave of nausea sweeps over me just as I am starting to fall asleep. I clutch my stomach and curl into a ball on the hard bunk, fighting the urge to vomit—out of fear of losing what little food I've eaten that is supposed to sustain me, and anxious about being exposed, stumbling onto the barracks floor in the dark to find one of the cans the kapos let us use that are always overflowing with urine and excrement. I press down harder, wishing I could tear out the pain but helpless to stop the constrictions. Finally I have no choice. I crawl off the bunk, wracking my brain to remember where I saw the closest bucket. Another constriction sends me to my knees as I grab my abdomen once again, but this time I can't hold back. Everything I've eaten spews out on the barracks floor. I keep retching, long after nothing more will come out.

A kapo storms into the barracks with his flashlight and club, cursing in Polish. I'm delirious, but still recognize the voice: Ivan the Terrible. He stumbles over me where I'm curled up on the floor, and he slips in the vomit. At soon as he rights himself, he's out of his mind, screaming, striking me with the flashlight, then with the club, on my shoulders, the back of my head. I try to crawl away, to pull myself up on my bunk, to climb to safety, but he won't let me. He grabs the back of my jacket and throws me onto the floor. Kicks me in the ribs. Continues the beating.

"Please. Don't," I cry out. I'm dimly aware of other movement, of someone rising from a nearby bunk, climbing down. This figure approaches Ivan from behind, grabs his arm to stop the beating. I clench my eyes shut, my jaw, my fists. I hear a gurgling sound, the sick noise a body makes when it collapses onto the floor. Someone drags the body away and leaves it sprawled in the middle of the barracks. Others climb down one by one, spit on the body, kick it with their wooden clogs, disappear back into the recesses of their bunks, the thin nest of blankets and straw pallets and frail bodies clinging to what little is left of their fading lives.

The body stays. The doors open. Lights blaze overhead. Guards enter, guns leveled at the prisoners on our bunks, huddled fearfully, blinking, silent. Other kapos kneel by Ivan the Terrible, lying in a pool of blood. His throat has been slashed. I shudder. I wonder if this is my fault. But of course it's my fault. I look for Henri, and see him, but he doesn't look at me. It is obvious he is avoiding my gaze. Will they somehow know this had to do with me? A kapo lifts something from under Ivan's body and holds it up to the light for the guards to examine. It is a bone from a human arm, only this one has been scraped down, filed to a point at one end. Covered in blood.

Again I seek out Henri, and again he won't look back. I remember the cadavers in the cellar.

The doors bang open as though forced by a great wind. More guards storm into the barracks, followed by Hauptsturmführer Kramer, the first time I have seen him since Antoine was murdered on the gallows. He marches to the body, takes the bone, keeps it in his gloved hand as though it is his turn next to use it as a weapon.

He barks an order in German. SS guards seize ten prisoners and drag them outside the NN barracks. The rest of us are ordered to follow. The ten are lined up against the side of the building, frozen at first in the glare of searchlights. The guards take their positions, ready to fire. One of the ten is Denis, his face twisted in terror. His knees buckle, but others hold him up. A final gesture of kindness. I am ashamed for having judged him so harshly, for having doubted him, for having thought him to be a mouchard, when he was only being—trying to be—a friend.

The Hauptsturmführer looks at his watch and waves the bone at the observing prisoners. "In exactly one minute," he says, still in German; one of his lieutenants translates into French. "These men will be executed. You will watch. The only way these lives will be spared is if the murderer identifies himself, and identifies anyone and everyone who is complicit in the murder of—"

He pauses. He doesn't know the dead man's name, or likely his nationality, or anything about him. Hauptsturmführer Kramer doesn't finish. But he doesn't have to.

Henri steps forward. "I alone," he says.

The Hauptsturmführer glares at him, but in a way that makes me think that he is more angry about being interrupted by the sudden confession than about the killing of the kapo.

But then he shrugs, signals to the guards, and they descend on Henri with their clubs. A scream dies in my throat. I wish I could do something, anything, but it is impossible. I'm helpless and can only watch as they beat him long after he has fallen to the ground. They lift him as if he is no more than a bundle of rags and carry him down the mountain. They take him to solitary confinement. They leave him there until the next morning, when he will be hanged at the gallows.

The Hauptsturmführer looks down at the bone, seems surprised that he's still holding it, hands it to his lieutenant. The aide asks what should be done about the ten men still lined up against the barracks wall.

Hauptsturmführer Kramer lifts his hat, wipes the band, replaces it on his head to sit just so, then responds, "Erschiebe sie alles."

Shoot them all.

17

DIX-SEPT

There is a new kapo in Block 6 who speaks decent enough French. Not a Pole. Most likely a Slovene. He holds the door open for me so I can empty the bucket into the sewage ditch outside, watching me the whole time, though there's no possibility of escape. He doesn't look at me with the same lewd expression as Ivan the Terrible, but I know to trust no one. After Henri was hanged—a week ago? a month ago? Time has blurred—I have been in a daze, drowning once again in guilt and grief. My hands work automatically in the Weberei. I stare ahead into nothing; I try to feel nothing—though there is no escaping the incessant hunger and thirst. And there is no escaping the loss of Henri, sitting next to me here, and singing with me and Albert and the others outside the NN barracks in the evenings. It is for Henri—an echo of the kindnesses that he showed me—that I keep rising to help the ones who struggle to lift the heavy bucket, the ones I know will spill on the way to the door, who will be beaten by the kapos. Perhaps even by this new kapo, who is younger, not yet hardened, not yet inured to the suffering, not yet one who instinctively inflicts suffering on the prisoners. This one opens the door for me, but I know it is only a matter of time before he learns.

He speaks to me, finally, the third time I help one of the old ones. "You can't save them, you know."

"I am only doing what I can," I reply. "That man, he couldn't lift the bucket. I was afraid he would spill."

"As you will spill," the new kapo says, "when you are too tired from trying to save them."

I don't know what to say, so I nod and return the bucket. The man I helped, though his eyes are sunk so deep into his skull that I can barely see them, manages to smile at me and bow his head in thanks. He doesn't close his mouth, not all the way, and I suspect he can't any longer, as though the muscles in his jaw have atrophied. He works slowly.

The new kapo notices and says, "He is not so long for this world."

I don't know why he's speaking to me. Perhaps he's bored.

This time I simply return to my seat on the bench. The kapo follows. The men on either side of me scoot away, almost imperceptibly, as if distance between us will protect them from whatever they fear this new kapo might do. He is an unknown quantity, as Papa used to say. *Quantité inconnue. L'impondérable.*

"Perhaps he will get better," I say, since it's clear the kapo wants me to say something.

"Then he will be returned to the quarry," the kapo says. The other kapos have wandered off somewhere, leaving this new man in charge of Block 6. It is an easy job. Everyone is docile. Too tired, too sick, too worn out, too frightened, too resigned to be a discipline problem.

"Do you worry that they will send *you* to the quarry?" I ask.

He sniffs. "Of course not. I will do whatever it takes to keep this position. Whatever the Nazis would have me do. And besides, someone has to be in charge of *these*." He sweeps his hand through the air, indicating all the beaten men, old before their time, wedged onto the workbenches. "It might as well be me."

The kapo yawns and stretches next to me. "You are wondering why I am even here, yes? It is the same story as everyone: The wrong friends. The wrong place. The wrong time. When the Nazis invaded Yugoslavia, they were convinced that we were partisans. Is this the right word? Partisans?"

I nod. The Resistance. In Yugoslavia as in France.

"Ha!" He laughs. "We were criminals, sure. But partisans? Who cares for what government. Nazis? Who cares. And after this is over, I will go back home." He taps his forehead. "With the job here as kapo, I learn so much about being the boss. Belgrade will need a black market. I will be the one to run it. I have big plans."

I can tell he enjoys having an audience, enjoys talking to a girl, even one who has had her head shaved, with cuts scabbed over from the clumsy hand that wielded the razor. I say what I'm sure he wants to hear: that I believe him. I think hard to come up with more flattering things to say, but the door opens just then, and the two Polish kapos announce themselves. The new kapo returns to his bluster immediately, turning his attention to the other prisoners, who suddenly need to be told that they are working too slowly, who suddenly need to feel the hard force of his fist on the backs of their heads, the smack of his club.

I lower my gaze and go back to work. Later, when the others have stepped outside again, the Yugoslavian kapo tells me his name—Draza. Once he starts talking, he doesn't seem to hold anything back. But of course he must know that I will agree with anything he says, that I will be sympathetic, or at least pretend to be sympathetic, because what choice do I have? Perhaps he doesn't care. Perhaps someone like him, someone who holds this power over the other prisoners, this power over me—but who is himself still at the mercy of the Nazis—must pretend as well.

"You remind me of my younger sister," he tells me one day. "Sofia. She was named for our stara mati, our grandmother. This name, Sofia, is supposed to mean *wisdom*, yes? But my Sofia, perhaps she will be wise when she grows up, but now is always silly, always making me laugh with her silliness."

I try to smile. And thank him, though I'm not sure for what. Perhaps if he thinks of me as his little sister, there is still some kindness in him.

But I couldn't be more wrong. Over time Draza becomes one of the cruelest of the kapos, even as he sometimes mistakenly calls me by his sister's name and slips me a crust of hard bread or a desiccated potato.

A few days later, when the Polish kapos are once again with him in Block 6, an older prisoner, André, making his feeble way to the bucket, accidentally bumps into his neighbor, jolting the neighbor's hand. The table blade slices off two of the man's fingers. Blood is everywhere. The neighbor, in shock, just stares at the bleeding stumps until I wrap his hand tightly in a fistful of dirty rags.

Draza is the first to reach André, who is beside himself with remorse, apologizing over and over to the injured man. Without saying a word, Draza clubs André to his knees, keeps clubbing him until he's prone on the floor, unconscious, blood pooling beneath him. I don't know if André is dead or alive.

Draza has a crazed look when he stands. The other kapos have watched everything, have hardly moved, even as I help the wounded man up from his bench and shepherd him toward the door. "Please," I say to them. "He needs help. Can he be taken to the infirmary?"

I'm surprised first that they seem to understand, and second that they nod their assent. One of the kapos takes the injured man by the elbow and drags him away. Perhaps to the infirmary, perhaps not. I never see him again.

I'm astonished when André, shaking his head as he regains consciousness, blood soaking the front of his tunic, pulls himself up to his hands and knees, and then to standing. Draza, unmoved, raises his club to strike André again, but the remaining Polish kapo snaps at him and Draza lowers his club back to his side. André totters over to the bench. He has forgotten the reason he stood in the first place—to use the bucket. He has soiled himself but is oblivious.

Later, outside the NN barracks, André finds me, standing alone at a corner of the building, shivering in my thin coat as the January wind whips through the camp. At first I think he wants to thank me for helping the injured man, not that I think I deserve any thanks. But André has another purpose. When he speaks, I have difficulty understanding him. His face is so swollen, his jaw likely broken from the beating by Draza.

He repeats himself. "I will endure this Natzweiler," he says through clenched teeth. "I will survive the war. I will find the kapo. Your friend Draza. When he is no longer protected by the Nazis. When he is powerless. So I can have my revenge."

I protest. "He's not my friend. I am only trying to survive."

André waves me off. He turns and drags himself back to the barracks entrance so he can be first in line when the NN kapos open the doors, and we can escape the biting cold outside and find the shelter, such as it is, of our wooden bunks.

André never gets his revenge. He can't eat with his broken jaw, can barely drink. A week later he dies in his sleep. Two prisoners are ordered to carry his body to the disinfestation building at the bottom of the mountain. As they're leaving, I stop them. I stare at his broken face. I do my best to memorize it, too.

I wonder for days about what André said to me, about exacting his revenge on Draza. I wonder if there can be justice after all this, true justice. In my heart and in my head I fear it is just as likely what Draza fantasizes will happen after the war: that he will survive Natzweiler, return to Belgrade, find his beloved sister Sofia, reunite with his parents, convince everyone that he was a war hero who fought the Nazis and suffered bravely in one of their concentration camps. Live the rest of his life as if none of this happened.

I hate Draza with all that is in me, and after André is taken away, I hate him even more, and entertain my own fantasies of revenge. But I still continue to accept the crust of moldy bread he sometimes gives me, the potato peel, because to reject these favors would be foolish, would be suicidal. More and more I come to realize, I am forced to realize—my emaciated, failing body knows even if my mind resists admitting it—that if I am ever to bear witness to these horrors, survival is everything. Survival is the only thing.

And it's impossible to know how far you'll go to survive, what things you'll do that were once inconceivable. Like how a month later, when a crow falls out of the sky and into the prison yard—falls for no discernible reason, but is clearly dead, and likely diseased—I join several others in tearing the bird into pieces and shoving it into my mouth: meat, feathers, bones, entrails. I am a feral beast, fiercely protecting what I have found, what I have fought others to seize and devour. But of course it all comes back out. Poison to my system. Indigestible. I vomit and vomit until there is nothing left but bile, and still retch violently even then, as if purging every dark thing that has grown inside me.

Every time there are new arrivals I study them to see if one might be Jules. Or the Stooges—Ángel, Frederic, Jean Pierre. Most have been brought from other countries, or are political prisoners from France but not members of the Resistance. These are assigned to the other barracks on the terraces below the special building for the Nacht und Nebel prisoners, all of whom, like me, have the cloth letters *NN* sewn to trousers and jackets, and a yellow patch with three black circles sewn over our hearts. The rest are made to wear triangles: red for the political prisoners; green for criminals; blue for emigrants (most of them from Spain); purple for Jehovah's Witnesses; pink for homosexuals; black for the mentally ill, alcoholics, drug addicts, beggars, and the Romani. Most of the kapos wear the green triangles.

Jules never comes. I hope that means he is safe, that he has not been caught. That he is still fighting back in ways that I cannot. I dream about him but remember little of the dreams. Bits and pieces. Hand grenades. Anxious moments confronted by Wehrmacht soldiers at checkpoints between arrondissements. Sometimes riding bikes and singing. More often finding ourselves lost in caves, running away, caught in quicksand, and then just me—suddenly alone.

There are days of despair, when I know in my gut, in my bones, that none of them have survived: not Jules, not Ángel or Frederic or Jean Pierre, not Yvette or Simone or Zuzu, not Charlotte. Not Maman, whose heart must be broken. The not knowing is what destroys me. It must be a thousand times worse for Maman. And I know all too well, all too horribly, what can happen to those who are caught by the Nazis. I have seen it already. The Ashers. Antoine. Henri. Denis. André. Me.

Time stands still, every torturous day like every other. They have forgotten about me, about the transfer to the women's prison, Ravensbrück. I say nothing. They might as likely kill me if I am a problem. The SS guards are furious when they are bothered by anyone or anything. They prefer to work their shifts in the guard towers, the disinfestation building, then retire to their quarters, their dining hall, their exercise gymnasium, their weekend leaves into Strasbourg, their furloughs home. The kapos know this and are more brutal at controlling us than the guards themselves would be. It often seems as if everyone hates the kapos worse than they hate Hitler.

It is still deep in winter, but I've lost track of the month. Requisitions must be running low. The thin gruel we're given to eat is at times no more than a watery broth, the extra portions long since ended. One afternoon, a caravan of trucks enters the camp, carrying dozens of women prisoners. Hauptsturmführer Kramer flies into a rage. He has no room for them. They are ordered to march up the mountain, into the forest above the camp. Out of sight. We are ordered to return to the NN barracks. The other prisoners, back already from the quarries, are sent to their barracks as well, though it's still early, still light out, but fading. The kapos bolt the doors, shutter the windows, but we still hear the automatic weapons fire all too clearly. The screams. The deathly silence that follows. A work detail is sent out to dig a mass grave. The dead-eyed men who go, when they return they are more ghostly even than before.

I am horrified, shaken. But also relieved that I wasn't taken as well, that I didn't meet the same terrible fate, that no one remembered that I am a girl. But what right do I have to still be alive? Henri sacrificed himself to save me, but why shouldn't he have lived instead? I am plagued by these thoughts, by the randomness of death in Natzweiler, by the senselessness of it all.

One evening a few days later, I am squatting on a dry patch of earth outside the NN barracks, a brick-like crust of Draza's bread tucked into my cheek. Not enough saliva in my mouth to soften it, not yet, so I wait. Henri's friend Albert, who I have avoided ever since Henri's death, shuffles over to join me. "May I have this spot of ground?" he asks with mock formality.

"Of course," I manage to say, and shift the crust to my other cheek, away from him. Albert wears wire-rim glasses, though one lens is missing and the other is cracked. He must need them badly to continue wearing them like that.

"We haven't spoken in some time," he says. "Since Henri . . ." He pauses. "Since he was murdered."

"Yes," I say. "I have been meaning to tell you how sorry . . ." I, too, trail off in what I started to say. This is too hard. This is why I've avoided Albert. What can I say other than it's my fault Henri is dead?

He nods. "You know Henri and I are from the same city, Lyon," he says. "The same school. We were arrested together . . . We were like brothers, did he ever tell you this? Not as teachers, not in the Resistance, though that as well. But growing up, as boys. We were inseparable. I miss him terribly."

He is tearing up. I wish he would stop. I can't bear this talk of Henri. This man, Albert, I pray he can see it in my eyes.

He presses on. "I have been meaning to speak to you, but it has been too difficult. And every evening, I am so tired from the work in the quarry. Anything besides eating and crawling into the bunks is beyond me. I lack the strength. That, at least, is what I have told myself. But the truth is I have avoided you. To speak of my friend now that he is gone, to use the past tense, is to acknowledge . . ."

He doesn't finish. It is my turn to nod.

"Henri—you know he was very ill?"

"Yes," I say. "I saw him coughing up blood. And I had to help him up the mountain the day we were ordered to carry a body to the disinfestation building, to the cellar."

"Tuberculosis," Albert says. "There is no treatment here. The guards, the kapos, they didn't know. He hid it from them, from everyone. But it was a death sentence. He knew this, of course."

"Why are you telling me?" I ask.

"Because he would have wanted you to know," Albert says. "We all blame ourselves for things that are not our fault. We take responsibility for things that are the choice of other people. Henri wanted to make one last gesture, and so he did. He would only want you to be glad for him that he was able to go out in this way."

"But they broke him with their beating," I say. "With their boots and their clubs. They hanged him at the gallows. How can anyone be glad for this? How can I not feel guilty for what I brought on him? If I had stayed in my bunk. If I had not put myself in harm's way. If he had not felt he had to save me . . ." I have managed to finish the crust of bread. My mouth is even drier than before. My voice is hoarse and raw.

Albert pauses again before answering. "But you see, everyone wishes to control as much of their life as possible, and especially they wish to control their end, to be the architect of their own destiny. I prefer to see Henri's death—and I believe he preferred to see it—as a tragedy, certainly. He was taken from his family. They haven't known where he is or what happened to him. The same as the rest of us in this Nacht und Nebel. But in his death he had triumph as well. Perhaps it is all a fiction. All accidents of fate. All pointless. But no matter. It is the story he was able to write for himself. Slaying that one in the barracks who was hurting you, who might well have taken your life if it had continued. And what beautiful irony, that one of the dead provided the weapon for this! In Henri's sacrifice, in any sacrifice, there is the gift of hope for those who remain. I believe this. I hope you can believe it, too."

I am sobbing now, silently, shaking. "But how can I ever repay that sacrifice?" I manage to ask.

Albert puts his hand on my shoulder. No other contact is allowed in the camp. "You live," he says. "You remember. You make certain that the world is never allowed to forget."

18

DIX-HUIT

The snows grow brutal in the Vosges. Almost overnight, the few meters of white powder we trample through every morning, turning it to muddy slush, becomes drifts half as high as the barracks walls. I pull down the blanket separating my sleeping space from the men, and now use it in the nights over the threadbare blanket, thin as a sheet, I have been using. Prisoners press their bodies to one another for warmth. A single stove in the middle of the barracks belches smoke, sending those with respiratory conditions into coughing spasms that keep everyone awake. For all of that, the stove gives off little heat. Still, men scrounge for anything they can burn: sticks, twigs, loose boards, leaves, tufts of dried grass.

Roll-call formation tortures get worse—the hour, the two hours, standing, freezing, jackets tucked into trousers to keep the wind from whipping the cold mountain air inside the loose-fitting uniforms. Those with clogs, or contraband boots, shift their weight from foot to foot to keep feeling in their toes, blood moving to their extremities. Those without—the ones with burlap bags tied onto their feet with discarded pieces of wire from the quarries—suffer frostbite. As winter deepens, I see blackened toes turn gangrenous. Some are amputated—a death sentence. Infections spread. I watch these men, unable to stand any longer, collapse during roll call. Twice more I am ordered to retrieve the stretcher and to take the body of yet another prisoner to the cellar below the showers at the bottom of the slope. My clogs have held up—I am one of the fortunate in that way—and the rags I was given to tuck inside to make them fit keep my feet warmer. But I shiver, at times uncontrollably, and can barely feel my hands. Like all the others, I have no body fat left, and my muscles have started to atrophy. But there is no way to avoid carrying out orders. Nowhere to hide.

On the second frozen trip to the disinfestation building, Albert and I can barely manage, staggering our way down the cellar stairs, grateful that we will leave the body there. But this time, a kapo orders us to stay. "Another job," he says, pointing to the putrefying stack of bodies. A naked light bulb illuminates the terrible scene. The furnace on the other side of the room has died down to embers. "You will load in the bodies," the kapo says. "When they have burned enough, you will load in more."

Albert and I look at each other with similar expressions: horrified, helpless. And in that moment, I understand what I should have figured out months before: that the bodies are what have been used all along to fuel the furnace, to heat the water to scalding temperatures in the boiler for the showers.

Once again, we have no choice. We do as we're told. At first we lift the body we just brought down the mountain, but the kapo stops us. "The rotting ones first," he says, pointing again, this time to the cadavers on the bottom. "I am sick of their smell."

I think about Henri when he killed Ivan the Terrible in the NN barracks—and have a brief fantasy of doing the same thing to this kapo, of shoving *his* body into the furnace. But the fantasy passes as quickly as it comes to me. I am too small, too weak. I have no weapon. I would be beaten, killed. And for what?

"Come, Nicolette," Albert says, wrestling free a half-buried cadaver. I recognize what's left of the face as I bend to help. It is a man I used to see in the barracks, but I never knew his name. As Albert and I work, I wonder if one day there will be others here—surely there will—assigned to this nightmare task, looking into the faces of the future dead. I can't help but despair, wondering if one of the faces will be mine.

A dozen fresh NN prisoners are brought to Natzweiler. I have been working in Block 6 for most of the past four months and have seen dozens of prisoners die in that time. To the Nazis it is a matter of logistics: more room for newer, healthier prisoners, who will in turn be worked and starved to death. It breaks my heart to see the new faces, to see the damage already done to these young men in torture and interrogations, to know that so much worse awaits them here.

But at least they bring with them—some of them—news of the war. In the barracks that night, I'm close enough to hear a whispered conversation among some of the older prisoners and one of the new ones, a Frenchman named Laurent. I took note of him when he arrived. He had been beaten so badly that the others were holding him up, all but carried him to his bunk. His nose is broken, twisted sideways on his face. Deep purple-black bruises circle his bloodshot eyes. He can barely move his jaw. He speaks through gritted teeth. It's clearly painful for him to talk. But he persists.

"Everyone anticipated the Americans would cross the English Channel and attack the Germans at Normandy," he's saying. "But they are in North Africa instead, fighting the Germans and the Italians there. In Morocco, Tunisia, Libya. In two days, they defeated the Vichy forces, and now the French in North Africa are on the side of the Allies."

This should be wonderful news but instead leaves everyone scratching their heads. Why North Africa?

Laurent is too tired to go on. We all are. We let him sleep. I pray he won't be sent to the quarry, not yet, not as weak as he is and so obviously broken. As it turns out, the snow is too thick for the trucks taking prisoners to the mines, and we're all assigned to shoveling crews instead. Laurent survives, primarily because others take care of him, holding him up when the kapos come around, shoveling where he is unable.

The next evening, in a rare hour when the kapos allow us to stand around inside the NN barracks and out of the wind and snow, Laurent is able to tell us more. It is March, and so much has happened in the months I've been here. "The Allied plan is to first defeat the Axis in North Africa," Laurent says. "Then from there—from Tunisia—they will invade Sicily, and then attack north, up through Italy, until they are at the doorstep of France and Germany."

"And what progress so far?" someone asks. "When did this invasion begin?"

"November," Laurent says. "So now four months ago. And they say it will be months longer before the Germans are driven out of North Africa and the Sicilian invasion can begin. But the Allies control the Mediterranean now, which means Germany and Italy can no longer resupply or reinforce their armies in Tunisia and Libya."

Most are encouraged. I am as well, for a while. But then I think about how long it will take—months, years, before the Allies reach us here, before Natzweiler might be liberated—if the Allies are even able to advance this far, are even able to defeat the Nazis and the Italian fascists in North Africa, where the British have been going back and forth against the German field marshal Rommel for years already, with no sustained success. I can hear the muted broadcasts even now—giving us some hope; dashing that hope—from when Maman and I sat huddled over the radio and hung on to every word that came over the BBC in the Ashers' apartment back in Paris.

I retreat from the crowd of prisoners and the hint of warmth from the stove to my lonely slab of bunk, the flattened, now-cushionless straw mattress, the flea-ridden blankets, the solace that only sleep might bring. Others follow. The kapos enter with their clubs to let the new prisoners know who is in charge. Laurent doesn't move quickly enough. They beat him to the floor, where he curls into a ball, covers his head, and whimpers. They leave him there. The lights go out. Men crawl down from their bunks to help him. In the morning he can't stand at all. He coughs up blood on the freezing trek in the dark to formation for roll call. His friends carry him, but they're not allowed to hold him up once there. He brought news of the war but will not live to see the liberation. He is the first of the new prisoners to die.

• • •

"We must honor him," Albert says a few days later. "He has given us the gift of hope."

"But don't you think this may all be wishful thinking?" I ask, flattened by all that has happened—the deaths of Antoine, Henri, André, Laurent. The deaths of so many others. The loneliness, and fear for my friends and family, that tears at my heart every day. Every waking minute of every day—and in most of my dreams.

"But you heard what Laurent said," Albert insists. "Also, the Nazis are still bogged down deep inside the Soviet Union. He told us this as well. Hitler has sent a million troops there, half the German army. And winter in the Soviet Union is murderous. The Nazis will lose as many men to the harsh conditions of winter there as they will fighting the Red Army."

"No one has been able to stop Hitler," I say.

"Remember your history lessons," Albert admonishes, not ready to give in to despair. "Hitler would have done well to study what happened to Napoleon and his Grande Armée when they invaded Russia."

We are lying next to each other in our bunks. He talks for a long time, though I am so tired, listening to him, that I fear I have given offense at times by falling asleep. But he doesn't seem to notice. He was a teacher of history in Lyon and considers me his student, whether I can stay awake to hear or not. Of course he has had sleepy students before in his classes. And of course he challenged them, as he challenges me, to see that the past is never simply the past. He quotes Shakespeare: "What's past is prologue." I have heard all this before, but there is something comforting in it for me as he intones about the 1812 invasion, the Russians' refusal to engage, their scorched-earth retreat, the ravages of General Winter, the half-million French casualties, the French army's own disastrous retreat, Napoleon's fall, his exile on the island of Elba.

For a few moments I am no longer in Natzweiler, no longer myself exiled deep in the Vosges Mountains. For a moment I am a schoolgirl back in Paris. For a moment none of this is real.

19

DIX-NEUF

The murderous Vosges winter has settled in so hard that breath itself turns painful, sleep all but impossible, hunger at times a twisted kind of relief from the freezing mountain winds, the snow that piles up to the barracks windows, works its way through cracks in the walls, accumulates in drifts on the floor inside, a dusting on frozen blankets. Faces ache. Extremities lose all feeling. Bodies fail at such an alarming rate that the kapos order a second stove brought into the NN barracks, take work parties out into the forests surrounding the camp, order wagons filled with fallen branches, and, when those are gone, trees felled by kapos forced by SS guards to labor with axes, not trusting the regular prisoners—and definitely not the desperate Nacht und Nebel prisoners—with weapons.

And still we are forced to endure the predawn formations, the interminable roll calls, the lost companions, too frail, too weak, too sick to last any longer. Bodies pile up to the ceiling in the cellar beneath the showers. The Germans' fears of lice and typhus grow as the weather turns evil, as transports to the quarries are shut down, the roads buried under so much snow that work crews can't clear them fast enough before they're buried again. And the prisoners dying every day. More and more all the time.

When the supply of materials to Block 6 is interrupted for a few days, I am officially assigned instead to a work crew "processing" the bodies in the cellar of the disinfestation building before they are thrown into the furnace to heat the boilers. At first I am grateful for the warmth, and hate myself because I am grateful for the warmth. But then I am handed a pair of rusty pliers by one of the kapos. He opens the mouth of one of the dead and pantomimes what I am ordered to do. I stand frozen in horror, unbelieving. Another NN prisoner, a quiet man named Ricard, perhaps thinking I don't understand the kapo, explains unnecessarily. He, too, has been given a pair of pliers.

"Before burning the bodies now, we are required to check for gold fillings to be pried out of the rotten teeth of these men," he says.

I can only nod. The kapo yells at me in his Slavic language. I kneel next to the other prisoners, next to the grotesque pile of bodies. The only light in the cellar comes from the open door to the furnace. We tie strips of cloth over our mouths and noses to protect from the stench.

I pry open the jaws of what is little more than a skeleton. It takes all my strength, and I half expect the jaws to snap shut when I release them, like a trap, but the mouth remains open. I am forced to bring my face close, centimeters away, to peer inside, to see the traces of dull metal that is presumably silver or gold, and I struggle to work the pliers under and around the fillings, grunting from the effort.

Ricard, working on a body next to me, grunts as well. Then,

perhaps to distract himself from the macabre work, he asks me where I'm from. "I have seen you in the barracks and was surprised that there is a girl here."

I am panting from the exertion, but I try to answer him. "From Paris," I say. "I was told there was a mistake, that I was to be sent to the women's camp."

Ricard scoffs. "Everyone thinks these Nazis are so organized, so methodical in everything they do, but I have found they are human just like the rest of us in that they, too, make bureaucratic mistakes. They, too, are often confused. I'm only surprised there aren't more sent here who were meant to go somewhere else."

He prattles on like this, saying nothing, really, and for a time it works to take my mind off what we are having to do, as impossible as that seems. But always I come back to the unspeakable horror of this. Always I come back to wanting to memorize what's left of the faces, to wishing I knew the names, to hating, hating, hating the Nazis for what they've done to these men, for what they're making me do.

Hours pass. It turns so hot in the cellar that we take off our jackets, though keep them close, tucking them under our knees where we kneel lest another prisoner, coming over to drag the bodies to the furnace, tries to steal them. Ricard, who has been assigned to this detail before, seems to know everything about what happens next.

"These fillings, they are separated out, then melted down and poured into molds for gold and silver bars," he says. "A chemist, also a prisoner, assigned to the infirmary, has this job. They say the bars are shipped to Berlin." He winks at me. "Or kept by the Hauptsturmführer."

Somehow we make it through the day. When the kapos tell us we're dismissed, I struggle back into my coat, exhausted from the hours of dark labor, and I pray that I'll never again be made to do this work. The shock of the cold outside, after ten hours sweating in proximity to the raging furnace, makes me dizzy. Ricard, too. We stagger as we make our way up the mountain. Everything seems sideways to me, every step a chore. I forgot to button my coat before leaving the cellar, and now my fingers are too numb. I wrap myself inside the folds of cloth as tightly as I can. It's not tight enough. I am frozen by the time we are let inside the fence that surrounds the NN barracks, can barely hold my cup for broth and water, shake uncontrollably under my thin blankets once the kapos let us crawl onto our bunks. Hours later, so deep into the night that it must be almost morning, the shaking eases and I fall into a deep, dreamless sleep—only to be awakened, still in the winter's dark, for roll-call formation in the field back outside. And so it begins again. A new day. A new hell.

Despite my prayers, Ricard and I are once again assigned to the disinfestation building. One of the kapos laughs when he sees us. In fractured French, he says, "You were so very good at what you did yesterday—not a single missed filling!—that you are rewarded by getting to do it again today."

We have just started when Nazi guards storm into the cellar. They grab one of the kapos, hold him at gunpoint, then order Ricard and me and two other prisoners to follow them outside. We are handed shovels, led to the gallows, and ordered to clear away the ice and snow. The kapo falls to his knees, crying and begging the guards, first in Polish, then in German. He is begging forgiveness.

"He tried to steal some of the gold fillings," one of the other prisoners whispers. "They were discovered buried outside."

I can't help feeling sorry for the kapo in his fear and desperation, for anyone facing execution, even if he has brutalized us in the past. Ricard, who seemed unmoved by the work we were forced to do in the cellar, is the same today. Even standing in the bald field that surrounds the gallows, forced to watch the kapo's body twisting in the wind, snow blasts burning our exposed faces, he maintains a stoic expression. When I ask him about it later, back in the cellar, back at work with the pliers and the dead, he doesn't answer except to quote a German philosopher, Friedrich Nietzsche. "When you gaze long enough into an abyss, the abyss will gaze back into you."

I don't understand him, not at first. Only later does it begin to make sense. But it doesn't matter in the moment, because the other kapos come into the cellar, inspect the bucket, see only a few gold fillings, yell at us for working too slowly, and beat us until my mouth fills with blood.

A week later, in the middle of the night, still fearful about a possible outbreak of typhus, the guards and kapos rouse all the prisoners in the NN barracks and force us down the mountain and into the scalding showers. Clothes are once again left in a pile outside, where they are thrown into enormous vats of boiling water. I cover myself with my arms and hands as I always do, still ashamed to be naked around the men, embarrassed, though most of them know me by now and look away—or are too exhausted to care. Once herded back outside, we are all left to stand on the frozen ground, amid snow drifts. An agonizing hour crawls by. Log fires rage beneath the vats, and we inch as close as we can to what little warmth we can capture. Finally the clothes are fished out and thrown to the prisoners, who have to find what fits, settle for what is left, and pull it on though still soaking wet and immediately freezing.

Barely able to walk in this frozen state, chilled to the marrow, teeth chattering so hard they threaten to break, I painfully climb the terraces back to the barracks, back to the insufficient warmth of thin blankets. I can't sleep. I am shaking too hard once again. I suspect everyone is the same. Hours later, at roll call, all the prisoners are still wet as we are once again ordered outside. Feet are blocks of stone. Fingers burn. Cheeks are caked with ice. Men fall. Pick themselves up. Fall again. I clench my hands into fists, but then can't open them. In the howling wind, I strain to hear the numbers called. Many don't answer. Can't answer. Half a dozen have already died in their bunks. Half a dozen more perish where they stand. I see Ricard standing next to two of the dead men. He still has that same stoic expression—from staring into the abyss, from the abyss gazing back into him.

The winter storm intensifies in the week that follows. For hours. For days. Surely it must be April by now, but here in the Vosges there is no sign of spring. No sign that there can ever be an end to the snows of winter. The quarries remain shut down. Men mill about the barracks with nothing to do, called away occasionally for a work crew for felling more trees for firewood, to carry another body down the mountain, to stumble to the infirmary. Few return from there. The supply trucks have somehow made it through to Natzweiler, so I am once again marched out in the mornings to Block 6, where I force my frozen fingers to work, where I no longer volunteer to help empty the slop buckets, where Draza still sometimes slips me food. He pats me on the head when the other kapos aren't looking, seeming pleased with himself and these fleeting moments of decency or humanity or whatever they are. I think I should feel guilty to have this when the others have nothing, but it is an abstract thought, one that flutters into my mind involuntarily, a habit of intellect or emotion, but it doesn't last. No longer.

I have lost my focus, spiraling down into this dark cave, and fail to even notice that I have sliced open my finger, cut it to the bone, until my neighbors on the workbench shout for the kapos, grab my arm, and wrap a dirty cloth tightly around the wound. The blood quickly soaks through and drips onto last night's snowfall as Draza leads me to the infirmary. I could be outside my own body as the doctor—Janssens, a Belgian prisoner from one of the other barracks—does his clumsy best to suture the wound shut. He cakes my bloody hand with white sulfa powder, explains in fluent French that it should help ward off infection, then wraps my damaged finger, and then my entire hand, in a cleaner cloth. It's never clear who is taken to the infirmary for treatment and who is left to suffer. Today I'm one of the lucky ones.

"There you go," Janssens says. "If it swells up, or if there is fever, ask the kapos to send you back. Who knows? Perhaps they will."

I look around the infirmary at the sick and the dying on cots, on straw mattresses, on blankets on the floor. A stack of stretchers in one corner. Suddenly my finger is shot through with sharp, throbbing pain, and I'm back in my own body, and there is no getting away from it, no matter what.

20

VINGT

Late one afternoon, already near dark, Draza leads me from Block 6, where I have worked for the past six months. "Aren't you the fortunate one," he says, smiling. He won't tell me why he says this until we're halfway down the mountain and stop outside the SS officers' hall. "Your new job," he says. "All of Block Six will miss you. No one left to carry their slop bucket."

He opens the door for me to enter but doesn't follow me inside. Immediately I think I could faint from the smell of food cooking in a kitchen somewhere I can't see. My knees tremble. My finger throbs. I am sweating and struck by how warm it is inside. How beautifully warm. A prisoner in a white jacket comes for me. His black hair, though short, is actually grown out some, not shaved like the rest of us. He is young, perhaps in his thirties. Handsome. Thin, but not skeletal.

"I am Christian," he says, and for a second I'm confused, as if he is telling me his religion. But of course it is his name.

He introduces himself further, tells me he is from the north, from Amiens, where he was a chef—and a communist. That is why he is here in Natzweiler. He was told there was a girl in the camp, and he requested I be sent to help him in the kitchen.

"Can you serve?" he asks. He is all business.

"Serve?" I'm not sure what he means.

"You are to be the new server for the officers. You will set their places, bring out and serve their food, fill their glasses, and remove dishes and cutlery when they have finished with each course." He sweeps his arm to indicate a massive oak table with a dozen heavy ladder-back chairs that take up most of the room behind him. A chandelier, unlit, hangs over the center from an exposed beam in the high ceiling.

"You will also help where needed in the kitchen," he continues. "But most important will be serving. And it must be done flawlessly. The SS officers expect everything to be done just so."

"Of course," I say.

He asks my name and I tell him. So few people have spoken it the past year that it sounds strange coming from my own lips, and even stranger coming from his. I only now realize that an SS guard, cradling an MP35 machine gun, has been standing in shadows during the conversation.

"Don't worry about him," Christian says. "He doesn't know French. And he is just a boy. Look at him. He's not much older than you." Christian rubs his hand through his hair. I wonder what that must feel like. It's been so long since I was able to do it.

"The Nazis are sending their children now to posts like this one," he adds. "Their old men, too. Surely you have noticed. The healthy SS guards have been conscripted into the Wehrmacht and deployed to the Soviet front. And now in Italy. I hear them speaking of this at their meals."

I say I haven't noticed. Mostly I am dealt with by the kapos. The Nazis—I don't see past their uniforms.

Christian says I must accompany him back to the kitchen, that he needs to finish preparing the evening meal for the officers and I must change. I follow him. The young soldier follows. "You will never be alone here," Christian says. "Usually there are two of them."

"Why?" I ask.

Christian smiles. "To make sure that nothing happens to the food before it is served to their bosses. To make sure no one comes in while the officers stuff their smug Nazi faces. To scrutinize you in case you should have an idea about stealing anything. To count the knives. The boy who preceded you, he thought he was clever enough to get away with certain things. He was wrong."

I understand immediately what Christian is not saying. Where that boy ended up.

As I step into the kitchen, I feel faint all over again, the delicious smells enveloping me, as if I've stepped into heaven. "Put this on," Christian says, handing me a white coat like the one he is wearing. I shed my striped jacket and fold it carefully, not sure where to put it. Christian points to the back door and tells me to leave it outside. The guard is right there as I do. He opens the door, points to an empty crate on the ground.

Christian directs me to the stove, hands me a wooden spoon, and tells me to stir. There is a pan filled with huge meat dumplings, the steam rising and bathing my face, making me delirious.

There are three kinds of sausages. An enormous pot of salted potatoes, another with spiced cabbage, smaller pots with simmering sauces. I have never smelled anything so wonderful in my life.

Christian curses. "That's all these Nazis will eat. This disgusting food from their homeland. They have no appreciation for gourmet cuisine. I could prepare for them even simple French dishes: coq au vin, flamiche, ratatouille. They would throw them out and demand to know why they hadn't been properly boiled."

I hardly know how to respond. Everything he is saying sounds foreign to me, trivial, absurd. How can he speak in frustration about gourmet dishes? How can there even be such things left on the earth when all I have known—all any of the Natzweiler prisoners have known—is watery stew, potato peels, crusts of bread as hard as stone?

Christian hails the young SS guard and tells him in German that I will eat now. With permission, of course. The guard nods, and Christian ladles a small serving of potatoes and cabbage into a bowl, a small cut of sausage added on top, and hands me a spoon. "Eat this. Then come back to help. We must get the table set before the officers arrive. They will want their beer and their wine right away. And their sausages."

I glance at the guard, afraid this might be a trick. I have only just met Christian, and though he has been nice, I know better than to trust anyone right away. But the smell is overwhelming and I decide I don't care. I press my face so close to the food that I could devour it all without using the spoon. There is no place to sit, but I don't mind. All I care about is the soft flesh of potato in my mouth, the salty broth that holds it, and the desire to keep tasting forever and never swallow because then it will be gone and I will be one spoonful closer to the end. But I can't hold back. I lift the bowl and drink it in gulps, let the slices of cabbage melt on my tongue, savor the unfamiliar feel of chewing and the taste of actual meat. I am crying. Christian sees this and laughs, but not in a cruel way. He knows. He can see how little flesh is left on my bones from these months of starvation.

"Slowly," he says, though I am nearly finished. "There won't be more. I am sorry." He nods toward the guard. He opens a large bread box on the counter and takes out a fresh loaf of black bread. With a serrated knife he cuts a thin slice and hands it to me. "To soak up what is left." In a moment that is gone, too. My stomach aches from the meal, so much more than I have eaten since the arrest. A wave of nausea breaks over me and I fear I will vomit. I panic at the thought, the possibility.

Christian pours a cup of water from a pitcher. I thank him and sip it slowly. It is better.

"Now to work," he says, taking back the bowl and spoon. I am reluctant to let them go, fearful that this might be my last true meal ever. But that is ridiculous. Surely there will be another tomorrow. And the next day. I have been assigned to paradise. I will do anything they want of me. Christian gives me a chef's hat to replace my striped cap, which is tossed outside with my prisoner's jacket.

My joy dissipates when the officers come in—a dozen of them, all at once, in their gray-green uniforms with sharp, pointed collars, death's head badges, Nazi-eagle emblems, bloodred swastikas, SS lightning-bolt insignias. I take their overcoats and carefully hang them to dry, place their black caps on hooks, fill their glasses with French wine or their mugs with German beer, struggle in with heavy platters of sausages, baskets of breads, bowls of fruit. When Christian tells me these are merely the appetizers, I am stunned.

The officers help themselves from the platters, but no one sits until they've milled around for half an hour, waiting, until the door opens dramatically—a junior officer barking, "Achtung!" And Hauptsturmführer Kramer enters. A dozen right arms shoot skyward with straightened hands in salutes and a chorus of "Sieg Heil!" The Hauptsturmführer surveys the officers, his gaze sweeping past me, or through me, as if I am invisible. He eventually gets around to a languid return salute, mutters his own "Heil" and throws his greatcoat from his shoulders, clearly expecting a junior officer to catch it, which one does. Tosses off his hat. Makes his way to the head of the table.

I am busy for the next hour carrying in trays of food, refilling glasses and steins, removing dishes, replacing silverware—too busy to listen to conversation, too weary anyway to translate much of what I do overhear. Christian makes a point of hovering near the door when he's not otherwise occupied over the stoves, arranging food on the plates and in bowls, pulling fresh strudel from the oven for the dessert course. The young guard and his machine gun have been joined by a second, both standing at attention, one at the entrance to the dining hall, the other at the rear door to the kitchen, like statues.

All along I have been deathly afraid of doing anything wrong: pouring a beer instead of wine, taking a plate too soon, bringing out a new course too slowly, dropping something, stumbling, coughing.

And near the end of the evening it happens, as if fated. I trip carrying a serving tray loaded with dessert plates of the strudel. Everything goes flying. I sprawl helplessly onto the hard floor, banging knees and elbows and my face. Dishes break. The tray skitters to the far wall. A cat I haven't noticed before slinks out of a dark corner to inspect the strudel and drag some away.

The conversation stops at once, stone silent as I pick myself up. I can't look at the table, the officers, the Hauptsturmführer. I cringe, knowing I will be beaten. I crawl to the spilled desserts and scoop them back onto what's left of the plates. My face is red with shame, and with fear. A chair scrapes away from the table. Boots make their heavy way across the floor. Someone takes my arm and lifts me until I am standing on trembling legs. A hand is tucked under my chin and lifts my face to see, looking down at me. Hauptsturmführer Kramer. He asks, in simple German, as one might address a small child, if I am injured. I shake my head and answer in German, "Nein. Danke, Hauptsturmführer."

He says, "Very good." Signals to the guards to retrieve the platter, instructs them to help me clean up the mess. Christian has come out of the kitchen by this time, and he, too, kneels to help. He is perspiring heavily. Takes the tray from the guard and draws me quickly away into the relative safety of the kitchen. I expect a kapo to suddenly appear, to attack me with his fists or his club, as always happens in the camp for even the smallest infraction, or for no infraction at all.

But there are no kapos in the dining hall, none anywhere in the building. And the SS guards, taking their cue from the Hauptsturmführer, just shrug. The moment passes. We hear the scraping of chairs, the scuffing of boots, the opening and closing of doors. We hear another chorus of "Heil Hitler."

"You are in another world now, Nicolette," Christian says as he sends me out to clean up the dining hall. "But you must always remember that nowhere is it safe."

21

VINGT ET UN

In this way, mindless day after mindless day, I escape the starvation that takes the lives of so many, the violent beatings by the kapos, the maulings by the Deutsche Schäferhunde, backbreaking work in the quarries.

When spring finally arrives, it brings with it rivers of melted snow and sewage cutting trenches down the side of the mountain, turning all of Natzweiler into a muddy, foul-smelling field. Planks are laid over the deeper trenches so we can cross. Some prisoners, unsteady under the best conditions, lose their balance and fall in. Some never climb back out. There is an upsurge of deaths, bodies at times left lying for days in the cesspools. Prisoners are returned to the quarries. Albert tells me much of their time is spent bailing out the flooded pits so the mining can resume.

The NN prisoners return one day caked in mud so thick I can't recognize them. Albert is speaking to me before I know it's him. "There was a flash flood," he says, leaning wearily against the damp barracks wall. "We had to scramble up the sheer face of the quarry wall. Some didn't make it."

I look around, try to do a head count. Many are missing. Survivors are sprawled helplessly on the ground, in the mud, too depleted, or injured, to stand.

Albert slumps to the ground with them. "I'm not sure how much longer I'll last," he says.

It's the first time I've heard him despair and I don't know what to say. Albert has always held on to at least a little optimism, even in the aftermath of Henri's death. Even after our assignments, carrying bodies to the furnace room. Even after everything. Until today.

I say the things one says—he'll survive; we'll both survive; we'll both get out of this alive. I know it. But I doubt he can hear me. Not really.

Weeks later, Albert sits with me again outside on the packed dirt when I come back from the officers' dining hall, where I have worked since sunrise. It may be June by now, we can't be certain, but the evenings are still cool. He has just been returned from work in the quarry and is trying, and failing, to weave some thread he teased out of his blanket into a belt to hold up his trousers. He can no longer cinch them tight enough to stay on. I take the thread from him and finish the job, then help him tie it around the frayed waistband. He stares at the weeping blisters and infected lacerations on his hands. All around us are the other NN prisoners from the quarries, many of them bent over at the waist from back pain, their limps so pronounced from injury that they can barely stand. I have smuggled a few bites of food for Albert from the officers' dining hall, as I do on those few occasions when the SS guards are distracted, and I slip it to him now, taking great care that others in the barracks don't see. There are spies, the mouchards. There are those who would be understandably resentful that I have brought these scraps for Albert while they have none. Those who, starving, would do anything for that extra crust of bread, that cold shred of cabbage, that rare mouthful of sausage.

Albert lets the meager scraps dissolve in his mouth so no one will see him chewing. He tells me there have been changes in the mines. "The guards are now calling the quarries die Sportplatz—the sports field. There are the Stairs of Death, a steep incline out of the quarry. Ten prisoners are selected at a time to climb while carrying blocks of stone on their backs. Fifty kilograms. The first to the top gets an extra ration of water. The rest, nothing. Well, not nothing. They are allowed to live. If one prisoner stumbles, the others behind him go down, like dominoes, some falling to their death. Those are the fortunate ones. The seriously injured are killed in other ways. Guards will force the prisoners to race up the stairs with their loads. They will execute those who lag too far behind."

He shudders. "The last time I was forced to climb, it was the man behind me who was shot."

He is silent for a few minutes, while I try to wrap my mind around the games of monsters. Then Albert continues. "There is a so-called Parachutists' Wall as well . . . Prisoners who are out of favor, which could be anyone at any time, are lined up at the edge of this cliff and given two options: to jump or be shot."

"But the work is already terrible enough," I say. "There was the flood. There were the drownings. There have always been accidents. Deaths. Why this?" As if any answer could be justification for these new levels of cruelty.

"A new officer, Koehler, was transferred here from Mauthausen, a concentration camp in Austria that has its own quarries," Albert explains. "He brought this 'sport' with him to Natzweiler. It is intended to motivate the prisoners to work harder. And to provide amusement for the guards. So we now have our own Stairs of Death. Our own murder races. Our splintered bones and broken skulls. Our own Parachutists' Wall. Koehler, Kramer, and the SS officers who carry out these orders—these are the men you are serving every morning at le petit déjeuner, every evening at le diner—"

The kapos interrupt, shouting orders for us to enter the barracks, beating and shoving those too slow climbing onto their bunks, shutting off the lights, locking everything down. My mind spins in circles, a dog chasing its tail. I have found my salvation in this prison, but at what cost? Am I betraying Albert and the other prisoners who labor—and die—in the quarries? But what can I do about any of it?

The answers are at once clear and not clear. Because of course there is nothing I can do, nothing anyone can do, to save all those who will die. I can't even be hostile, or distracted, when I serve Hauptsturmführer Kramer and the other officers, because I, too, will die. And isn't that what they want? For us all to perish? For us all to be erased? Already under Nacht und Nebel, we have been disappeared from our families, from our friends, from our world. Disappeared with no trace, no clue. Disappeared from Maman and Papa. But I cannot let them erase me altogether. It's the one thing I will refuse to do. I remind myself that I must continue quietly serving, smiling, bowing, doing whatever it takes to survive.

A week later Albert is dead—one of those forced to stand at the edge of the cliff, the Parachutists' Wall, and given the choice to jump or be shot. It is the stoic Ricard who tells me: "Everyone was forced to watch. No one saw Albert's transgression. But it didn't matter. His transgression was to have been a prisoner of the SS."

I can't speak at first. I am grasping for something, anything. "I hope Albert at least felt free in his last seconds as he fell to his death," I finally manage, thinking of what he told me when Henri was murdered.

"That is a romantic notion, but you shouldn't think in that way," Ricard says in disagreement. "It is false, and it is demeaning. We should only speak the truth."

"What, then?" I ask. "What do you suppose he felt at the end?"

"Terror," he says. "I think only terror."

I no longer have it in me to cry, but the sadness is still overwhelming. I think of the last time Albert and I spoke about anything of consequence—the night he told me about the newest ways the Nazis dreamed up to murder prisoners in the quarries. Did he know he was telling me his own future? There were a few more evenings after that, fleeting moments as we sat together in silence at the end of a day, evenings I wish I could have back, to cherish more his friendship, his kindness, his company, to ask questions, to learn more about the life he led—and the life Henri led as his friend—as boys in Lyon, as teachers, raising their families, joining the Resistance. So I could keep more of their stories alive and in my heart. So that one day, when I survive all this, I can share their stories with a loving world that must still exist somewhere, and that must still care.

Christian sees my stricken face the next day in the kitchen and asks me what has happened. He listens patiently as I tell him about Albert, how he was murdered at the quarry, how he had been my friend. I don't stop there. I tell him about Henri. About Denis, who we falsely suspected might be a mouchard. I tell him about a handful of others who I knew in the NN barracks, perhaps just a little, who perhaps shared with me, or I with them, a small gesture of kindness. And who perished.

"Everyone who is my friend, everyone who tries to be my friend, they all die here," I blurt out.

Several silent moments pass between us. Christian busies himself chopping vegetables. Then he stops. Lays down his knife. Turns to me. I am expecting him to tell me something understanding, supportive, sympathetic. Instead, he says, "And so what? Does this mean you are bad luck? You think I will be the next? I should write my will?"

I know he's not serious, but I can't believe he's making a joke of what I've just said. And yet it makes me smile, just a little, this gallows humor.

"Perhaps so," I say. "You should be very careful."

Christian laughs, forcing me to laugh with him. "I thought I *was* being careful, in my life before, but clearly I wasn't careful enough or I wouldn't have ended up here—where, apparently, I am next for the guillotine, thanks to you? C'est relou! How annoying!"

I ask Christian later, after the morning meal service, once the SS officers are gone to their posts, how he came to Natzweiler.

He considers the question, looks around for the guards, sees that they're far enough away that we can speak freely, and tells me, "In your own resistance work in Paris, you heard of this underground network, Réseau Comète—the Comet Line?"

I shake my head.

"We were based in Lille, near the border, and Brussels. A rescue operation for Allied soldiers and airmen shot down over the north of France and in Belgium. I was a happy restaurateur until my friend convinced me that I could easily hide a British pilot in my truck when I drove out to the village markets in the countryside. Deliver him to the next guide. So we constructed a false bottom in the truck where these men could hide. I would deliver my cargo, purchase whatever meats and vegetables and fruits were to be found, and return to my family in Lille."

"How long before you were caught?" I ask.

He shakes his head. "I was never caught. Or at least I was never caught in the act. Someone else in the Comet Line must have been captured, though. Someone who betrayed me, and probably others. Someone who named names."

My own shame at having given up the names of my friends and family comes flooding back over me. I tell Christian this. I say I'm so sorry.

"There is nothing to be sorry about," he says. "Everyone talks. It can't be helped. One can stand only so much of the pain of torture. We are all aware of the risks of what we do."

He doesn't say anything more for a while and neither do I. We busy ourselves wiping down the kitchen, putting away the dishes and silver on their proper shelves, scouring blackened pans.

Later, he returns to the conversation. "The greatest pain," he says, "is my wife not knowing what has happened to me and my not being there for the birth of our child. Not knowing if I'll ever see them again. You must feel this way as well about your family."

I nod, unable to speak.

"But come," Christian says. "Enough of this depressing talk. I had meant to be cheering you up and instead I have managed to bring us both down."

I try to smile again, to let him know I appreciate his trying. But I can't manage it.

"Here is what I think," Christian says. "When this war is over, and when we are free. When we have been reunited with our families and our friends, you will come to Lille for a visit, to meet my wife, Elena. She is from Belgium, but promises our son or daughter will speak French as a first language, though it wouldn't surprise me if she has also taught Flemish to our little one as well. And when you come, I will make for us all my favorite meal that I always loved as a boy. It's not gourmet, but even now it is the food I dream about most when I think of home."

"You can't make it here?" I ask.

Christian scoffs again, shakes his head again emphatically. "I would never share this with the Nazis. No torture ever devised could force me to do that."

He launches into a description of the dish, carbonnade flamande with a side of pommes frites, making me so hungry that by the time he's through, my mouth watering like an open faucet, it feels like a kind of torture itself, hearing about this meal but not having it before me.

"Chunks of tender beef in a dark beer and thyme gravy," he says. "Butter, onions, garlic. Bay leaves. Perhaps some boiled carrots, whole. A light snowfall of flour. Flavored with mustard and brown sugar. Tangy and salty as it's eaten, with a sweet, lingering aftertaste."

Christian has closed his eyes as he's talking, perhaps imagining himself back in Lille as a boy, or preparing a carbonnade flamande for his own little family.

I think of the dishes Maman prepared for us when I was a child, in happier times, with Charlotte and Papa and Maman and me. In my memory, all of them have a sweet, lingering aftertaste of their own.

In August, there is a new influx of prisoners to the NN barracks. One of them, a watchmaker from Chantilly named Michel, had built a homemade radio to monitor the BBC and was arrested for spreading information about the war. He reminds me of Albert, because his glasses have one lens missing and the other is cracked. Michel is squeezed into the bunk next to mine, and after he shares his story, and I in turn share mine, he tells me the great news—that the Allies have driven the Axis forces out of Tunisia, out of North Africa altogether.

"And not only that," he whispers. "They have crossed the Mediterranean. They're in Sicily. Perhaps even on mainland Italy by now." He is breathless with excitement despite his capture, despite having been beaten and tortured by the Germans, and despite disappearing in Nacht und Nebel. Michel tells me that he was always a quiet person, even timid, but that his work for the Resistance gave him a sense of purpose. And even this incarceration in Natzweiler, and whatever will become of him now, can't take that away.

Over the next few days, the news of the Allied invasion of Italy spreads to others. I overhear some things from the SS officers during meals but am too busy to learn very much. Christian eavesdrops as well and tells me that the Nazis, too, are consumed by the developments, fearing that the war has turned against them. For a brief time there is something like hope among the prisoners, and with it a kind of resistance, a slowness to respond to orders from the kapos, and even from the SS guards.

Word gets back to Hauptsturmführer Kramer. He is incensed, announces a ban on all talk of the war by prisoners. Spreading rumors—Gerüchte—is now a crime punishable by death. If the SS guards find out that it is continuing, the kapos will also be punished. So the kapos become even more ruthless in beating confessions out of prisoners and bribing their network of mouchards, fabricating incidents. Draza seems to be everywhere, chief among the kapos, leading many of the assaults. One evening he enters our barrack and, with no warning, drags Michel off his bunk and beats him to his knees. Michel is slumped, cradling his face in his hands, blood dripping through his fingers.

In his rough French, Draza spits out a warning to us all. "The next one caught speaking news of the war ends up on the gallows. And by the time he is taken there, after we are finished with him—much worse than what has been done to this one—he will be grateful to be hanged."

Draza turns to leave. When he sees me, he smiles, as if I truly am his sister Sofia. I am sickened and helpless.

Even with the warnings, for two weeks there are daily hangings. Soon, no one trusts anyone in the barracks. But some still fight back. A suspected mouchard turns up dead in the night, impaled on a sharpened splinter later discovered to have been pried from a cracked wooden post.

Reprisal is swift. As before, ten prisoners are selected, lined against the barracks wall, and shot. Once again I would cry, but once again I can't. Not any longer. Not even at this brutal and senseless taking of lives. I have just returned from the dining hall when I'm ordered to help dispose of the bodies. Michel, with his broken spectacles and mostly healed from his beating, takes one end of the stretcher. I guide us down the mountain at the other. He has been working at the quarries and has all but succumbed to exhaustion, yet somehow manages to push on. I vow to steal some food for him, even a bite, even a forbidden morsel, the next opportunity I have.

We try to speak but are soon out of breath and forced to give up the attempt. The weight of the body, the deep weariness from struggling down and then back up the mountain, the wet bloodstains on my striped trousers and jacket, the stench of the cellar and the furnace, the lost hours as the tasks take us past the gloaming and into thick night darkness, have me wishing I could become like Ricard, that I could somehow will myself to be immune to the horrors and the suffering of those around me. I am desperate for sleep, for the release it brings from the terrors of Natzweiler. The Allies might have invaded Italy, but will any of us still be alive by the time they're able to fight their way here to France?

22

VINGT-DEUX

One day in September, as summer gives way to the first frosts of autumn, Christian hands me a package, brown paper tied with twine. "You are to wear this when you serve, on orders from the Hauptsturmführer," he says. Then he shrugs. "I'm told there are guests expected."

Inside I find a long, dark green skirt. A white blouse and bodice. An apron. I recognize the outfit, of course—a dirndl, the German peasant costume. I hate it right away, frown when I put it on and Christian sees, hate it when he laughs.

And yet. The feel of clean cotton, the smell of new fabric, not seeing dirty stripes when I look down at my body: After a while I can almost think I am pretty. I'm playing a role for the officers and guests—I know this—but perhaps I can pretend for myself as well. They all notice that evening when I enter the dining hall, smile as I serve Hauptsturmführer Kramer and two guests, both of them in formal civilian attire. They even compliment the way I look in my lovely German dress.

It's the usual menu of sausages and sauerkraut and heavy vegetables and black bread and also oranges—oranges! I sweep into the dining hall with the trays and platters. Before, I always hated skirts and my long hair for how they made it harder to ride my bike, but now I'll gladly take them. Because, for a brief moment, I feel some sense of who I was before. Human.

The guests stay with the Hauptsturmführer for an hour after the others are dismissed, which means I must wait as well, anticipating when to offer more wine, more beer, more food. They have me clear away everything and wipe down the table. Hauptsturmführer Kramer calls me over to introduce me, something that's never happened before. I'm embarrassed but stand at attention and do my best to smile and bow. To perform as expected.

"This one, as you can see, was sent to us by accident," the Hauptsturmführer tells the guests. "A rare bureaucratic error. But these things happen. We have found her useful, and so have chosen to keep her with us. For the time being."

He doesn't tell them my name. I'm sure he doesn't know it.

"She is quite efficient, I have noticed," says one of the guests, a lipless man with a scarred mouth, perhaps from an accident or a war wound. He has a high forehead, beady, recessed eyes, a pinched face, a nervous tongue that darts in and out of his damaged mouth like a frightened rabbit.

The other guest says nothing, doesn't acknowledge me in any way. He is younger, almost handsome, but frightening with his fierce gaze, jutting ears, and strange, thick eyebrows that stand out boldly on his forehead, then take a sudden downward turn on both sides.

I am dismissed.

As I remove what remain of the dishes and utensils, I glance at the blueprints they have spread out before them. I whisper to Christian in the kitchen, out of earshot of the guard. "Do you know what this is about?" He has been in and out of the kitchen as well, has also seen the documents.

Christian is packing away his knives, placing them carefully in a wooden box with velvet lining. Stepping over, the guard affixes a lock, lifts the box out of Christian's reluctant hands, and takes it to a cabinet that can also be locked. He keeps all the keys.

"One of the guards said they are both professors from the medical college at Reich University in Strasbourg," Christian says quietly. "The ugly one with the scar is August Hirt, an anatomist."

"And the other?"

"A virologist. Otto Bickenbach."

I'm not sure what to make of this. So one studies anatomy and the other viruses.

"And the blueprints?" I ask. I already have an awful feeling, another premonition of terrible things, though that is what I wake up to every morning in Natzweiler.

"Construction projects," Christian says. "One is a crematorium. The Hauptsturmführer says he can't dispose of bodies quickly enough in the furnace at the disinfestation building. People in the villages have complained about the smell."

I shudder but press on. "And the other blueprint? What is it for?"

He hesitates. "There is an annex to a Struthof hotel, a small building not far from the main gate. It is to become a laboratory, with an examination room. And a gas chamber."

• • •

Every morning in early October, a detachment of prisoners is marched down the mountain and out of the camp to work on the gas chamber, a densely insulated room with a thick steel door that we're told can hold a dozen prisoners at a time. A small crematorium goes up quickly as well, inside the camp, next to the infirmary. Other prisoners are forced to do that work, under the watchful eye of Hauptsturmführer Kramer, who has taken a personal interest in the construction, or so it appears, though Christian says the Hauptsturmführer is just taking the opportunity to be outdoors more during the balmy fall days.

The two professors are frequent guests at the officers' dining hall, are often seen with the Hauptsturmführer walking out of the prison gates, following the workers to the hotel annex to inspect the work being done there.

In the evenings, when he has been drinking too much, Professor Bickenbach regales the Nazi officers with his stories. "In the Great War," he says, "there was so much suffering in the trenches, yes? From the mustard gas, the chlorine, the phosgene. Highly toxic. Highly effective. Too effective, you might say. When our side first deployed it, the winds blew too much back into our own trenches. We lost our advantage! And then of course the Allies developed their own to use against us. Impure forms, I should add. Mustard gas, for example. Odorless and colorless in its pure, liquid form, but with these impurities, it took on the color of mustard, and the odor of garlic or horseradish. Low mortality rate, but a powerful irritant that led to many, many casualties.

"But as I am a humanitarian, and a scientist, and because our revered leader is also a notable humanitarian—though he gets no credit for this in the international community—I have turned all my research over to finding the antidotes to the poisons we are certain the Allies will attempt to use once again—and our own need to deploy them in response. But if our brave soldiers can be protected from the ravages of the gases, and if at the same time we can protect our noncombatants, our women and children, who are, after all, the future of the Reich, then won't we have done a great service both to the war effort and to all of humanity?"

Professor Bickenbach says his particular focus for his research at Natzweiler is phosgene gas. "I have enough right now to kill every prisoner in the camp!" he boasts.

"And the officers and guards?" the Hauptsturmführer asks.

"But of course we will take great care to insure that none of them are ever exposed," Professor Bickenbach responds.

While Bickenbach has their attention, Professor Hirt glances over and sees that I have been listening from the door to the kitchen. He looks at the Hauptsturmführer, then back at me again. I am nervous all of a sudden, as if I've been caught doing something wrong, instead of standing where I am assigned, waiting to slip in to remove empty serving dishes and silver and plates and glasses and mugs. I make a show of doing just that as Professor Bickenbach continues.

"And with your gracious permission, Hauptsturmführer Kramer," he says, "prisoners will be selected, weighed, measured, inspected . . . If they are deemed too weak, too small, too sick already, of course they will be sent back to their work in the quarries. The heartier prisoners—those are the ones we need for the experiments. It will be through them that we will learn how best to protect our German soldiers from the ravages of phosgene and what the field doctors call dry-land drowning."

The Hauptsturmführer thanks him for the information, though he says it in a way that suggests he's heard it all before and is tired of the repetition.

It's Professor Hirt's turn next to speak to Hauptsturmführer Kramer, although their conversation is private. At first I'm afraid Professor Hirt might be telling the Hauptsturmführer that I was eavesdropping, but neither of them looks at me again and I'm relieved. Perhaps Professor Hirt the anatomist is planning his own terrible experiments. I busy myself collecting dirty plates, filling glasses and beer steins, bringing out pastries and fruits and steaming pots of coffee. But I can't help worrying about what is to be done to the prisoners in Professor Bickenbach's gas experiments, wondering if I should warn them back in the barracks. As soon as I ask myself the question, I know the answer, and I'm swept by a wave of despair. Even if I told every living soul in the camp, it wouldn't make any difference. They do whatever they want to us in Natzweiler. Even this.

I continue to work in the kitchen through the days and weeks that follow, changing out of the dirndl into my striped trousers and jacket and cap every night, putting it on when I return in the mornings, stumbling down the mountain on stiff legs after the interminable roll calls that always seem to be in the middle of the night, hours before sunrise. By now, the apron is food-stained, the sleeves spattered with grease, green skirt torn in two places. The bodice still sags. I haven't magically blossomed into a perfect Aryan country girl with long blonde braids and wide blue eyes. I am still the malnourished French girl with protruding ribs, sunken cheeks, sallow complexion, stubble of dark hair half-hidden under my new kerchief.

But this charade has caught the eye of Professor Hirt, who still comes to Natzweiler every few weeks. One night, he asks Hauptsturmführer Kramer if I could be allowed to work for him in the annex in the spring, when Professor Bickenbach is finished with his work, and when subjects can be shipped to Natzweiler for Professor Hirt's experiments, whatever those might be.

"You are an industrious young woman," he sayings, beaming at me while I am horrified. "And surely can be trusted with, eh, sensitive tasks. Would you agree, Hauptsturmführer Kramer?"

The Hauptsturmführer looks at me as if he's appraising my worth. He is noncommittal. "We will see."

Professor Bickenbach starts his research shortly after at the beginning of November. Several prisoners are selected from the NN barracks for the experiments, and despite Professor Bickenbach's grand assurances that he will only select the strongest prisoners, Michel is one of those taken. He is gone for two weeks—so long we think he is surely dead. But eventually, from across the camp one evening, we see him drag himself slowly up the terraced mountain, his breathing labored, his voice a raw whisper.

Someone gives him water when he makes it back to the barracks. He eases himself to the ground, where he sits, leaning against the outer wall in a light dusting of snow. The prisoners crowd around him—so we can hear and so we can provide at least the illusion of protection.

When he catches enough of his breath that he's able to speak, Michel tells us what happened. "The SS guards marched us out of the front gate to the gas chamber and laboratory, perhaps one kilometer away," he says. "We were measured by the assistants in the laboratory, and they wrote everything down in their logs, under the watchful eye of Professor Bickenbach. Some were given injections. Others, nothing."

He pauses to sip more water from the snowmelt. The shock of the cold makes him cough so hard that he struggles to continue. But he perseveres.

"We were ordered inside the chamber," he rasps. "It had white-tiled walls, a concrete floor, a glass peephole in the door. It smelled like acid and old hay. I heard three bolts thrown on three locks to seal the door. The light was on. We waited, sure we were going to be killed. One prisoner banged his fists on the door. Another began sobbing. Something rolled through a pipe that extended through the wall—this was the poison. It landed in a basin of water and became the gas. The acid smell, much stronger now, rose from the floor with the fumes. All the prisoners, we went crazy—flailing, screaming, biting, clawing the wall, trampling one another."

He has been speaking quickly, as if afraid he will run out of breath, or time. Now he stops again, wracked for the next several minutes with lung spasms. Finally he can go on.

"After an eternity of this, there was a noise like a vacuum. The room was cleared of the gas. I was in a delirium, but I still managed to breathe. The door was opened. I was pulled out of the chamber. We had been packed in so tightly, there was no escaping. I was covered in excrement. They cleaned me off with a pressure hose. Two of the men were dead. They had suffocated. I heard them as it happened, the sound of their lungs filling up with fluid. Three others—I didn't know them; they were from a different barracks and didn't speak French. They didn't speak at all. They lay on their mats, in great pain. They coughed up blood and the shredded remains of their lungs. They, too, died. But it took a long time."

His breath has become even shallower, his sentences shortened. "The rest of us were kept for tests. Given electric shocks." He holds up a heavily bandaged arm. "They cut the tendons. And they broke my hand. I don't know why."

He is shaking his head and says nothing more. We help him onto his bunk, gently lay him on his side and prop him up on shared blankets to help with his breathing. Someone gives him another sip of water.

Miraculously, Michel once again lives. He is spared from the quarries and sent to work at Block 6 instead, though I can't imagine how he is able to do the work there one-handed. But he is one of the few who survive the experiments of the men marched out of the camp to the annex and herded into the gas chamber. The antidotes, the vitamins, the various treatments all fail in the end, we are told, causing consternation and grief for the humanitarian Professor Bickenbach.

23

VINGT-TROIS

1944 arrives, but there is no celebration for a new year. This second winter in the camp is the same as before, bitter cold and seemingly impossible to survive. We stand outside the NN barracks in early January snowdrifts half a meter deep, shifting from foot to foot in a vain attempt to keep warm through minimal exertion. Most of the men who have toiled since before sunrise in the quarries are too zombie-like even for that. There are morning stars, eclipsed every few minutes by the sweep of searchlights from the guard towers. We watch as yet another contingent of new prisoners is marched up the terrace to the wire surrounding the NN barracks, bayonets jabbing their backs to hurry them through the gate where they are released once inside. I am aware they have come, but only barely. I am incurious, empty. Ricard, when he is not too tired, has been trying to teach me the constellations, those we can see in the early night sky. But I keep forgetting their names. Forgetting where to draw imaginary lines to connect them into mythical figures. Forgetting so many things.

"Look, there," he tells me for what seems like the hundredth time. "Orion's Belt. The three brightest stars." He's not pointing so much as he's jabbing his finger at the sky, as if he can actually touch something. "And there's Orion's Sword. And see, he's being chased by the scorpion that kills him, those stars there."

I nod but still can't see it. I dimly remember some of the myth. That Orion was a famous hunter. Fell in love with a girl, but her father, some king or another, didn't approve, so he had Orion's eyes put out. The only thing that could restore his vision were the rays of the rising sun. I'm not sure where the murderous scorpion came into the picture.

"I think I see it all now," I tell Ricard, though it's a lie. But stoic that he is, I know he still likes it when he thinks he's taught something, anything, to me or any of the other younger prisoners.

And then everything changes. Someone says my name—says it as a question, an exclamation. It is lower, deeper than I remember, but I recognize the voice right away.

"Jules!" I cry. My own vision is blurry from staring at the elusive constellations. Now I struggle to focus, to see him, to seize proof that he is truly here, that I'm not hallucinating. I stumble toward the voice while a young man who was once Jules limps from the scrum of new prisoners and throws himself at me. We hold each other, overwhelmed, speechless, sobbing. I take his face between my hands and stare into the still-familiar eyes. He seems to have doubled in size—now tall, broad-shouldered, lean. But it's him! My Jules! I have never been happier, and at the same time never more heartbroken with the realization that he, too, has been captured, has been disappeared from the world, imprisoned now with me in the horror that is Natzweiler.

Michel is kind enough to make room on the bunks so that Jules can sleep next to me. Though he's spent the last several weeks assigned to Block 6, Michel has been slow to heal from the severed tendons and broken hand—and especially the damage to his lungs from the phosgene gas.

"I know you want to catch up," he rasps as we wrap ourselves as tightly as we can into our thin blankets. "But please, first, is there any news of the war?"

Jules lifts himself onto his elbows, peers into the darkness around us to see if anyone is listening in. Others have asked this as well, but I have warned Jules about the dangers of mouchards in the barracks and the Hauptsturmführer's edict banning any news of the war. I assure him that Michel can be trusted.

"I don't know a great deal," Jules whispers. "I have been with the Maquis in the wilderness, and we have had only patchy radio connection. But we have heard that the Allies are now in Italy. You know this already?"

"Yes, yes," Michel says. "But has there been much progress?"

"Only a little," Jules answers. "But there has been other news. The Red Army has retaken the city of Kyiv from the Nazis. This is supposed to be a major victory on the eastern front. And the other thing we have heard—this you won't believe—but the Royal Air Force managed to send dozens of their pilots on a night mission to bomb Berlin. Hitler must have been beside himself with rage."

Jules has nothing else to offer, and soon Michel is snoring

softly, despite the freezing temperature already inside the NN barracks. Jules and I stay awake, whispering long into the night. "I thought I'd lost you," he says, and he keeps saying. "First my father, and then you. It was too much." He starts and stops. Starts and stops. Has trouble finishing his sentences. Talks in circles. Jumps back and forth in time. But eventually it comes out. He has been with the Maquis since escaping Paris a year ago, a few months after I was abducted. "Jean Pierre was the one who told me, who warned all of us. I'm not sure how he knew that you had been taken. He raced from apartment to apartment that night to tell us. I knew I couldn't stay or else I could be caught as well, and my mother and Margaux would be in danger. I hid underground for weeks. Coming to the surface only when I needed food, like a rabbit hiding in his burrow. Until I was able to escape the city and join the Maquis."

He has to stop, to collect himself. But he continues. "My comrades were killed in an ambush last week, and I was caught. Only a lookout managed to get away, to warn others. We were operating outside the city, south, in the forests of Gâtinais."

I reach out in the dark and lay my hand on Jules's shoulder. He places his hand on top of mine.

"Before I left the city, I went to your apartment," he says. "I wanted to speak to your parents, to tell them what little I knew—that you had been captured by the Nazis. But I was certain I saw figures in the shadows, watching the building."

"So you have no news of them? No news of Charlotte?" I have to ask.

He shakes his head. "I was afraid to go back. Afraid to approach them on the street. It was too dangerous. And afterward, I was working so hard just to survive in hiding. There was no food, no water, nowhere to sleep except on the rocky underground. When I surfaced for the last time, I had with me the remaining hand grenades and a Luger. If they caught me before I could get out of the city, I was determined I would fire the pistol until it was empty and then detonate the hand grenade, and kill as many of them as I could and also kill myself . . ."

He keeps trailing off. And he is trembling. Perhaps remembering more. Perhaps reliving the terrors of that time.

I tell him about Antoine. "He was killed the day I arrived here," I say. "At the gallows."

Jules squeezes my hand tighter, whispering that he is so sorry. "But you say you know nothing about Charlotte?" he asks.

I shake my head. It's too dark for him to see me at all, even lying next to each other. But he must feel it.

"Charlotte and Antoine must have run with a different cell, perhaps in a different province. There is a loose network. They may have been sent west of Paris. Given missions attacking supply lines from the north. There are Maquis all over," Jules says proudly. "The Resistance is growing. I'm certain of it. But so are the risks and the retributions. And the betrayals."

The next morning, we are awakened as always before sunrise, herded out of the barracks, and made to stand in the snowy field halfway down the mountain. Jules moves stiffly, and at some point I realize he can't lift his arms above his head. I try to ask him about it, but he shrugs off the question. We're freezing in the harsh wind that slices down the mountain, and desperate for any warmth when we're released back to the barracks for our morning rations of water and stale bread and broth. After, Jules is marched off with most of the other NN prisoners to trucks at the Natzweiler entrance to be transported to the stone quarries. I am taken as usual by one of the kapos down to meet Christian at the officers' dining hall. I only just got Jules back last night and it worries me that he's in the mines. All day I despair about the Stairs of Death, the murder races, the Parachutists' Wall, and it's all I can do to keep from shouting my relief to see him return that evening, to know that he has survived the day.

We talk a little that night in our bunks but are both worn out from lack of sleep, from the cold, and Jules from his hard labor at the quarry and his injuries, which he still avoids discussing. Michel, lying next to us, struggles for air more than before, but at last seems to sleep—only to wake us later in the night gasping, flailing, desperate for air in what must be his worsening blocked lungs. Jules holds him, whispers to Michel that he'll be all right, that he must relax, that breath will come.

But he's wrong. Michel stops breathing. Suddenly. Stops flailing. Stops moving at all. Jules feels for his pulse, but there's nothing.

"I'm sorry," Jules says, though I'm not sure if he's whispering to Michel or to me. We lie there in stillness for a few minutes. Then I lift off Michel's blanket and spread it over Jules and me.

"If we can hide it in the morning, the kapos might not know we've taken it," I say.

"But what about his body?" Jules asks.

"We leave him," I say. "Until the morning. Otherwise we'll be ordered to carry him to the crematorium tonight."

It feels cruel, but this is who we have been forced to become.

I burrow closer to Jules, hoping for a little more warmth and hoping to forget the terrible choices we must make in the name of survival.

A few nights later, when we are forced into the showers after reports of an outbreak of lice, I see burn marks all over Jules's body. Perhaps because he knows I've seen, he tells me it's from when the Nazis tortured him. "I don't know why they didn't kill me," he says. "Many in the Resistance are sent to these prisons. But the Maquis, there is no mercy shown, if mercy is even the right word for any of this. The only reason for keeping me alive after they murdered the others was to force me to give them names."

I want him to tell me he refused, that no amount of torture could break him, but of course I broke easily when they interrogated me. The beatings. The isolation. The sleep deprivation. No food or water. Why should I think it would be any different with Jules?

"I gave them the names, of course," he says. "But they were noms de guerre. My closest friends among the Maquisards, I knew none of their real names. And we all changed our identities so often, it was impossible to keep up at times even with my own." Jules manages to laugh when he says this, as if it has all been a game. But the laughter gives way to a profound sense of sadness, of grief and loss, that I can feel emanating from his face, from his soul.

24

VINGT-QUATRE

In February, dozens of Soviet prisoners are crowded into one of the lower barracks. We see them, or the shapes of them, in their tattered uniforms, soon replaced by equally tattered prison stripes. Many are shoeless, made to stand in the predawn formations with strips of cloth tied around their frozen feet. Others have only their trousers and shirts but nothing else, not even the thin prison jacket everyone else is issued. They are sent to the quarries, where Jules finds himself working alongside them.

"They tell me there are more and more Nazi defeats on the eastern front," Jules whispers to me in our bunks at night. "That must be why the SS officers are so brutal with them. Even worse than with the rest of us. No heat at all in their barracks. Starved, beaten daily, forced to work even longer days and into the nights at the quarries under arc lights. Some of them are eating frozen grass, dung, worms in the mud of a little spring that still manages to bubble up through the snow and ice."

Jules is so angry, he's grinding his teeth. "I can't begin to count the number who have already died here. Who have already been killed. Every day. The stairs. The wall. I have been speaking to one of the Soviets who knows a little French. I have gotten him to trust me. He tells me there is already talk among them—of an insurrection, a mass escape. It will take much planning. They will have to find a way to disarm the guards. There are automatic weapons trained on us at all time. And kapos who are more brutal even than the SS guards, who think nothing of assaulting prisoners—their fellow prisoners, after all—for little reason, or no reason at all. To make an example. For exercise. To impress the Nazis. To earn extra rations. They, too, will have to be neutralized."

I am alarmed at Jules's enthusiasm and try to convince him that it would be futile to try, a death sentence if word of these conversations got out. "You can't be involved," I tell him. "Please. You don't understand how it is here. You could be killed just for having listened to this talk. They'll find out. They always find out."

I hate how I sound, how compliant, how pathetic, but there's no room in my heart for losing Jules, not after I've just found him, just gotten him back in my life. Already I am taking my own risks, smuggling him more food than is safe from the kitchen. Noble Jules tells me we should share it with others, though it is still meager fare, but I beg him not to. There are too many who are starving, too many who would sell us both out if they thought it would put more in their own bellies.

Jules assures me that he will be careful, but I don't believe him. He acts as one who is not afraid to die, and that frightens me more than anything. I vow that I will save him, no matter what. Even save him from himself. I will steal all the food I need to steal, regardless of the risk, if that's what it takes to keep him alive. Already he is wasting, as they are all wasting, from the brutal labor in the mines. At night when he wants to have another of our whispered conversations, I try to insist that he sleep instead, though I love nothing more than to hear his voice, the voice I feared was gone, and he wants desperately to talk, to tell me his stories of life with the Maquis, of their running and hiding, their bold attacks on Nazi patrols, how they destroyed telephone wires and telegraph cables and the same bridges over and over, and, once, even an ammunition train. He whispers to me about a boy named Anders from the Netherlands who fled to France and joined the Resistance, and who loved him.

I know he tells me these stories to give me hope.

But as much I love him for it, and as much as I want to believe the encouraging reports about the war, I can't help feeling that we're losing. In every way. As Anders has lost his life. As Jules has lost his freedom. As I have lost myself.

In March, late one afternoon, work is halted early for the day, and the prisoners are all ordered to the snow-packed field near the gallows. Christian and I are brought there by one of the guards at the dining hall. Thirteen young college students have been brought into Natzweiler from Strasbourg, arrested for the sort of crimes Jules and I committed hundreds of times in Paris. Their faces are beaten and bruised. Some, blinded, their eyes swollen shut, have to hold on to others to find their way forward. They've all been beaten, probably tortured. And now, a Nazi officer announces, they are to be used for target practice.

Eleven of the thirteen are tied together in small groups and herded into a sand pit near the gallows, surrounded by SS guards, while we are forced to watch. Jules is shaking with rage. I hold his arm, my fingers biting hard into the flesh.

An Unterscharführer named Fuchs gives the order. The SS men are to aim for arms and legs with their Karabiners. There is no escaping the sounds, the anguished cries of pain, the volley after volley, the begging, in French and in German: "Tue-moi! Töte Mich!"

It is Fuchs himself who finishes them off with his Luger, one shot each to the head, though most are surely dead already. The muddy pit absorbs the blood and tissue, the red-soaked sand turned under by prisoners with shovels once the bodies are removed.

The two partisans who were spared are ordered to carry what remains of their friends to the crematorium. Fuchs follows closely behind, his Luger still drawn. For convenience, he waits until they reach the steps of the new crematorium before he executes them.

It takes the rest of the day and into the night for all the young partisans to burn because the furnace room in the disinfestation building is already full, and the new crematorium is too small. So someone has to climb inside after each cremation and sweep out the ashes. Perhaps because I am smaller, I am one of those ordered to do this. I struggle to fight off waves of horror and claustrophobia the whole time I'm inside. I hold my breath for as long as I can, but there is no way to avoid inhaling the dust of the dead.

Jules is assigned to carry the ashes down the mountain, outside the gate, to the Hauptsturmführer's house, fertilizer for his garden. I beg him not to do anything—I start to say *foolish,* but that isn't the right word. I struggle to come up with something to convince him, and fail. But I can't lose Jules, not again, not ever, so I just tell him I need him to live, to survive. With me. No matter what.

As I return to the officers' dining hall, as I change into the dirndl and kerchief, as I clean and prepare and serve, as I force myself to smile at Hauptsturmführer Kramer, what echoes in my head aren't the sounds of gunshots, but the voices of the doomed students as they are used for target practice:

"Tue-moi."

"Töte Mich."

Kill me.

Professor Bickenbach has long since finished his experiments, and so, with the annex available—the laboratory and the gas chamber—it is Professor Hirt's turn. He appears at the SS dining hall with Hauptsturmführer Kramer one frozen night a couple weeks later, and I am filled with dread the minute I see him. I had hoped he'd forgotten about me, but after the meal and the other officers are dismissed, Professor Hirt asks again that I be given to him to help with his research—temporarily, of course, he assures the Hauptsturmführer.

"What we have planned is, ah, delicate work," he explains to Hauptsturmführer Kramer, as I stand, waiting to pour them more wine. "There is nowhere convenient to house my assistants from the university, and some things are best kept secret from the villagers. You understand. But most important, many of the subjects who are being sent here for my research will be women. It would be good to have a young woman like this one—to keep them calm, to reassure them, so they will be compliant."

The Hauptsturmführer acquiesces, though I doubt he cares very much, if at all, what the villagers in nearby Natzweiler and Struthof think about *anything* that is allowed to happen here.

Christian is worried, and not just to be losing me for a couple of weeks. He is worried about what I'll be made to do. "These 'subjects' he has mentioned," Christian says. "Has he said anything about who they are? What he intends?"

But I have no answers.

Jules is worried as well, though more about how this will affect his plans with the Soviet prisoners. I've been told I'll be kept at the annex during the research, taking meals and sleeping on a pallet on the floor there. "I'll miss you," he whispers as we lie awake deep into the night in the NN barracks. "But I'll know where to find you, if things move forward at the quarry before you return. I promise that whatever happens, I won't forget you. I'll come for you."

He says half the Soviets are on board with the insurrection. The leaders are cautiously approaching the others, worried about who might already have turned against them, might already have become mouchards for the kapos and the SS guards. "It will be difficult to get close enough to the machine gun emplacements," he says. "Our only weapons will be pickaxes and stones. But we'll have superior numbers. And hope that the other prisoners follow our lead. Surely they will, once we gain the advantage. If we can take even one of their Knochensäge—their bone saw guns—we can take out the rest."

I'm so frightened by the prospect of Jules and his Soviet

friends trying—and surely failing—to overthrow the Nazis that I can't respond. I want to beg him again to let it go. To keep his head down. To stay away from trouble. To disavow any knowledge of the insurrection. I can't think of how I could continue without him.

A few days later, I am escorted along with two young Frenchmen out of the camp by two guards and led to the annex. Professor Hirt is already there, fuming. He tells us eighty-six Jewish prisoners—he calls them his "specimens"—have arrived in transport trucks, sent from other camps in Germany or Poland. They're being kept isolated from the rest of the Natzweiler prisoners, but he is upset about the conditions. A dozen Jews have been squeezed into each of a handful of cells, even though he requested more spacious, and certainly more hygienic, accommodations.

"I need our Jews to be at least relatively healthy," he tells us. We are standing before him in the lab, shifting uneasily, heads bowed, waiting on his orders.

But Professor Hirt isn't through. He loves to talk and insists on an audience. "I ask you, what good to us are damaged specimens?" he says in a loud voice, as if he's addressing a roomful of students instead of just me and the young men, Matthieu and Sébastien. "It will be your job to reassure them, the women especially. If they are calm, if they are sedate, if they are cooperative, things will proceed much better. Much, much better. Tomorrow we begin. Tomorrow you will be instructed in how to make molds, how to make casts of their heads. This will be vitally important. From these measurements will come once and for all our scientific understanding of the defining physiological characteristics of the Jews. They will no longer be able to lie about what they are, and once so clearly and publicly identified as Jews, no longer able to procreate with the cleaner races. Do you understand this?"

I tell him what he wants to hear, even as I'm swept by a crushing wave of fear of what is about to come.

25

VINGT-CINQ

We spend the rest of the day organizing the lab according to Professor Hirt's specifications, not that there is much to organize. Pens and notebooks. Measuring tape. Calipers. Hypodermic needles and syringes. Instructions for how to draw blood. Vials and stoppers. Food is brought in for us that evening, a feast for Matthieu and Sébastien, but we're all too anxious to talk. The floor is hard underneath our thin pallets, but the annex is kept warm—so much warmer than the barracks—and we are grateful at least for that.

In the morning, shortly after Professor Hirt returns from Strasbourg, SS guards bring in fifteen women in striped sack dresses. They crowd together against the far wall, clutching one another, fearful, their eyes wide and straining with apprehension. They have been brought here from Auschwitz, Professor Hirt tells us, specially selected for his anatomical studies.

"You will first take blood samples and anatomical measurements, exactly as you have been shown," he says. He points to the tray of syringes and rack of test tubes, then the notebooks we are to use for our records. He has brought other papers with him. "The identification numbers are already listed. You will match those on the sheets to the numbers tattooed on their arms. There are thirty women altogether who are to be processed. Fifty-seven men. Nicolette, it is your job to keep them calm, as I explained to you before. Use your most soothing voice, even if they don't understand what you're staying. You don't speak Polish, do you? We have a great many Poles. Try your French and your German if not. There are going to be a few who speak those languages, a few from those countries, mixed in with the others—the Poles, the Greeks, the Norwegians, the Belgians, some Dutch."

I tell him I don't know any Polish. Matthieu, short and dark-haired, and Sébastien, a teenager around my age, both say the same. "As I suspected," Professor Hirt says. "Well, do keep in mind that our work is only beginning here. After the blood samples and the measurements, molds and casts must be made of all the heads. The final stage, to come later, at the laboratory in Strasbourg, will be disarticulation of the bodies, followed by reconstruction. Now, are there any questions?"

I don't fully understand what's he's saying, what his plans are, but it feels wrong. Something bad is coming, and my heart races furiously, pounding so loudly in my chest that once again I'm surprised no one else can hear it. I force myself to breathe deeply, slowly. Sense that the guards are growing impatient, just standing next to the door with their weapons trained on the new prisoners. Professor Hirt turns away to examine other papers, but I can't move. When he sees that we haven't started, he barks, "Well? What are you waiting for?"

I steel myself, approach the women, and speak to them in simple French, though none seem to understand. "I am Nicolette," I say. "There is nothing to be afraid of. We are only here to do a study for the Germans." I hold up a cloth measuring tape that Professor Hirt has given me. Select the first woman and demonstrate on her. Matthieu records the measurements while Sébastien has the women step on a scale. He calls out the weights, and Matthieu records those, too.

The women relax a little, begin whispering among themselves, even speaking some to me in their mix of languages. They are gaunt, haunted, clumsy from illness and malnutrition. The signs are obvious: the sunken eyes, the protruding bones, the overlapping bruises, the festering wounds. Despite that, I can see they are healthier than most prisoners in Natzweiler.

Professor Hirt keeps a watchful eye on us for the first few hours as we take the various measurements of the women, and the next ones after, before moving on to making plaster molds of their heads and faces. At lunchtime, he leaves for the dining hall and we're left alone with the women. We continue to do as we're ordered, but once Professor Hirt is gone, I repeat my name—pressing my hand to my chest and saying "Nicolette, Nicolette"—and asking them theirs. We don't speak the same language, but we still manage. It seems important that I at least know who they are.

Bella. Emma. Palomba. Nette. Sara. Sophie. Maria. Katarina. Allegra. Ernestine. Jeannette. Alice. Martha. Marie. Sarina.

It takes all day to complete the work, but it is a distraction from what we know—and from what the women must fear—is going to happen next. They steal glances at the door to the gas chamber, but no one says anything in any language about what might await them inside.

When we're through for the first day—no more food is brought to the annex—they lie draped on top of one another on the stone floor, the only place offered to them to sleep. Sébastien, Matthieu, and I roll out our mats and blankets on a different section of floor. New SS guards come in for their twelve-hour shifts.

"Even you young French must appreciate the importance of our work," Professor Hirt intones on the second day as we resume, elbow to elbow in the cramped laboratory. "Reichsführer Himmler himself has given his endorsement, you know. In fact, the selection of and requisition of these specimens"—here he gestures toward the women, most of whom are still huddled together on the floor—"were personally approved by Himmler. It has become difficult to find undamaged subjects among the Jews. Most have been *spoiled*, one might say, due to a variety of factors, conditions, necessary reductions. The race of the Jews is being dealt with. There are plans, bold initiatives. But only through careful anatomical and physiological study can we determine what to do about the Mischlinge, the half-Jews of future generations, so that they can be also dealt with appropriately. Perhaps sterilization. Or perhaps more severe measures may be called for. But that is policy, and policy is not our concern. Our concern is simple, and that is to carefully, scientifically, measure and evaluate and determine racial truth."

I am disgusted, listening to him, wondering if he truly believes what he is saying, or if he is working hard to convince not just his prison audience but himself. Hirt leaves again for lunch and, later, for dinner in the SS officers' dining hall back at the camp—meals I can picture: rich, salty potatoes and juicy, seared sausages—while once again, none of us are given anything to eat.

Matthieu, Sébastien, and I have finally finished with the last of the fifteen women when he returns late that evening. I've been repeating their names quietly in my head while we work, as if somehow that will keep them alive. Professor Hirt examines the notebooks, studies the molds, and pronounces them acceptable.

Then he summons his driver, speaks quietly to the SS guards, and tells us that Hauptsturmführer Kramer should arrive soon. "You will receive further instructions from him."

Sébastien and Matthieu have said little over the past two days, and they don't say anything now. We stare after Professor Hirt as he leaves and then glance at the door to the gas chamber.

But as soon as Hirt is gone, the women from Auschwitz begin speaking, even shouting, imploring us in their various languages and with gestures and the desperate expressions on their faces to help them, please—

The guards bark at them, aim their weapons, and things quiet down. But my mind continues to race. We all know, have known all along, what will happen once Hauptsturmführer Kramer arrives. And we all know there's nothing we can do to stop it. These women will be killed. What little is left of our humanity will die with them.

Soon enough, the door opens again, letting in the night and the Hauptsturmführer. He stands at the entrance, the door half ajar, and surveys the room: the fifteen women, the rough casts of their heads and faces that would be watching over them if the eyes weren't squeezed shut in the molds. He speaks crisply to the guards, one of whom goes to the gas chamber and unbolts the door.

Hauptsturmführer Kramer barks another order, and the guards drag and shove the women inside. Some go quietly. Some fight and claw at the guards. But they don't have the strength. Or perhaps they're too tired. But just when I'm thinking that, a young woman, the girl named Emma bolts past them, flings open the door the Hauptsturmführer has neglected to lock, and throws herself out into the black night.

The guards follow quickly, and shoot. Or maybe it's the Hauptsturmführer who unholsters his Luger and fires. Emma only reaches a low, decorative wall surrounding the cottage, which is where she falls. The guards leave her there, sprawled in the grass, and herd us back away from the door while a dispassionate Hauptsturmführer Kramer picks up a telephone to call Professor Hirt for instructions on how to proceed. He is told to dispose of the body, that it is now "spoiled" and will no longer be needed. I want to vomit. To scream. But for them, Emma's death, her murder, is nothing.

"He needs his Jew specimens to be perfect," Hauptsturmführer Kramer says to the guards. He shakes his head. "For his skull and skeleton collection." He gestures out the annex door toward Emma. "Take that one to the crematorium. You know what to do with the others."

He turns back to the other women, pressed together in the gas chamber. "You worry for nothing," Hauptsturmführer Kramer lies to them in simple German, though the words are most likely lost. "No one else will be hurt. You are only to be disinfected. That's all. Now you must remove your clothes."

I am ordered inside to coax one of the women to disrobe and to indicate to the others that they are expected to follow. Once they are all naked, I collect the pile of dirty striped uniforms, damp and soiled and reeking of urine. I can't look at their faces. As I go to leave, two women grab my arm, try to hold on to me, as if I can help them. I want to do something, anything, the desperation clawing inside me, but we are all prisoners here. The SS guards start beating them with the butt of their guns until they release me. As soon as I am out and the door is locked behind me, the women scream. Sébastien and Matthieu cover their ears. Both are crying silent tears. But I stand away from them, willing myself to see and hear everything.

The Hauptsturmführer draws a vial out of his pocket, breaks the wax seal, and pours it down a funnel that empties inside the chamber. There is a peephole in the door, and after turning on a switch to illuminate the locked room, he watches. It only takes a minute before we hear them, one after another, go silent and fall to the floor. I am frozen, empty of all purpose, despairing. Sébastien and Matthieu continue to weep.

Hauptsturmführer Kramer turns on the ventilation. After five minutes, he orders the door unlocked. He peers inside but doesn't enter. He turns back around. "They are all dead," he says, looking at no one in particular, speaking to no one in particular.

SS guards bring in wooden crates filled with straw. My instructions are to pack the casts of the women's heads, which by now have fully dried and hardened. A delivery van arrives not long after. Hauptsturmführer Kramer instructs Sébastien and

Matthieu to bring in a hose connected to a faucet outside the annex. They are to clean the bodies and wash out the chamber.

"The bodies and the crates are to be loaded into the van," the Hauptsturmführer says. "There is to be no trace of these prisoners left in the annex. They are to be transported to Strasbourg, to the Institute of Anatomy at the medical college at Reich University. You will receive further instructions there from Professor Hirt and then you will return here immediately. Tomorrow the work will continue. There will be fifteen more specimens to be processed, and more after that."

Sébastien, Matthieu, and I sit in silence in the back of the delivery van with the SS guards. It is dark. There are no windows. We are thrown back and forth as we wind down the mountain roads on the hour drive to Strasbourg. We see none of the city, only feel the descent at what turns out to be the end of the journey, backing down to a hidden loading dock. Professor Hirt, clad in a white surgical gown, directs us where to bring the bodies inside a cavernous room.

I try not to think about what we're doing when I see what is there: Metal autopsy tables. Trays with scalpels, bone saws, forceps, shears.

The casts of the women's heads and faces are left buried in straw, packed inside the wooden crates, stacked against the far wall.

I take note of where we are. I promise myself—I promise the victims—that I will find my way back here someday, somehow. That they will never be forgotten. That the world will know what happened here. That I will always, always remember.

• • •

I develop a tremor in my hands and am unable to draw blood the next day on the second group of women who are brought in. Sébastien and Matthieu take over for me. I am in anguish all day. I fight to control the voice in my head that only grows louder and louder, shouting to me that I am complicit. That promising the dead that I will make sure they are remembered—this isn't enough. I try to convince myself I have no choice but to follow orders, no matter how ghoulish, no matter how gruesome.

And yet a part of me that I so desperately want to deny is grateful that it is not me or Jules. We are allowed to survive, even though survival is its own form of torture. But how can I be so selfish as to even be thinking about myself when I am helping to prepare these poor women for their deaths—deaths they don't deserve, horrible, painful deaths, no families to be with them in the end, no one to hold them, to remember them, to avenge them.

Again and again—four more times over the next two weeks—we are forced to be witnesses to the cyanide murders, to gather the clothes of the dead, to wash clean the gas chamber, to load the bodies and the plaster casts into the delivery van, to accompany the SS guards when they drive the corpses into Strasbourg under the cover of early morning darkness, the bodies still warm, their eyes wide open and glassy. When I fall asleep on the laboratory floor, I am plunged into a sleep so deep and hard—and so devoid of dreams—that I wake disoriented, as if I've been emptied, as if I'm some Lazarus brought back from the dead. I don't know how I got here, where I am, my name.

And then it floods back over me and back through me—the repeated nightmare we are living. It becomes increasingly difficult for me to maintain my own footing inside the chamber. I'm claustrophobic even with the door propped wide open, the harsh light on, the exhaustion fan sucking out any lingering traces of acid air. The floor slopes just enough so we can wash all the filth down a drain the designer thought to have installed at the center of the room. We scrub the white tile walls, and they, too, come mostly clean, though there's nothing I can do about the scratch marks the victims leave where they try frantically to claw their way out in their last, desperate seconds. I find broken fingernails embedded so deeply I have to go to the SS guard for pliers to pull them out.

Some days the only thing that gets me through what I am made to do is the bottomless hatred in my heart for these men—the Hauptsturmführer and the professor. I fantasize about locking them inside the white-tiled chamber, releasing the lethal chemicals, watching them die. It will never be enough. I know that. But at times it feels like the only thing keeping me alive.

Sébastien, Matthieu, and I return from Strasbourg for the final time to clean the annex, "disinfect" the gas chamber, and remove all trace of the eighty-six. I still tremble so much that I drop whatever I try to hold: the mop, a box of syringes, a bag of plaster that tears open and spills out a cloud of white dust that settles on everything, making more work for us all. I stand frozen, unable to move, in the middle of the annex until Matthieu touches my elbow and leads me to a corner. "Sit here," he says in his gentlest voice. "Until you are better. We will clean this up."

Sébastien nods. Nothing more is said. We can't speak about what has happened, about what we're doing, about what we've done. I am numb. Mercifully numb. But only for a little while. Then the shame and the guilt and the horror flood back over me and into me, and I think it must be the same for them as well.

Afterward we stumble our way under guard back to the NN barracks. Starving. Exhausted. Broken. Jules and I lie together once again on our hard bunks. He has survived the past two weeks of backbreaking work in the quarry, but I can feel how thin he's already gotten from the hard labor and the lack of food. Like so many of the others, he can't close his hands into fists. We whisper deep into the night, and I tell him everything.

"How am I supposed to go on?" I ask him. "After what I've done. I held their faces in my hands. I breathed their same breath. Until they had no breath. And I could do nothing to save them. I only tried to give them comfort, and what a lie that was! As if I was the one leading them to their deaths . . ."

"No!" Jules tells me emphatically. "No. Never. You survived. You had no choice. They had no chance. None. From the moment they were selected at Auschwitz. And even if they had stayed in Auschwitz, do you think they would have survived there, either? You can't blame yourself, Nicolette. You can't. You are a witness. That is your job. It is as you said: To remember them. To remember their faces. To remember their story. When this is over. When we prevail."

I break down when he says this—break down as I have been unable to the past two weeks. Jules puts his arms around me, though it is forbidden for prisoners to touch each other. If a kapo walks in with his flashlight and sees, we will be beaten. But I know Jules is beyond caring about such things, which is what frightens me, too.

“Soon enough, as soon as the first snowmelt,” he whispers. “When we’re able to move quickly against the guards. That is when we take over the quarry. Then the prison itself. We avenge these murders. We destroy Natzweiler and everything in it.”

I no longer try to dissuade him. I know that I am helpless to stop what will happen next, just as I was helpless to stop the deaths of the Jewish prisoners. At first I despair, thinking that for all his bold talk, Jules has lost the will to live, that the insurrection they have planned at the quarry is suicide. But the more Jules talks, the more the excitement in his voice tells me that I’m wrong. That what Jules understands, but few others ever do, is that the only way he can fully live is to be free, and to accept death however and whenever it comes.

“Nicolette,” he whispers. “You have to promise me that no matter what happens, you will live through this. You will survive the camp. And if anything happens to me, you will tell my mother and my aunt. Tell them I love them. Tell them I was brave as Papa would have wanted me to be.”

“You have to promise that you will survive as well,” I say, but Jules just says it again, admonishing me, making me swear. So I do.

A week later, just before the first snowmelt, the insurrection is crushed before it even begins. A mouchard informs on the conspirators. Dozens of the insurrectionists are shot at the quarry. An interrogation room is set up in the Soviets’ barracks.

I pray that Jules was one of those killed, that death for him came quickly. That he's not one of those still alive inside the barracks, where the organizers have been bound, their hands behind their backs, strung up to the ceiling by their tied hands. For a week, we can hear, all over the camp, the torture of those spared from execution at the quarry. They tell the SS guards whatever they want to know. They name names. Some lose their minds and begin to sing. The prisoners in neighboring barracks are unable to sleep because of the continuous cries of those being tortured. Hauptsturmführer Kramer seems pleased at reports that the prisoners are telling one another this, that the news has spread everywhere through the camp.

"What better way to maintain discipline?" he says in the dining hall, to murmured approval from the other officers. "In this way, they control themselves. My prediction is there will be no more talk of a prisoner revolt. Or if there is, we will hear about it before the prisoners themselves!"

The torture continues until the SS guards grow tired or bored. Those prisoners who have somehow survived are finally cut down. Most can no longer walk. The rest of the Natzweiler prisoners are once again ordered to gather at the gallows, where the condemned Soviets are hanged with short rope.

I have shut down. All my emotions. Though I am one of the few in camp who still has some flesh to cover my skeleton, I fear I am becoming Muselmann like so many others. Like Sébastien and Matthieu, who have been returned to the quarries and who can't look at me anymore, just as I avoid looking at them. Like even the stoic Ricard, the only friend I have left in the camp besides Christian.

For hours we stand and watch the hangings, one after another, until it becomes routine. Until the last one, who is Jules, who I can see, who we all can see, has already died from his injuries. They hang him anyway. I don't move. I don't try to speak. I don't make a sound. I don't cry—not now, not for a long time. But I feel as though I'm falling. Inside myself falling. Into a void falling. So much deeper into despair than I thought possible falling. Falling when I didn't think I could plummet any further after what occurred, what I was made to do, in the annex. Falling because I had foolishly let myself believe that even the Nazis couldn't invent any greater horrors than those murders of the eighty-six people. I am even more broken than before. We are all broken.

Some of the bodies are carried to the new crematorium and disposed of there; some are taken to the cellar of the disinfestation building and burned in the furnace to heat the scalding water for the showers.

I lie awake night after night, clutching the remnants of Jules's blanket, surprised that it gives me some comfort, sometimes pretending that it's him, that it still holds his smell, his warmth, even his voice. I miss him, and I miss Maman and Papa and Charlotte, so much that it becomes a physical ache, a torture itself—not just from what was done to Jules, but from my desperate need to know that Maman and Papa and Charlotte are still alive, that one day I will be with them again, and that somehow they know that I, too, am still one of the living, still breathing, still holding on, even if only by a thread.

But over time, that desperation starts to fade as well, and I can feel myself losing the faint hope that there might be something left of the light once this nightmare is over, the pathetic belief that this nightmare can ever end. Better to give up. To go through the motions, no longer care. Better to accept death. Jules's. Maman's and Papa's. Charlotte's.

And my own—whenever, however it comes.

26

VINGT-SIX

My second winter in Natzweiler crawls to an end. By late spring the snowmelts have cut new streams through the prison—streams that still freeze over at night, and even disappear at times under late snows. There are more wet deaths—when feeble prisoners fall into the ditches and are too weak to pull themselves out. When we stand for hours in the freezing rain for the interminable roll calls. When we are forced from our bunks again and again in the middle of the night, marched down the icy terrace steps to the showers, stripped, shaved, our clothes boiled for lice.

The guards are fearful of typhus, which we're told has swept through other Konzentrationslager. They blame the lice but do nothing about the overcrowded conditions in the barracks, the starvation, the hours of enslaved labor that destroy prisoners' bodies. After the showers, we stand barefoot and naked in the mud or the snow until given the signal, then scramble to retrieve our clogs, to find and wring out our steaming uniforms. My fingers burn at first, then quickly turn blue. I stab my limbs into the wet trousers and coat, jam a sodden cap over my bare and bleeding scalp, then line up for the trek back up the muddy mountain, slippery with patches of ice, struggling against the harsh night winds.

Christian has been happy to see me since I was returned to the officers' dining hall, but he hasn't asked about what I was made to do for Professor Hirt. He must have his suspicions. There must have been talk about the Jewish prisoners from Auschwitz. Natzweiler is a small camp. Nothing is secret. I have not spoken with him about Jules, either, though surely he knows about that as well. I can't. Not yet. Perhaps not ever. I am grateful for his kindness, that he looks after me not by asking questions, not by prying, but by keeping me busy. There are sausages to be ground. Knives to be sharpened. Cabbages to be shredded and fermented for sauerkraut. Anyway, Professor Hirt is gone, as is Professor Bickenbach.

And then, one day, Hauptsturmführer Kramer is gone as well, transferred to Auschwitz-Birkenau prison.

A stranger to the camp—a thin SS officer in a loose-fitting uniform, his high forehead glistening with sweat—shows up at the officers' dining hall to make the announcement. He introduces himself as Obersturmbannführer Fritz Hartjenstein, the new Kommandant of Natzweiler-Struthof.

"I myself have just come from Birkenau," he says. "I expect only that here will be maintained the same exacting level of discipline as there, and as everywhere demanded of us in the Third Reich." He pauses. "Regardless of what rumors you may have heard about the direction of the war. The rule is simple: Prisoners will work. They will obey every command. Or they will be executed. Officers, and SS guards as well, will do their jobs.

Will obey every command. Or they will be dealt with firmly. Is this understood?"

He is answered with a chorus of "Heil Hitler" and Nazi salutes.

Later, once we have finished with the serving, the cleaning, what preparations can be done in advance for tomorrow's first meal, Christian and I stand in the doorway, looking up at the night sky, which is clear and brilliant with a thousand stars. The officers are gone, and the guards have grown too bored to care much what we do—despite the harsh speech earlier by the new Kommandant. Christian lights a contraband cigarette, not even bothering to hide what he's doing. "This new Kommandant," he says. "He looks like an accountant, I think. Someone needs to iron his uniform."

I only nod. I am thinking of Papa, who always smoked his pipe after our meals back home. When I was little, he sometimes let me clean out the old ashes before he packed the bowl with fresh tobacco. I could always smell it on his clothes, a certain cherry scent that belonged to him alone.

And I am thinking about Hauptsturmführer Kramer, wondering if he has escaped whatever punishment, whatever justice, whatever revenge he is due—from me, for Jules, for the eighty-six, for Henri and Albert and the hundreds, the thousands of other prisoners.

Christian smokes his cigarette down until it burns his fingers, and even then takes one last puff before crushing it out in his hand and returning with it to the kitchen, to add it to a bucket of compost—crusts, apple peels, eggshells, a sausage casing fallen on the floor, a wilted leaf of rotted cabbage—thrown-away food that the prisoners would fight over if ever given the chance. But this will go to livestock, a handful of hogs kept in a slaughter pen just outside the camp.

In the past, I would steal from the compost when I thought I could get away with it. Now, though, even in front of the guards, Christian urges me to take clean food, whatever I can tuck into my waistband or inside my cheek to share with Ricard back at the NN barracks. The guards say nothing, perhaps because they have been helping themselves to the officers' forbidden food as well.

"What will happen to Hauptsturmführer Kramer?" I ask Christian, my voice a hoarse whisper.

"Whatever it is," Christian answers, "I only know it will never be enough to be called justice."

A week later, in a fierce night storm, the electricity goes out. Two prisoners with stolen wire cutters attack a kapo and beat him unconscious before prying up loose floorboards in their barracks so they can crawl away without being seen. They manage to elude the searchlights and the guns, cut through the double wire fences, and make their escape, though they leave a trail through a new dusting of powdery snow as they drag themselves down the mountain, hoping to disappear into the forest.

The escapees have one hour of freedom, no more, before they are caught by SS guards. Dogs are unleashed. The screams carry back up to the camp, where all prisoners have been ousted from our bunks and made to stand in formation as the late snow turns to freezing rain.

Guards return with the two bodies of the escapees. Obersturmbannführer Hartjenstein the Accountant orders both of the men to be hanged. We follow to watch, as ordered. Wait while a prisoner detail shovels away a snow drift under the gallows. I gaze elsewhere—on the stars in the suddenly cleared night. Perhaps ironically, if darkly so, I fixate on Sirius, the dog star, the single brightest of all in the winter sky, as Ricard has taught me. Perhaps there is some significance to this. Or just a distraction from the strangling sounds of another slow murder in the frozen night.

Overnight, it seems, more prisoners begin falling down during the predawn roll calls in the muddy fields. Not long after the executions of the escaped prisoners, three men tottering near me suddenly pitch to the ground. Ricard, who is standing close by, mutters, "Typhus," and I automatically recoil.

"It begins with exhaustion, with severe weakness," he tells me later. "But the swelling, that is the telltale sign. Did you see it on those men? Their hands, their feet, their ankles, their legs. It is called edema."

Two of the men die there in the field. A third is taken to the infirmary, which is already filled with the sick and the injured and the dying. The next morning, Ricard and I are ordered to carry another fallen prisoner to the infirmary. The man is lying facedown in the mud but still alive. Right away I notice what Ricard described—the swelling. We do our best to avoid contact with his flesh, gripping what we can of his torn trousers and striped jacket. Long, gaping, festering lesions cover his arms and legs.

"There," the Belgian doctor Janssens tells us, pointing. "In the corner on the floor. Next to the others."

I'm afraid to touch anything or anyone, afraid to breathe the fetid air inside the packed building. All around us are men with similar lesions and swelling. Their hands covered with sores. Protruding cheekbones. Soiled-sunken faces. Fever. Chills. Panicked breathing. Confusion. Disorientation. Crying. Whimpering. Begging for mercy.

We drop off our prisoner and quickly leave, not bothering to take the stretcher, which has been stained with pus and blood.

After that, the victims are kept at arm's length, forced to get themselves to the infirmary, until there's literally no more room. Then to a quarantined barracks. Food and water are left at the door. Inside, the victims fend for themselves. Kapos have meter-long tongs they use—or order prisoners to use—to clamp around the necks of those who have stopped breathing and drag them outside, haul them into wheelbarrows to be taken to the crematorium or the disinfestation building, where the bodies are needed more, to stoke the constantly raging furnace to heat the showers.

The death rate climbs. Christian tells me the SS officers are debating other measures, beyond the quarantine. There is talk of a boneyard farther up the mountain where the Polish women prisoners were buried in a mass grave the year before. Perhaps the typhus prisoners can be disposed of there.

Obersturmbannführer Hartjenstein and the SS officers speak of these things—as if the dead and the dying are mere inconveniences, disruptions to business as usual, a problem of logistics. Even in my numb state I am horrified, and surprised that I'm still capable of feeling the emotion. Any emotion. And angry. As if a small ember has been kept alive somewhere buried deep inside me, and still burns despite the Nazis' best efforts—and at times my own—to put it out.

Most who have contracted typhus die quickly, already so emaciated that it doesn't take much for the disease to finish them off. A few survive. Once they are healthy enough, a miracle—or a different kind of curse—those few are given the job of scouring the barracks clean. And then they are executed, to be sure no trace of typhus can possibly survive.

The NN barracks has been spared. I have been spared. But for what?

We are issued new blankets. The old are to be burned in an enormous pyre at the center of the camp. The ground thaws, rivers of winter melt racing down the terraces, undermining foundations, creating muddy waterfalls. I pray that the entire mountainside will be eroded and Natzweiler-Struthof destroyed in a massive avalanche or mudslide, carrying everyone and everything, every trace of the camp, into the valley, into the villages whose people have been able to pretend that the horrors above them could never have happened, couldn't still be happening.

The new blankets have been woven from human hair.

27

VINGT-SEPT

By June, the typhus infestation has largely passed. The quarantine barracks, though cleaned over and over by those who survived, is demolished. The prisoners assigned to live there—new arrivals from Poland and Yugoslavia—are ordered to work quickly and efficiently to rebuild it. They sleep on the ground in the late spring cold for the weeks it takes to pour the new foundation, erect the frame, raise uninsulated walls, build floor-to-ceiling bunks, hang the tin roof. A squad of kapos, led by Draza, administers daily beatings to hurry the project along. A dozen prisoners are killed.

A few evenings later, while the SS officers mill around the dining hall, waiting for the Obersturmbannführer, and for their dinner, they begin talking openly, agitatedly, about recent developments in the war. Clearly something big has happened. They seem even more worried than before, and angry. Because I am in and out of the dining hall, I hear some of what is said. Christian hangs close to the door from the kitchen and hears some as well. We piece it together later. "The Allies have landed on the beaches of Normandy," he whispers. "A thousand ships. Half a million men. They're saying Hitler hasn't moved enough troops to adequately defend the coastline. The Nazis are outnumbered.

"Of course they're saying their comrades are fighting heroically, to the last man, refusing to surrender, only grudgingly retreating when ordered by their gutless superiors hiding out in bunkers under Berlin. But they're also wondering how long the Nazis will be able to hold Normandy. How long they will be able to hold Paris. All of France. How long before even Strasbourg, even Natzweiler, are liberated by the Allies."

I can hardly believe what I'm hearing, and I can tell Christian is also in disbelief. Obersturmbannführer Hartjenstein storms into the dining hall and the conversation immediately stops, though for a brief moment it seems as if the voices of despair echo on. Then the Obersturmbannführer, who has heard enough to send him into a rage, explodes. He sweeps a tray full of beer steins off the table and onto the floor and yells at the officers, spitting and fuming until his face is purple. He threatens to have them court-martialed—anyone who is a defeatist, anyone who is critical of the conduct of the war, anyone who spreads false rumors, anyone who dares question the Führer!

Christian and I hide in the kitchen. Despite myself, I begin to feel something like hope, though in the past that has only led to more crushing disappointment. Voices are lowered in the dining hall, but we can still hear the Obersturmbannführer for the next hour as he berates his officers. The food grows cold. The officers are finally dismissed, the food left uneaten. I smuggle as much as I can back to the NN barracks for Ricard. And for Sébastien and Matthieu, although we can't bear to speak of things, but who, when I press bites of stolen pork into their palms, nod and then look away as they slip it into their mouths. I bring the news, too, about the Allies and Normandy. About the distant prospect, however faint still, of the liberation of Natzweiler.

In the days that follow, the guards and kapos respond by once again raising the level of brutality, if that's even possible. The crematorium spews white smoke day and night. New rope is requisitioned for the gallows. The Obersturmbannführer's garden, in full summer bloom, can no longer hold all the remains of the newly dead.

Within weeks, Allied planes are roaring overhead. They are bombing Strasbourg, fifty kilometers away. Some nights I can see it, faintly in the eastern sky, like the aurora borealis. The prisoners are no longer mining pink granite for Hitler's grand architectural plans and monuments in Nuremberg. Now they are carving out a massive tunnel, large enough to hold an underground factory beneath the Vosges for repairing bomber engines for the Luftwaffe. That is the official declaration as the days are lacerated by explosion after explosion, the kapos ordered to set the dynamite, and the prisoners forced in afterward to remove the newly freed rock.

I worry about Ricard, who is Papa's age, though with every subsequent week in the quarry now, in the factory tunnel, he ages more and more—gaunt, stooped, limping, trying to hide his limp, whether from me or the kapos or the guards or himself, who is to say? He no longer has the strength to stand outside in the evenings before curfew and instruct us on the constellations—me and a handful of other NN prisoners who joined us in the past because it was a distraction. Sometimes I sit quietly with him in the gloaming after slipping him what scraps I've managed to steal. One of those times, early in July, he talks about his family, a subject he's never mentioned before.

"I have a daughter who is your age, you know," he says. "She must wonder whatever became of me. Why I abandoned her. Why I disappeared from our town, from her life, without a word."

I am quick to reassure him. "But surely she would suspect it had something to do with your work with the Resistance," I say. "Even if she doesn't know about the Nacht und Nebel."

"I would like to think that," Ricard says. "But here I must confess something. I was never involved in the Resistance. Nothing so noble as that. My arrest was a mistake. I was at a café late, as usual, drinking. I made a mistake of making conversation with some Resistants whom I knew only casually. But a drinking companion is a drinking companion. And for the drunk I was then, it didn't matter who I was with, especially if they were the ones buying."

I lay my hand on top of his. "But you must have done something against the Germans. Said something. Helped someone they were after," I say.

Ricard shrugs. "The café closed. My companions invited me with them to the house of their friend. I thought I was so clever. I had been to university, after all, though I had done very little with my life afterward. Perhaps that's why they wanted me along. For drunken entertainment. I should have gone home instead, to my daughter, to my wife, though they must have had quite enough of me by then. When the arrest came, I was too drunk to understand what was happening. I thought the Nazis had come to drink with us, too. I was the one who opened the door to them, who invited them in—not that they would have waited for an invitation."

He lapses into silence for a while, then continues. "There are so many others here you could be helping. So many others who are more deserving. I never told you this—it is foolish, after all—but at times, I have pretended that you were my daughter, because who else besides a daughter would be so considerate to someone so undeserving? Perhaps it was a pathetic attempt to convince myself that I might have some worth in my daughter's eyes, if she were to ever see me again, if I could ever explain what became of me. If I could ever apologize to her enough for being a poor father. A poor husband to her mother. If I could ever atone for having abandoned them."

I take his hand in both of mine. "In your own way, you *have* been a father to me," I say. "Teaching me about the stars. Showing strength in your stoicism, your refusal to complain. So many here have given up, and I don't blame them for that. It is beyond them to continue. So many others have turned on one another, have cooperated with the guards and the kapos. For them, I have nothing but contempt. But you have never done this. And in helping you, and in helping the others before you—Henri and Albert and the others, and my friend Jules, all of whom did more for me than I could have ever done for them—I have had a purpose. Perhaps that is what keeps me alive. Perhaps it is what keeps any of us alive. And perhaps this—surviving Natzweiler, returning to your daughter and your wife, making up to them for every way you have failed them in the past—this is your purpose . . ."

I trail off, hoping I haven't said too much. I can't imagine ever speaking to my own father in this way, even if they are things that had to be said.

But Ricard isn't offended. He gives me a weak smile. "Merci, Nicolette," he says. "Merci. I will hold on to these thoughts. And I will always remember your kindness."

He pauses. "At the risk of becoming maudlin, there is one thing I would like to ask of you." He doesn't wait for me to respond. It is the same request I had from Jules. The same I would have gotten from Henri and Albert and so many others. If only there had been enough time.

"If I don't survive whatever time is left here," Ricard says. "Perhaps you can find them one day, after the war. My family. My daughter. Perhaps you can tell them for me what was in my heart."

A few days later, four middle-aged women are thrown from the back of a truck at the entrance to Natzweiler and clubbed by guards as they're forced to climb to the gallows. They are dressed in civilian clothes, like shopkeepers. Like Maman and Madame Asher. The women aren't French, Obersturmbannführer Hartjenstein announces. Though when they were caught, they were pretending to be. They are British. Spies. Special Operations spies. Saboteurs.

One has been beaten so badly that she remains unconscious even as guards hold her up and the noose is fitted around her neck. We have seen this before. One weeps openly. One stands erect, clearly defiant. One begs for her life. We have seen all of it before.

All are killed.

I try to find out their names.

A few weeks later, near the end of July, a British pilot is dragged into the prison. His plane, one of the bombers that has been attacking the Nazis' stronghold in Strasbourg, was shot down. All the others on board died in the crash or were shot trying to escape. The Obersturmbannführer himself administers a last beating and death, there on the gallows platform. Though I have never been one who often prays, I pray that night, and I pray now every night, that if they are not able to liberate us soon, that the Allied bombers will target Konzentrationslager Natzweiler. That even if it means we must all perish, they will find a way to wipe the camp and all the Nazis and kapos who run it off the face of the earth.

The murders continue, but the Nazis can only do so much. The war is getting closer and closer. We hear it every day, every night. I hear others praying, too, out loud, and perhaps we are getting our answer. Perhaps there is reason for hope. The SS officers must sense it as well, and must fear they will one day be held responsible for what they have done here. And so must destroy the evidence. Late in August, Obersturmbannführer Hartjenstein gives the order for the guards to kill as many prisoners as they can. Transport vehicles will be arriving soon to take the rest to another camp called Dachau, close by, in southern Germany. Christian and I start warning others, as many of our fellow prisoners as we think we can trust, despite knowing we can do nothing to stop any of it.

Ricard is one of dozens selected for execution in Natzweiler. As he is being led away, out of the camp, up the mountain with one hundred fifty others, he sees me and manages to smile—only the second time I have ever seen him do this. It is a show, however slight, for my benefit. He is my last friend in the barrack besides Sébastien and Matthieu, and it tears at my heart in ways I didn't think I could still feel. I want to shout to Ricard, to ask him all the things I need to know but that I forgot to ask: *Where are you from? Where is your family? You didn't tell me! What are their surnames? What is yours?*

But I'm too late. The guards carry tripods and cartridge belts and Knochensäge machine guns. The prisoners know what is to come. The firing goes on for an hour. It takes a long time to kill so many men. I collapse onto the floor. I can no longer stand as it goes on and on. It is too much to bear.

"There are too many of us to kill outright," Christian tells me that evening. "And even if they could, there would be too many bodies to dispose of. Too much evidence left behind. The crematoria here are too small for such numbers. The boneyard is full. We can only hope the liberators reach us before the transports get here. From what I have heard, the only escape in the places they're taking us is through the chimneys. Is through death."

Christian seems to take it all in stride, seems fatalistic about our dim prospects for survival as the war winds down, even as we dare become optimistic about the Allied victory and the Nazis' impending defeat. I think this one minute, but then in the next, Christian says something hopeful, reminds me of his invitation and my promise—that I will bring my family to visit him and his wife and baby in Lille, near the Belgian border. That we will break bread together in celebration of having survived the war. That he will prepare for us all this wonderful, wonderful stew, carbonnade flamande, about which he dreams every night, with a perfect side of pommes frites.

28

VINGT-HUIT

One hundred three-tonne Opel Blitz trucks arrive the next morning, announced by the grinding of gears up steep mountain roads, the high-pitched sound of straining engines, a rising cloud of exhaust. The convoy parks just outside the camp entrance. One by one, starting at the bottom of the mountain, the barracks are emptied, kapos forcing prisoners down the terrace steps and into the back of the dilapidated trucks, under the cover of torn canvas shells. The transports are meant to hold ten, facing one another on benches, but the kapos and the SS guards force forty inside. The benches have been torn out. Everyone stands, clinging to the metal frame, rips in the canvas, one another as the trucks lurch forward for the trek back down the mountain, bound for Dachau. With the trucks comes word that Paris has been liberated. De Gaulle has returned; the French army has entered the city, chasing out the occupiers without firing a shot. The Nazis are in retreat. Natzweiler must be emptied before the Allies come, before they can learn what has been done here. Despite what Christian has said about where we are to be taken, I feel an unfamiliar rush of excitement that I can't explain.

The NN barrack is the last, positioned as it is on the highest terrace and farthest from the entrance and the line of trucks. Despite everything, my mind is filled with thoughts of Paris, a free Paris, Maman and Papa, Charlotte. But Paris is west. Freedom is west. We are being taken east, into darkness, a descent into the underworld. Our shoes are confiscated before we are marched down the terrace steps to the convoy of wheezing trucks. I feel every pebble, every stone, every patch of damp earth. I look frantically for Christian but don't see him anywhere until we reach the camp entrance. He is climbing into a transport several trucks ahead of mine. He doesn't look back, though I try to will him to, so I might see him, and be seen by him, my last true friend, one final time.

Draza is assigned to my truck, one of the remaining transports. The camp is all but empty. Only a skeleton crew of SS guards, a handful of officers, stay to destroy documents, dispose of evidence, dismantle the crematorium.

"Little sister," Draza says. "I have missed seeing you."

I can feel the condemnation by the other prisoners for this recognition by Draza, for my association with such a notorious kapo, for the possibility in their minds that I, who they have protected in the barracks, might have been a mouchard. I'm wedged in the back of the truck with three dozen others. None look at me. No one speaks. The kapos slam the tailgate shut behind us and climb onto the back of the truck. The SS guards follow in a jeep. The driver cranks up the diesel engine, and we are immediately engulfed in exhaust.

But our truck breaks down only a kilometer from the camp. There is discussion about having us walk back to Natzweiler, but in the end it is decided that we will wait with the kapos and the guards until a mechanic can be summoned for repairs. The rest of the convoy, the last five trucks, pass around us, other SS guards jeering at their friends who are left behind. I'm ordered out with the other prisoners and lined up in a wet ditch on the side of the road. The man beside me says he's afraid there may be an order to execute all of us here, but that doesn't happen. I see, just down the road, the hotel annex—the gas chamber. From here it looks like a small country cottage with its white walls and red roof and quaint shutters. The windows are boarded over. There is no indication of the nightmare that went on there.

The excitement of leaving Natzweiler, finally, after these two long, terrible years, vanishes abruptly at the reminder of the eighty-six who were murdered, of what Sébastien and Matthieu and I were forced to do, a foreshadowing of the certain death that awaits us all. But something changes. One minute Draza and the other kapo are smoking cigarettes with the two SS guards, laughing and talking in German. The next minute the kapos have overpowered the young, unsuspecting Germans, clubbing them to the ground, seizing their weapons. It all happens so fast. The kapos order the guards to take off their black boots, uniforms, and hats. The guards, terrified, do as they're told, and the rest of us can only watch, unsure what this means for us. Then the kapos march the barefoot guards into the woods off the road. I hear the sharp report of automatic weapons. Only the kapos emerge back into the sunlight, now dressed in the Nazis' uniforms.

Draza climbs behind the wheel of the jeep. The other kapo takes the passenger seat. Prisoners are already pulling themselves from the ditch, already running, hobbling, limping, down the road or into the woods or toward the villages below, away from where the kapos just executed the guards, away from Natzweiler-Struthof. Draza shrugs. He smiles and waves to me. There's no one left to stop them as he and his friend race off in their stolen uniforms and stolen jeep to whatever version of freedom may lie ahead.

No one has waited for me, but after the friendly greeting from Draza, why would they? In a daze, I wander over to the annex. I try the door, but it is locked. I don't know what I would have done there anyway. I don't know why I would ever want to go inside that house of horrors ever again.

It's just that standing here, alone, suddenly free—even with the great danger of someone coming from the prison at any minute, drawn by the sound of gunfire—despite all my dreams of liberation, I don't know where to go.

Finally I force myself to move, following the narrow lane to the outskirts of Struthof. Down there, on a busier road, the retreating Nazis are everywhere. Columns of trucks, tanks, artillery, ambulances, beleaguered Wehrmacht soldiers streaming past. They pour through the villages and towns that populate the Vosges range, all heading east, toward Strasbourg and beyond, to the border, across the Rhine and back into Germany. For hours, for what remains of the day, every time I try to go west, over the mountains toward Paris, I have to stop and hide until they pass. But then more come, and more after that, until I'm forced to accept that I have no choice but to make my way east instead, ahead of them, to Strasbourg. My hope is to disguise myself there and find food and shelter and wait and pray that

Strasbourg, too, will soon be emptied of Nazis fleeing the Allied advance.

A few hours later, I am wading through a waist-high field of green corn to a red-roofed farmhouse to ask for help, for food, for shelter. An angry agriculteur steps out into the sunlight, shotgun aimed, and shouts for me to leave. If the Nazis find me here—an escaped prisoner—they will destroy his farm, he says. They will kill his family. I retreat through the field.

Two days later, still wandering vaguely east, following a small mountain stream, staying clear of roads as much as I can, I hear the soft lowing of cows. Another farm. The stream pours out onto a clearing, a green, rolling meadow, dozens of dairy cows. There are two burned-out barns, but a third still standing. A broken farmhouse with a sagging porch roof. A man, a woman, four children toiling in the yard and in the pasture. I haven't eaten since Natzweiler, though my belly is swollen from drinking so much of the clean water. I try again, fighting off waves of dizziness and fatigue, stepping out of the forest with my arms already raised. The late morning sun burns overhead. I am bathed in sweat, though whether from the heat of the day or from the onset of a fever I can't say. I force myself to keep going, to call ahead: "Monsieur! Madame! S'il vous plaît!"

The woman orders me to halt. The children stop what they're doing to watch as she crosses the field, clutching a pitchfork, strands of hay dangling from the tines. Her husband, like the first farmer who threatened me and chased me away, retrieves his shotgun from inside the barn.

I tell the woman my story before she can turn me away, before she can ask me anything. Prisoner. Natzweiler. Escaped. I hesitate, then add, "La Resistance."

The woman stops me. Tells me to not utter another word. There is a small cabin, she says, pointing to where the stream reenters the forest on the far side of the farm. It is not much, but it is shelter. There will be food, a blanket, clothes brought in an hour and left nearby. If I am there, so be it. I may stay, only for a few days. But I cannot be seen. I cannot speak to the children, to anyone. I cannot have any contact with the woman, her husband, the farm. If they are questioned, they can deny I was here.

I whisper "Merci," but she has already turned away, marching back to her husband and her children and the barn and the house with the sagging porch roof.

I find the cabin easily enough. It is an abandoned, one-room hut with visible holes in the roof and a rotting, leaf-strewn floor. There is no glass in the windows, no door, no furniture. But there is water close by, and I am able to stumble down to the stream, drink my fill, bathe my fevered face, then drag myself back to wait.

An hour later, I hear someone entering the woods not far away. After they leave, I find blankets, as promised. A boy's clothes—canvas shoes with soles bound in place by thin wire, wide trousers, stained work shirt, men's jacket, black wool beret. Cheese, milk, half a baguette, sausage, a small bunch of carrots pulled straight from the soil. I eat too quickly, not bothering to carry the food back to the cabin or wash off the carrots. And I vomit it back up immediately. My first impulse is to scoop up the vomit and force it down again. I've seen it done a hundred times in the NN barracks. I've done it myself there. But no. I have more food. I will make myself eat slowly. I will bathe in the stream, scrub myself red and raw with pebbles and mud, no matter how cold the water there, bury my prison uniform deep in the forest where it can never be found, wish I could burn it, burn every vestige of Natzweiler-Struthof.

A week passes in the hidden cabin. Someone from the farm continues to leave me food under cover of darkness. My fever breaks. My hair is already beginning to grow out, and the places where it hasn't are easily hidden under the oversized beret. I am still gaunt, and know I look like a boy, a starved, beggar child, a figure from *Les Misérables*. So in that sense the clothes are a perfect fit, even hanging off me as they do, even with the twine I must use to hold up the trousers. I spend hours sitting in shadow at the edge of the forest, staring across the pasture at the cows, at the family, at what could be mistaken for normal country life, except for the bombers continually flying overhead, the echoes of explosions in faraway Strasbourg. Or I find myself weeping, uncontrollably weeping, in the middle of the dark nights. Or I am trapped in a recurring nightmare about the eighty-six, surrounded by the plaster casts of their faces, their eyes slowly opening to reveal their terror. Their mouths won't open. They can't speak. It's only the eyes, the eyes, the eyes.

They want something from me. I owe them something. I don't know what it is. I turn to Jules to ask him to help me, grateful that I'm no longer alone. But of course he's not there, either. No one is there. For most of the past two years, I haven't dreamed. Sleep has been an escape from the horrors of Natzweiler. But now that I'm free, there seems to be no escape even there.

• • •

I awake one morning to the sound of an automatic weapon firing, fast and loud, like cloth being ripped. I hear screams—animal and human—somehow rising above the cacophony. I make my way to the edge of the pasture. A Wehrmacht patrol is mowing down the dairy herd with an MC-42 machine gun mounted on a tripod—a Knochensäge—one soldier aiming, not that it takes much to aim at the helpless cattle in a small pen, another soldier feeding in the long belt of high-velocity rounds. It is too much weapon. At close range, most of the cows are cut in half, carved into pieces. They must be slaughtering the cows for their meat, but anyone can see that what's left of the beef will be ruined by the overkill.

The firing stops, as the Knochensäge has overheated, the barrel turning red. Smoke lifts into the morning air. Trucks pull up to the pen, and soldiers leave their shoulder arms in a pile and load the meat—hooves and heads and all. The French family, including the sobbing children, are forced to help. A few of the cows aren't yet dead. The father speaks to an officer, who nods. The father goes to the barn, returns with his shotgun, and puts down the suffering animals.

The officer takes the shotgun when the father has finished, demands the extra shells, and confiscates them all. The trucks leave, trailing a river of blood that follows them out of the pasture until they're obscured by the one standing barn. I remember the sand pit at Natzweiler. The young partisans bound together and used for target practice while the prisoners were forced to watch. The bodies removed. The red-soaked sand turned over.

After the Nazis leave, I approach the parents. But they don't want their blankets back; they just wave me away. The children are busy shoveling clean soil over the blood-soaked earth, though there doesn't seem to be any point to it. They'll have to give up the farm. Anyone can see that. There's nothing left for them here. Even their vegetable garden is in ruins. The Nazis drove their trucks through it on their way out.

I am on the move again, east toward Strasbourg. The nights have grown cold—too cold to sleep outdoors, though for the next few nights I have no choice, so I wrap myself in my blankets, wedge myself under shelves of rock, bury myself under piles of fallen leaves, craft beds of pine needles, and still it's not enough to keep me warm. But I know better than to call attention with fires, even small ones. I try begging when I find isolated houses, other small farms. Most have been ransacked by the retreating Nazis. Some turn me away, even threaten me, but a few are willing to share what little they have, and even invite me to stay, to share my story. But I am afraid that if I start talking about what has happened, if I open that door, I'll never be able to close it again. So I thank the people, accept a warm corner to sleep in for the night, promise to repay them someday for their kindness, and continue on to Strasbourg.

29

VINGT-NEUF

When I finally reach Strasbourg, in late September, it is a chaos of bombed-out buildings and traffic jams. No checkpoints, no one demanding papers, no one noticing me at all. I still freeze every time I pass the wandering patrols, pull the oversized beret as far forward as I can to hide my face, shuffle down broken sidewalks and ruptured cobblestone once they pass. I realize I am invisible to them—twice they brush against me and don't even bother to yell or curse—and this understanding helps me calm my racing heartbeat. An old street merchant sees me staring hungrily at the handful of desiccated apples, which are all he has left on his stand, perhaps all he has had for days. He offers me one but gets angry when I bite into it and only then tell him I have no money to pay. He yells at me, but even in my weakened state, I have no problem getting away.

The streets are busy with troop movements, though they seem to be heading in all directions at once—advancing, retreating, driving in hapless circles. No one seems to know anything, except that the Allies are closing in. The advancing armies have come as far as the Saverne Pass and now have a clear path south to Strasbourg, not that the bombers have to wait for the armies. I hear talk that it is the reconstituted French army, with support from the Americans, who are marching on the city. The Wehrmacht are under orders to fight to the last bullet, but I doubt that will happen, judging by the pandemonium. Most of the Nazis I see are standing around in clusters, or sitting outside abandoned cafés, smoking, drinking, in despair. A French civilian I meet on the street tells me some have already been shedding their uniforms and donning civilian clothes, making their way on bicycles, on horse-drawn carts, on foot out of Alsace and across the Rhine, back into Germany.

I've only been to Reich University in the dead of night, in the back of a pitch-dark van, but it's not hard to find in the daylight—south of la Grande Île, the city center with its circle of canals and stone bridges and quays and white buildings, many of them still blanketed with Nazi flags and banners, or bombed into rubble. The medical college stands unscathed, empty except for a handful of frantic men in lab coats. Piles of documents have been burned to cinders in the foyer. Boxes and papers and books and journals and other laboratory equipment have been abandoned in random piles. All the signs are in German, but I'm still able to find Professor Hirt's anatomy lab, deep in the bowels of the building, through a labyrinth of narrow halls. No one has bothered to lock doors. The last one I open leads to the white-tiled room, bare except for the three dissection tables, covered stainless steel vats, drains in the middle of the floor, and a small office to the side.

I expect to see the plaster casts we had to make and Hirt's

gruesome collection of Jewish skeletons. But I don't see the casts anywhere, and if the skeletons were ever here, they're gone now.

I spend an hour in the small office, ransacking drawers, pulling open file cabinets, afraid that what I'm looking for has already been destroyed. Much of it has—there is a trash can still smoldering in the hall, filled with the blackened remnants of charred papers—but much is still here. I find scattered pages from the notebooks Sébastien, Matthieu, and I were forced to fill with notations, measurements, details on each of the eighty-six. There are folders with documents that I'm unable to read, copies of letters, official correspondence, requisition forms. A partial list of numbers, but no names.

With trembling hands, I stack everything carefully on top of the desk. Professor Hirt has abandoned his laboratory, abandoned his research, abandoned his life here. Surely the next to visit this unholy place will be the Allies, seeking answers. And so I will make sure they find them.

I return to the autopsy room, the dissection tables, the drains, the bright overhead lights that illuminate everything. Even in remote corners there are no shadows. None. There is a storage closet I overlooked before. Inside are tanks of synthetic alcohol. Sealed jars filled with tissue samples. A collection of actual human skulls, gleaming white, perfectly formed. I close the door quickly and sag to the floor. I stare at the covered vats but can't yet bring myself to approach them. I already know, fear, what I'll find inside.

But I brace myself to check. To once again bear witness to what has happened. I check the first vat and find the body—half of the body—of someone inside. A man, his features no longer recognizable. The number tattooed on his forearm is 107969.

It becomes difficult to breathe. I want nothing more than to be out of this place of such horrors. Out of my own skin.

But I make myself keep going until I've checked every one of the covered vats. I want to cry for these lost people, for all those who suffered at the hands of the Nazis. But I know if I start, I'll never be able to finish. Once I'm done, I scrawl a note: *Here are victims of anatomy murders by Professor August Hirt and Natzweiler Hauptsturmführer Josef Kramer. There were eighty-six Jews selected from Auschwitz.*

I find Hirt's home late that afternoon, the address on a letter from his office. I still need proof—that Hirt is dead, or if he is alive, that there are traces of him that can be found, clues to where he has gone, so that one day he can be caught and exposed and made to pay. I have passed block after block of destruction to find this address, or what I think is the right address. There are no street signs here—in German or in French. No landmarks. Only rubble and a sun that has ghosted the wintering sky. But I'm certain I'm in the right neighborhood.

I am standing in the middle of the street. There is no traffic. Only broken bricks and stone and shattered glass, the shredded remnants of Nazi flags. An old woman clenching the hand of a small child approaches. They stop close to me, as if studying the bombed-out houses next to a stranger is the most natural thing to do. I can see the woman isn't old after all, just worn out by this war. She points to another pile of rubble just down the street. "There is ours," she says.

"And this one?" I ask.

"The Hirt family," she says. The child begins to cry. The woman doesn't seem to notice. "The mother and the son were killed when the bombs fell."

"And Professor Hirt?"

She shrugs. "If he was lucky, he died here as well."

The fruit merchant, the one from whom I stole the apple, is surprised when I return. I have coins I found in Hirt's office.

"I had no money before," I say, placing the coins in his open palm. "I was very hungry."

I turn to leave, but he tells me to wait. "You have overpaid," he says, and he hands me another apple, his last. Then he gestures to a stool next to his stand. "You may sit here to eat if you would like. You look tired."

I have no intention of accepting his offer, but as soon as he says it, perhaps in response to his kindness, I collapse onto the seat and sag back against the wall. My arms feel too weak to lift the apple to my mouth.

The fruit merchant gently takes it back, and with a small paring knife expertly cuts it into sections. I manage to eat, one wedge at a time. After, I sit there for an hour, just watching, at times dozing off, as the fruit merchant conducts his business. He has brought out a small tub of berries that he sells by the scoop. Customers bring their own containers, or cup their palms together and eat the berries directly from their hands. The fruit is soon gone.

At one point the merchant tells me his name—Monsieur Toussaint—and I tell him mine. "And do you have somewhere to be?" he asks.

I shake my head. "I'm only trying to make my way home," I say. "Back to Paris. Back to my family."

He doesn't ask anything more, but as the late afternoon turns into cool September evening, as the frenetic street activity dies down and the soldiers and citizens scurry to safety from the nightly air raids, he invites me to share the floor of his "apartment." It is a grand name he uses for the storage shed where he keeps his empty crates. He rolls out a straw-stuffed mattress there at night and heats an evening meal of soup and bread on a small stove. I still have my blankets from the dairy farm.

Monsieur Toussaint is quiet and welcoming. Once I returned with deutschemark for the apple, all was forgiven. I am his friend now. He tells me he doesn't have many friends. He is one who goes unnoticed, he says. He shares his soup and bread, apologizing because he has so little to give. I explain that in Natzweiler-Struthof, this would be a feast. There are those who would kill for so much food.

It is the first time I've mentioned the camp. He nods in recognition.

"I, too, was in the war," he says. "Not this one, of course. I am too old. But the last one. The war that didn't end all wars. Many of my friends died. We were young then. Too young to understand."

"To understand what?" I ask, but he only answers, "Anything."

We talk about other things for a while. The occupation of Strasbourg. The complacency of so many. I tell him about the young partisans from the university, the thirteen who were murdered. The target practice. Perhaps they stopped at his fruit stand. They must have had lives before the war. Ordinary lives.

Families. But then I start talking about the others, my friends from Natzweiler, the ones I want to remember. The ones who gave me purpose—to share their stories, to make certain they're not forgotten. I tell him about Henri the music teacher, leading us in song. Albert, his friend from childhood, who couldn't hold a tune but sang with us anyway. Michel, the watchmaker, who built his own radio and gave his life to make sure the rest of us had news of the war. Ricard, who taught me about the stars. And Christian, who has promised me the most wonderful meal one day. I try to tell him about Jules, but the words catch in my throat. I can't. I am silenced by my grief. Perhaps one day I'll be able to tell the story of Jules, and of Jules and me, in a way that will honor him, in a way that will do him justice. But not yet. Not today.

Monsieur Toussaint washes our bowls and spoons, then blows out the one candle. I hear bombs falling elsewhere in the city and burrow deeper into my blankets. For the first night since Natzweiler, I sleep without nightmares. I dream instead of Maman and Papa and Charlotte, of nothing really, of a morning when I was younger, bowls of hot chocolate, warm baguettes from the Ashers' boulangerie, creamy butter and sweet raspberry preserves, œufs brouillés.

In the morning, I tell Monsieur Toussaint that I am starting my journey home, that I don't think I can wait for the Nazis to leave Strasbourg or for the Allied advance to reach here.

He nods. "Your family," he says. "Of course they must be missing you."

He says he will make a gift of the one thing he has of value, though it is so old, it's likely not worth very much. A bicycle. "It is rusty," he tells me, "but the tires are good." And he also has a kit for patching should one go bad, and a bicycle pump, bent but still able to work.

"Merci," I whisper. I have known kindness in Natzweiler, and sacrifice. I'm still surprised. And grateful. I get right to work repairing the bicycle as Papa taught me. I roam through the city looking for parts I can pirate from broken and abandoned frames. A spare set of tires and tubes that still have some wear. Brake cables, frayed, but only a little. Pedals to replace the cracked ones on Monsieur Toussaint's. A replacement chain with barely any rust, and oil and rags for cleaning. In a deserted bike shop, the shelves stripped bare, I still manage to find some tools—pliers, a spoke wrench.

When I am finished with repairs, Monsieur Toussaint ties on my blankets, wraps his scarf around my neck, and tucks it inside the oversized coat. He has a worn set of panniers he fills with what little food he has and attaches to the old bicycle. Insists that I take the few deutschemarks he has, and, in case anyone is using French currency again now that the occupation is ending, some francs.

"It is not much," he says, still apologizing. But it is—it is a lot to me. I thank him. Then we shake hands, a formal goodbye. His eyes are rimmed with tears. I think perhaps he is crying not so much for me, but for all of France.

I walk the bicycle slowly through the bombed-out streets, avoiding potholes and craters and burning vehicles. Paris is west, five hundred kilometers, through the Saverne Pass, where

I will meet the advancing Allied armies. It will take weeks to get home, and I'm afraid of what I will find. Who is dead. Who is broken. Who is left.

At the outskirts of Strasbourg, where I once visited with Maman and Papa and Charlotte and Jules and his family on that long-ago cycling tour, I climb onto Monsieur Toussaint's bicycle. It feels heavy and unbalanced, but after a few easy pedals, I feel certain I can manage. The going is slow. The highway has been damaged by tank treads and bombs. I have to pull off to the right to make room for columns of retreating Wehrmacht. Refugees and farm families, their crops and livestock destroyed, line the road and beg for food from the listless soldiers. Long caravans of trucks and ambulances are loaded with stretchers carrying the sick and wounded and dead.

I can almost feel pity for them, these German casualties of war. But then in my reverie I return to lost moments with Henri, Albert, Jules, Ricard, and I can no longer be sorry for what I am seeing now.

Ricard once taught me a Greek word, *katabasis*, a descent into the underworld, to describe the prisoners' work in the quarries. He taught me another word, too—*nekyia*: summoning ghosts to question them about the earthly future. They often go hand in hand, he told me—katabasis and nekyia.

But I have to wonder, what do the dead have to teach us that the living shouldn't already know?

I ponder this for a while, but then let it go. The road is steep here in places and can be treacherous. It opens up and is even empty for a few kilometers of anyone but me, and just for a moment, coasting downhill, it feels as though I'm flying once again. So I continue my long journey home—out of the underworld, out of the night and fog, back to Maman and Papa and, I pray, Charlotte.

Back to what's left of the light.

HISTORICAL NOTE

While the stories of Nicolette, Jules, Charlotte, Antoine, Maman, Papa, the Ashers, Henri, Denis, Ricard, Christian, Albert, and many of the other characters in *Stolen by Night* are fiction, the events are drawn from the actual history of occupied Paris during World War II and the documented horrors of Konzentrationslager Natzweiler-Struthof, the only Nazi-run concentration camp on what is now French soil.

The Paris occupation began on June 14, 1940, one month after the German army, the Wehrmacht, invaded France. Wehrmacht troops entered the city with very little resistance and soon held total control. Shortly after, France signed an armistice with Germany, setting up a puppet French state with its capital in the provincial city of Vichy. Though much of the French military had been defeated or surrendered, Free French forces under the leadership of General Charles de Gaulle, exiled in Great Britain, joined the Allied cause and provided support and encouragement for the Resistance movement inside occupied France.

Hundreds of thousands of French people, including tens of thousands of teenagers, worked tirelessly in the Resistance, fighting the Nazis and their Vichy collaborators. Many were caught and imprisoned. Many were tortured. Many were executed. Thousands were "disappeared" in the Nazis' Nacht und Nebel program—Night and Fog—the women sent to Ravensbrück prison in northern Germany, the men to Natzweiler-Struthof.

More than 22,000 prisoners were murdered at Natzweiler during the war. The few hundred women sent there were all executed within a few days of their arrival. In real life, Nicolette would not have survived her time in the camp.

Hauptsturmführer Josef Kramer served as Kommandant of Natzweiler-Struthof for three years, from April 1941 to May 1944. Among Kramer's many atrocities there were the torture and executions of thirty Soviet prisoners who had planned an insurrection in the mines before they were betrayed, an event included in *Stolen by Night* with the fictional character of Nicolette's friend Jules. Kramer was also responsible for the deaths of eighty-six Jewish prisoners, brought to Natzweiler to become anatomical specimens in a Jewish skeleton collection housed by Professor August Hirt at the Institute of Anatomy at Reich University in Strasbourg. At his trial after the war—for crimes against humanity—Kramer confessed to the murders.

In May 1944, Kramer was transferred from Natzweiler to Auschwitz, in southern Poland, to manage the gassings of new prisoners. After a few months, he was transferred again, to his final post, Bergen-Belsen, in northern Germany, where his brutality earned him the grim nickname the Beast of Belsen. He was responsible for the suffering and the deaths of tens of thousands of prisoners during his time there, including two German sisters from a Jewish family who had been hiding for two years in the Netherlands, in a secret annex above a spice business in Amsterdam.

One of the girls was Anne Frank; the other was her sister, Margot. Their mother died in Auschwitz, starved to death from passing her meager rations of food to her daughters—dropping bread crusts to them through a hole in a floorboard, lifesaving gifts they were unable to refuse. Anne and Margot were transferred to Bergen-Belsen after their mother's death. The new Kommandant, Josef Kramer, was driven to his post there in a Mercedes-Benz 770. The sisters were taken by cattle car. They contracted typhus shortly after their arrival. Margot was the first to die. In her delirium she fell from her bunk; the shock was too much for her disease-ravaged body and frail heart.

Anne, bald, emaciated, shivering, burning with fever, was recognized by two friends from Amsterdam who were also in Bergen-Belsen, in a different section of the camp, separated by barbed wire. One of the friends, Hanneli, scrounged a packet of food for Anne, but when she threw it over the fence, another prisoner caught it and ran away as Anne screamed and screamed. She died two days after Margot. They were buried in a mass grave.

War criminal Josef Kramer was eventually hanged, in December 1945, his body left only for a short time on a wooden gallows in Hamelin Prison, not unlike the gallows still left standing today at Natzweiler-Struthof.

Professor Otto Bickenbach, a virologist at Reich University, was captured after the war and put on trial for his chemical experiments on Natzweiler prisoners, for the suffering and the deaths. Several of his victims survived long enough to testify against him. After a few years in a French prison, those witnesses by then missing or dead, Bickenbach was granted a retrial in which he claimed that all the Natzweiler-Struthof prisoners who participated in the experiments had been volunteers. A German research assistant testified for him at the second trial, and with no counterevidence, a tribunal vacated his sentence. He was returned to Strasbourg and allowed to practice as a physician, a respected member of the community until his death on November 26, 1971.

Anatomy professor August Hirt wasn't killed by the bomb that destroyed his home and his family. He had left Strasbourg ahead of the Allied invasion in a mass exodus of the medical institute faculty. The French First Armored Division, led by the Free French general Philippe Leclerc, followed by the American Seventh Army, took the city of Strasbourg in November 1944 with little resistance. Instead of fighting to the last bullet, the remnants of the Wehrmacht threw their ammunition into the river and pretended that they'd run out and so had no choice but to surrender.

Leclerc's men were the first to report the horrors of Hirt's laboratory and the remains they discovered there of fifteen of the eighty-six Jews who were murdered. Hirt and his assistants had disposed of the other victims after disarticulating their cadavers to more easily transport the remains to the city's crematoria. Hirt knew that the Allies would not understand his work, would think him a monster, so he ordered his assistants to destroy it. But, for reasons we may never know, his instructions were not followed, and so evidence was left behind of his horrific actions. In *Stolen by Night*, Nicolette finds and leaves documentation to help identify the victims. In reality, it took decades for researchers to discover all the names of the dead, starting with the prison numbers tattooed on the arms of the fifteen bodies found in Hirt's lab.

There were two young Frenchmen who were forced to help Hirt with his antisemitic anatomical "study" at Natzweiler; however, the characters of Matthieu and Sébastien are fictional. No young woman like Nicolette was ever involved.

After the war, Hirt hid for seven months alone in the Black Forest in Germany. When finally discovered, in the village of Schluchsee, months after he was sentenced to death in absentia by a war crimes tribunal, he chose to take his own life instead and died on June 2, 1945.

The eighty-six Jewish prisoners who were murdered at Natzweiler, what could be found of them, were buried together in the Jewish cemetery outside Strasbourg. One young woman, called Emma in the story, was shot trying to escape at Natzweiler, but her actual identity isn't known. More than fifty years after the war, researchers led by the historian Hans-Joachim Lang were finally able to learn all their identities, and a memorial with their names was erected at the burial site in 2005. Lang devoted most of his professional life to uncovering not only their identities but their stories, which were published in his book *Die Namen der Nummern* (*The Names of the Numbers*).

In advance of the August 25, 1944, liberation of Paris by the Free French Second Armored Division and the US Fourth Infantry, workers throughout the city went on strike, and those members of the Resistance who had survived the war emerged from underground and began openly attacking Nazi troops and installations. Dietrich von Choltitz, the Wehrmacht general charged with defending the city against the Allies, had been ordered to destroy all the great landmarks and burn Paris to the ground, but at the last minute, as de Gaulle's troops closed in, he surrendered instead.

And after four terror-filled years of Nazi occupation, the City of Light—la Ville Lumière—was once again free.

ACKNOWLEDGMENTS

I couldn't have written *Stolen by Night* without the dozens of sources that I read and reread—books, articles, websites, and archived material dedicated to preserving records and documenting the horrors of Natzweiler-Struthof and telling the story of the thousands of young people who fought so bravely and sacrificed so much in occupied Paris during World War II. Essential sources that I strongly recommend, and to which I owe an enormous debt, are: *When Paris Went Dark: The City of Light Under German Occupation, 1940–1944* by Ronald C. Rosbottom; *Necropolis* by Boris Pahor; *KL: A History of the Nazi Concentration Camps* by Nikolaus Wachsmann; *A Train in Winter: An Extraordinary Story of Women, Friendship, and Resistance in Occupied France* and *Village of Secrets: Defying the Nazis in Vichy France* by Caroline Moorehead; *Auschwitz and After* by Charlotte Delbo; *And There Was Light* by Jacques Lusseyran; *The Diary of a Young Girl* by Anne Frank; numerous articles, documents, and photographs posted online by the Holocaust History Project and by the United States Holocaust Memorial Museum's *Holocaust Encyclopedia;* "How Should Children's Books Deal With the Holocaust?" by Ruth Franklin from the July 23, 2018, issue of the *New Yorker*; and *Investigation Report on the Life in a German Extermination Camp (Natzweiler) and the Atrocities Committed There*

(1941–1944), which can be found online through the Jewish Virtual Library.

Many thanks as well to my friends Susan Steska and Janet Holley, language teachers at Mountain View High School in Stafford, Virginia, who reviewed the manuscript to help correct my uses and frequent misuses of the French and German languages. Any errors that survived their vetting are mine and mine alone.

Jody Corbett has once again been the most wonderful of editors as we worked together through multiple drafts of *Stolen by Night*. Thank you also to Janet Marshall Watkins, my first reader and partner, and to Kelly Sonnack with the Andrea Brown Literary Agency, who is the driving—and guiding—force for so much of what I've been fortunate to do as a writer and author, and without whom this book would never have come to be. Thanks also to the folks at Scholastic who made sure *Stolen by Night* became an actual book: Melissa Schirmer, production editor; Chris Stengel, designer; and Kassy Lopez, editorial assistant. Thanks as well to Jana Hausmann and the Clubs and Fairs for all their support.

ABOUT THE AUTHOR

Steve Watkins is the author of the young adult novels *On Blood Road, Juvie, What Comes After,* and *Great Falls,* as well as the middle-grade novels *Down Sand Mountain, Sink or Swim,* and the Ghosts of War series, including *The Secret of Midway, Lost at Khe Sanh, AWOL in North Africa,* and *Fallen in Fredericksburg.*

A former professor of journalism, creative writing, and Vietnam War literature, Steve is the cofounder and editor of Pie & Chai, a monthly magazine that you can find and read online at pieandchaimagazine.com.